ALSO BY STEPHEN DIXON

PHONE RINGS

A NOVEL BY STEPHEN DIXON

PHONE RINGS

RINGS

A NOVEL BY
STEPHEN
DIXON

 MELVILLE HOUSE PUBLISHING
HOBOKEN, NEW JERSEY

©2005 STEPHEN DIXON

PARTS OF THIS NOVEL HAVE APPEARED IN THE FOLLOWING
MAGAZINES: BELLEVUE LITERARY REVIEW, BOULEVARD,
CALL, IDAHO REVIEW, KONUNDRUM ENGINE LITERARY
REVIEW, PEQUOD, QUICK FICTION, RBS GAZETTE, STORY
QUARTERLY, TRIQUARTERLY AND WASHINGTON SQUARE
MAGAZINE.

BOOK DESIGN BY DAVID KONOPKA

MELVILLE HOUSE PUBLISHING
P.O. BOX 3278
HOBOKEN NJ 07030

WWW.MHPBOOKS.COM

ISBN: 0-9761407-8-0
FIRST EDITION

LIBRARY OF CONGRESS CATALOGING-IN-PUBLICATION DATA

DIXON, STEPHEN, 1936-
   PHONE RINGS : A NOVEL / BY STEPHEN DIXON.-- 1ST ED.
       P. CM.
   ISBN-13: 978-0-9761407-7-1
   ISBN-10: 0-9761407-7-2
   1. JEWISH FAMILIES--FICTION. 2. NEW YORK (N.Y.)--FICTION.
   3. BROTHERS--DEATH--FICTION. 4. BEREAVEMENT--FICTION.
   I. TITLE.
       PS3554.I92P48 2005
       813'.54--DC22
                           2005017528

THE NOVEL IS DEDICATED
TO MY SISTER PAT, ONE FOR HER ALONE

1

Phone rings. "It's for you," his wife says. "Manny. He doesn't sound—"

The phone rings. "Should I get it," his wife says, "or do you want to?" "I'll get it," he says, and picks up the receiver and says hello. "Uncle Stu," his nephew says, "it's about Dad...."

Phone rings. He's lying on his bed reading and thinks "Why didn't I shut the ringer off?" and yells out "Anyone going to get it?" More rings. Nobody answers him. One or two more rings and the answering machine will come on. He yells "Damn, you got a portable phone, what're you using it for?" and jumps off the bed and picks up the phone just as the answering machine comes on. "Hello," his older daughter's voice on the machine says, "you've reached four-ten, three-two-one—" and his nephew's saying "Uncle Stu? Janice? Are you there? It's Manny." "Just a second," he says, "I'm trying to shut this thing off, but I don't know how," pressing some buttons. Nothing stops the message till it's over, and then the beep to speak and he says "Finally, though we're probably being recorded. Don't worry; I'll erase. How are you, Manny? What's up?" and Manny says "It's Dad. I've some very bad news."

Phone rings. "Will someone answer it?" his wife says. "I dropped my portable phone and can't reach it," and he says "Anita's still out. I'll get it," and jumps out of the chair he's reading in in the living room and runs to the bedroom and picks up the phone.

He last spoke to his brother two days ago. "Just calling to see how things are," Dan said. "I've nothing new to report on my end." Stu said "With us, among other disasters, it's the damn van again. Today. The sixth flat in seven months, a new world's record for a van that only runs on normal paved roads. I've counted them, can tell you where and when each flat was," and Dan said "Sure it's not the tires? Bald, or the pressure's too low, or the same sharp object's still in there and the guys who fixed it never got it out?" and he says "Different tires, and they're all fine. No, these are all accidents. Two flats ago, it was a ballpoint pen stuck in the tire. Mechanic said he'd never seen anything like it before. One today was a long mirror sliver. It's a joke, for what's a broken mirror piece doing on the road?" "Could have been from a car accident and the debris wasn't entirely swept off the road or street. Or the sanitation men when they're dumping the cans into the garbage truck," and Stu said "I didn't think of that; you could be right. Before the ballpoint pen—okay, probably tossed out a car window when the pen ran dry—roofing nails, which could've come from anywhere, but two in one tire and dug in deep." "Maybe it's sabotage, all done by the same person," and Stu laughed. "I'm serious. Have you been in an argument or made anyone angry—something that goes back seven months? A neighbor; colleague? You can be a tempestuous guy, I hear—runs in the family on the male side, except for Dad and Jay, though I think my temper's ameliorated considerably the last ten years. I'm practically a puppy now; it's retirement and my age," and he said "No arguments with anyone in years other than with Janice, and she'd never resort to sabotaging the van to get back at me. She needs it so I can transport her." "One of your students, present or past? I'm just tossing out possibilities. Unfair low grade, the kid thought, and he's getting even?" and Stu said "I'm a notorious high grader. You have to work hard at doing poorly in my classes to get a B+. And my neighbors and colleagues, though we rarely socialize, are neighborly and collegial, as I am to them." "I was the same way at work—didn't mix much—and still am that way with my neighbors. I hate parties and don't like eating out anymore except for the rare celebratory event with Melody and the kids and their spouses and children. Then it's lots of fun." They talked about the Manhattan brownstone they and their two sisters have owned since their mother died five years ago. Dan collected rents from their mother's old apartment and the rest of the tenants in the building and looked after things. "I think the optimum time to sell is now," Dan said, "and Harriet and Natalie, for once, agree with me. Not that we need unanimity to sell it—that's not in our corporation's rules—but I'd love for you to go along with us on this," and he said "Sell, sell; whatever decision you make I know is well thought out and will benefit us all. And we could use the money. Our expenses the last few years and in the near future—medical, Meera's college, Anita's soon-to-be, cost of the converted van and it breaking down every other month, plus IRS, which is always nabbing me for five or so thousand more than I tallied we owe—are killing me."

Manny tells him on the phone that the police and doctors aren't sure how Dan died. It could have been a tree that fell on him while he was running. Or he could have tripped on a tree root or rock and banged his head so hard he got a blood clot and died. Or a heart attack or stroke while he was running. Or else tripped, got up fast to continue his run—"you know Dad"—and tripped much harder this time because he didn't know he'd broken a leg in the first fall, and then hit his head. Or he could have tripped and broken a rib, which also could have made him fall, and it pierced his lung and he bled to death. Or he could have been jumped by one or a couple of guys, fought back—"again, you know Dad"—and was hit on the head with a branch or bat, for his head was severely bruised. A man saw him on the ground just barely alive, this man thought, and got an ambulance, though they had to carry him a quarter of a mile to it because this area was in the most remote part of the park and the path was too narrow for the ambulance to drive on. They think he might have died on the way to the hospital. Or else while he was being carried on a stretcher to the ambulance—a gurney, they said, would have been too bumpy a ride for him. Nobody was around—unless it was a mugging—when he fell. He was probably on the ground for an hour, which they determined by the dried blood around him and the color of his bruises, before this man, walking his dogs, saw him and ran back on the path screaming for help, till a woman near the entrance to the park loaned him her cell phone to call 9-1-1. The two-fall theory, Manny said, when Stu asked, came about because there were two impressions of his body on the ground close to where he had crawled to, one just a few feet from the other and both heading in the direction he'd been running.

The phone rang. He answered it. It was Dan. "Hi. Just checking in with you, seeing how things are. Janice? The girls?" "They're all fine." "You? Feeling okay?" and Stu said "I'm fine, I feel great. Nothing's new or changed. Everything's going well, even the van, except that Anita got her driver's license today. She in fact just came back from the road test." "Oh boy," Dan said, "now you're in deep trouble. Actually, she's a smart kid, so I'm sure she's a good driver," and Stu said "It's funny you say that about my troubles now. Because—the driving school took her for the test; I just gave my blessings and a check for the driver's license—and while waiting for her to call if she passed or not, I paced around the house for about three hours. I was worried she'd be depressed and feel defeated and all that if she failed. You know how you get involved in your kids' lives and that what's happening to them it's like it's happening to you. I only have the two—not *only*, but you know—while you have four, all adults now, so I can't imagine what it was like," and Dan said "Yeah, but with two wives, and the two families separated by a few years, and the first kid I did less for because I mostly didn't live with him, so I bet it comes out to the same thing, yours and mine." "Anyway," Stu said, "I not only forget what I was getting at but I also didn't ask how all of you are doing," and Dan said "Everybody—couldn't be better. And you were pacing back and forth before you got lost. Then, I suppose, Anita calling, so you knew it had to be good news since they never call telling you they failed. And it is good. Sooner they drive on their own the better, because that's how they become experienced at it. It also gives them more independence and self-confidence and takes some of the driving burdens off you, and you can use all the burden-lifting you can get." "But I didn't mind driving her anytime she wanted. We'd talk; she let things out in the car she didn't anywhere else. I don't know what it is about it. And then, one more year and a few months and she's in college and gone, you can say, for good." "So the independence and self-confidence and other elements of it then," and Stu said "But that's my point. I'm elated, for her sake, she passed, but now worried that before she becomes experienced at driving she won't be experienced enough. She'll make rash or wrong decisions that most adults wouldn't. She'll put a tape into the player or try to locate a radio station or drink a soda while she's driving and lose control of the car. And when it snows or the road's icy, what'll she do if the van, or let's say a car, if we have to buy her a car—and that's another thing; the money for it and insurance for her—starts skidding?" and Dan said "Slam the brake down too hard like the rest of us. No, I don't want to worry you more. As I said, she's smart. Teach her what to do—cover every eventuality if possible—and she'll be fine. And be honest; half, or whatever figure, of adults driving are lousy at it. They drive too fast and don't follow the rules of the road and take ridiculous chances." "That's true. On our road? You're supposed to go twenty-five max, but seven out of ten of them—I once counted—go fifty or more. Once in a blue moon someone goes thirty. I can't push Janice along the road—she likes to take walks, we call it—without fearing for our lives sometimes, since we're on a curve where the visibility's poor no matter which way we go. We can cross the road and go up the street there, but then it's hill all the way, though with fewer cars on it and less room to speed, so much safer. But on the road that runs past our house, and I wish you'd come down here once and stay with us. More than once, but at least a first time, and for as long as you like. I want you to see our house; we've been here for seven years. And you and Melody, of course," and Dan said "Don't worry, some day we'll take you up on it. Or just I will, since she isn't keen on going anywhere but the city to see the kids and grandkids, or to Europe with one of our girls." "Good," Stu said, "and I hope soon. But where was I again? Oh yeah, our road. Cars speeding on it, and especially between five and six when people are returning home from work...."

Years ago, more than forty. Dan was working in DC and got Stu a job there with a news outfit six months after he graduated college. Dan and Melody—she was his girlfriend then—invited him for dinner at Dan's apartment. Friends of Dan were there, mostly colleagues. During drinks Stu was attracted to a woman who'd come with one of Dan's friends. When the woman went into the kitchen for ice for her drink—it was a sticky night and there was no air-conditioning and the ice melted fast—Stu said "Jeez, I think I need ice too—anybody else while I'm in there?"

They all said they were fine and he went into the kitchen and started a conversation with the woman about where they worked and what they did and how long they'd been in Washington and then he said—they were alone—"Excuse me. You might find this a totally inappropriate question, and if you do and you want to please reprimand me, but how close are you and your friend in there, Gene?" "We've been dating a few months." "So there's no hope you'd see me for lunch or something?" "There might be. What do you have in mind?" "What I said, lunch or something." "'Something' meaning dinner or a drink?" and he said "Sure, either of those." "I think Gene would mind that, but I don't see why he'd have any objections if I had lunch with you." "You don't have to tell him, lunch, dinner or a drink." "But I'd have to. I wouldn't want to hide anything like that from him." "Maybe you don't know what I'm saying." "I know what you're saying. Let's just have lunch." "Lunch, then. When?" "This Saturday or Sunday?" "Sunday's good." "You can meet me at my apartment or the restaurant. I know of a nice inexpensive place around the corner from me." "He doesn't stay with you weekends?" "Sometimes, and me with him, but he'll be on assignment this weekend. And this isn't a date we're having, you understand. It's just lunch, and we go Dutch, or I'll pay, since I'm sure I earn a lot more than you." "Nothing else; just lunch. And Dutch suits me fine. I'll pick you up. I like to see people's apartments for the first time." They set a time and she started giving him directions by car. "I don't own one. I don't even have a driver's license. Dan's going to teach me how to drive and help get me one." "I know how to get there by bus or streetcar too." Then they went back to the living room and resumed sitting with the other people. Actually, they continued talking about their work and the news assignment Gene would be on next weekend—he was a television producer—when she said "I think we should go back. People will wonder." "Let them." "But I don't want them to." "You go back first. I still have to get ice. That was my excuse to come in here so I could speak to you. But know what I'd really like to do before you go back?" "I can imagine." "Kiss you. Would that be all right?" "Don't be a silly boy. Of course it wouldn't be all right." "Does that mean you'll never kiss me?" "I didn't say that." "So, let's kiss now; just one." "I don't want to." "I want to, but okay. And I know I'm acting silly. I'm sorry." "All right, you want to kiss so much, I'll kiss. I could use a nice kiss." "Why, Gene doesn't kiss you?" "Of course he kisses me. We kiss a lot. Just, maybe it's the second drink in me speaking—your brother makes them too strong. And you know, you two look nothing alike. He's short, you're tall. He's got all his hair, you've lost half of yours. And different-shaped faces. What happened? Anyway, it'd be nice to have a long kiss. Are you ready for a long one?" "Longer the better." "Let's get away from the door so nobody sees us if they walk in, especially Gene. That'd be terrible. Even let's go into the pantry there." They went into it. They kissed. He felt her buttocks and breasts. They kissed several times. "I don't know why I'm doing this," she said. "Jeopardizing a perfectly good relationship with a very sweet guy whom I like a lot. And for a kid! But I like kissing you. Maybe I just like kissing. But don't get any ideas. We're just having lunch this weekend, because I've nothing to do and I like talking to new people and you seem reasonably intelligent and you're kind of funny and I can always use a laugh. Come on, one last kiss, but short," and they kissed. "Whew, that was some kiss," he said. "You're a real kisser. I'm glad I followed you in here." "Oh, this is so stupid," she said, smiling at him. "How do I look?" "You look fine." "My hair?" "It's okay." "I gave you my address and directions to get there?" "Yes. Take your drink with you." She took it, smoothed down her dress and left the room. He got ice for his drink, some more vodka and tonic and squeezed a fresh lime wedge into the glass, and started for the living room, stopped and yelled "Excuse me, but long as I'm in here I can also get refills for anyone who wants." "You'll have to get our glasses if you do," Dan said, "so come on back." He went into the living room. Gene was looking at him when he came in as if he was on to what happened in the kitchen. Dan didn't seem too happy either, staring at him, one eyebrow raised. The woman, Beatrice, was sitting with her legs crossed, looking over her shoulder at the window. "So," Stu said, "anyone want me to get them a refill now?" "Don't bother," Melody said. "We're about to sit down for dinner." Next day Dan called him at work and said "Did you make a pass at Bea last night?" "Not a pass. We got to talking and then I asked her out for lunch this Saturday because we both have nothing to do. Or Sunday; I forget. I'll have to check with her. But to talk and nothing else." "Don't give me that," Dan said. "When she returned to the living room she was flushed and looked a little messed up as if you two had been going at it in the kitchen, and you didn't look that pale or tidy yourself." "It was very warm in there, that'd account for the flush. No fan, the window open but with zero circulation. You have this thing against air-conditioners, that could be the result." "Come on, out with it. What'd you two do in there?" "We talked and then, all right, kissed, but just for fun. We were both a little high. She even commented to me how strong you make the drinks. Then, after that one simple kiss, we realized it was ridiculous what we were doing, and stopped." "Don't you know she and Gene have been seeing each other for months? They've even discussed marriage. He told me. Nothing set yet, but he thinks it's in the bag. Worse, out of anything, he's a close friend of mine and my colleague and a terrific guy. I invited them to dinner with you and the others because I thought you'd all be good company together, not so you could try to stick your prick in her first chance you got. Okay, she's old enough to know what she's doing. She's in fact about ten years older than you. Still, you knew they were together. You should respect relationships. You shouldn't try to move in and put the make on every pretty woman you meet. I've seen you. You're too goddamn horny and filled with yourself sometimes. If she had come alone and wasn't attached, then I would have said do what you want with her in the kitchen, within reason. But there are consequences to what you did. Gene could find out and be hurt. Maybe he already knows—it seemed so by his quick mood change when Bea came back—and is being discreet. Or he could say to me 'What's up with your brother?' You'd lose his respect. You're losing mine by what you did. Not Melody's. She thinks everyone's fair game in sex till they're married or publicly engaged, which doesn't make me feel too good. But Gene would never pull a stunt like that on you. So you're charming; so you're good-looking and a smooth talker and get hot rocks for women more than other guys, or as much but just act on it more. So show some restraint." "Okay, I get the message. I was wrong. I'm sorry. I'll cancel the lunch date." "Do, and don't see her even if she contacts you later. Don't tell her you spoke to me either. Tell her you didn't think the lunch date, innocent as it was, was a good idea because Gene is such a close friend of your brother." "Will do." "No, don't say that; she'll see through it and recognize my hand in it. Just say you realized, looking at your calendar, you had something doing this weekend and you're sorry and you'll take a rain check on it, but you don't." "I got you." "No, don't say anything about a rain check or that you'll call again. Just say you've news work all weekend and you're sorry. She'll catch on. And damnit, start thinking more of other people's feelings. There are plenty of unattached single girls in DC, most in your age range or a couple of years older, and half of them working in the Capitol building where you mostly are. It would have been different if you two had flashed on each other and Gene and she were breaking up and had just come as friends and you knew that. But all you wanted was to get her in bed, and the hell with what it would have done to Gene if he had found out, right?" "No. To have lunch, talk. I found her intelligent, elegant, pretty for sure, and other things, and then, eventually, long down the road, if it resulted, we'll say, in—" "Bullshit, whatever you were about to say, and you know it. Use your head from now on, will you? Foremost, be more moral." "Okay, I will, but I have to go." "I'll speak to you later this week," Dan said, and hung up.

The phone rings. Manny says he has very bad news, the worst imaginable. "I'm sorry, I don't know how to say this, even though I practiced before I called, but my mother asked me to tell you." "It's Dan. The worst. He's dead."

This also happened in Washington. Same kind of summer night: hot and muggy. Dan invited him and two women on his news staff over for dinner. This was before Melody. They were drinking margaritas. "Dinner's almost on the table," Dan said. "I got a great bottle of Chianti. And Jane," one of the women, "brought over a very nice Beaujolais, so we've plenty to drink. Lizzie's salad, Stu's bread, French pastries from downstairs; so we're set. Appetizers. Good God, I forgot the appetizers I prepared. They're in the refrigerator when they should've been taken out two hours ago. We'll have them with dinner. I'll get the sauce on the spaghetti and we'll eat." He went into the kitchen. Seconds later: "Oh no," he screamed, with such pain in his voice that Stu thought he was hurt. "What's wrong?" and he ran into the kitchen. Dan was smiling. "You won't believe this. Everything appears normal, right? Nothing broken, spilled or on the floor. It's too ridiculous to explain." The two women came in. "What happened?" one said. "The spaghetti; ruined." "How? Overcooked? We can still eat it. One more margarita and we won't care what its texture's like." "Worse. I knocked my ex-wife's bottle of perfume into the spaghetti after I'd poured the sauce in, one I've been working on all day." "What was her perfume doing by the stove?" Stu said. "Good question. My brother; you can tell he's had lots of journalism experience. The spaghetti was in the pot, a small flame under it to keep it warm while I got everything else to the table. The perfume, which she left on the stove shelf more than two years ago—I don't know why she put it there. Maybe she didn't and the cleaning lady found it and put it there. Anyway, it's been there untouched for two years—I certainly didn't leave it there to remind me of her every time I boiled water or cooked—and when I reached for the pepper mill on the shelf I knocked the perfume into the pot. That's what these reds spots on my shirt are from." "Fish the bottle out carefully," Stu said. "If the stopper didn't come out, the spaghetti won't be ruined." "I already got the bottle out; the stopper's still in there somewhere. It's ruined, believe me." "Not if the perfume evaporated in the two years," one of the women said. "Let me taste." She tasted it with a spoon, made a face. "So what's for dinner?" Stu said. "I'm starved. How about, since you worked hard enough on this, I boil up more spaghetti and toss it with garlic and olive oil? All of you go inside, have another drink and the appetizers, and I'll call you when it's done. Let me set the table too." "No, thanks," Dan said. "One mistake invariably leads to another mistake unless you completely change the pace. You're all my guests at Chez Mangez downstairs." "And the appetizers?" "Leave them. We'll get mussels and pâté at Mangez. Everybody ready?" "You shouldn't have to pay for everyone," one of the women said. "We'll split the check four ways." "Don't argue, I'm treating. I invited you for dinner here and was careless. I should have dumped that Chanel No. 5 two years ago when she left." "You don't dump good perfume," the woman said. "It's too expensive. You give it to someone who'll appreciate and wear it." Stu finished his drink and Dan changed his shirt. The women brought the drink glasses into the kitchen and washed them and dumped the spaghetti and cleaned the pots and hung them up, and they all walked down the three flights to the restaurant. Had a great dinner, finished off two bottles of wine with it, then desserts and Dan insisted they all have cognacs and café filtre after. Then Dan and one of the women went upstairs and Stu walked the other woman to her car. "I didn't know they were seeing each other," he said. "When did that happen?" "Most likely tonight. I didn't see it coming either and she never spoke about it, so how they worked it out to just say goodnight to us, as if they lived together, and walk upstairs to his apartment is a mystery to me too. I'm sure it was prearranged. But all she told me at the dinner table when you were in the men's room was that I didn't have to drive her home as I'd planned to, so I thought she was taking a taxi to spare me the long drive." "Good; she's nice; I'm glad for my brother." When they got to her car, he said "Would it be too much for you to drive me home? I live a mile from here, off Columbia Road, but it's mostly uphill and I feel kind of beat. Besides, my neighborhood can get a bit dangerous around this hour." "Sure," she said. After she pulled up to his building, he said "Like to come up for a drink?" "I'm sorry; I'm dating someone. I'm just not with him tonight." "That's okay; thought I'd ask. And I really didn't mean anything by it except a nightcap and talk and I'd walk you back to your car."

"No thanks," she said, "but nice try. It's been fun," and she stuck out her hand and they shook hands.

2

Phone rings. What he'd want now and for it to be Dan. "Hello," he'd say and Dan would say "Stu?" with the "u" drawn out. "How's it going?" and Stu would say "As Mom used to say, 'Okay, I guess.'" "Yeah? What's wrong?" "Sometimes, hate as I do to say this, taking care of Janice can get too tough for me. I don't usually mind the day-to-day stuff, getting her up, exercising her in bed, in and out of chairs and so on, and same in reverse the before-bed stuff, and during the day too, all the little chores. Okay, I've got it down to a science. But one mishap, something goes wrong, more work than I'm expecting to do—my science gone awry, you could say—and it gets to me, and sometimes I go a little crazy. Let's face it, as Mom also used to say, I get tired faster and I'm weaker because I'm getting old and I know that contributes to the mishaps. I can't lift her or set her down as easily as I used to, for one thing." "Come on, compared to me you're a youngster." "But you're in much better shape. You run and exercise a lot more." "Because I'm retired and have the time and have been running like an idiot the last forty years. But you're in good shape, or last time I saw you, and those things don't change so fast." "I must sound awful, because I don't mean to complain." "Why, why shouldn't you? Let's face it, as you say Mom used to say—I don't remember her saying it, but I'll take your word—you've a lot to do. Janice, the kids, house, teaching, your writing, and that damnable van. Just slow down, don't try to get everything in at once. Little here, there, it all gets done eventually. And if there's anything I can do—anything, I swear to you; I've got all this free time—just say the word and I'll drive right down. But it's not easy for you, I know that. How you've handled it so far, I really admire you for. I doubt I could have done it." "Oh God, I feel like such a drip now, as if I asked you to say that." "Come on, don't be a dope."

Phone rings. Or he'd want to call Dan. For one thing, to tell him how hard it's been for him lately, just to tell someone. Doesn't want to tell Janice because it's mostly because of her he's so exhausted, and he doesn't want her to feel worse than she already does. Guilty; worse. So he calls Dan. If he could, he'd say "Hi. Just checking in with you to see how you and your family are." Dan usually said "Great, great, no problems, everything going well," and then would tell him what his kids were up to and then a couple of things about himself. Reading a lot. "Mornings, afternoons, evenings till I'm too tired to—it could be the wine—so I take an hour's nap in my reading chair here, and then later in bed before sleep I read some more." "I remember Dad," Dan once said. "I never saw a book or magazine in his hands other than a dental journal, till he got sick and was forced to give up his practice. Then he started reading books, mostly novels. It was that or staring at walls and driving Mom nuts. I've always read but nothing like I do today. But give Dad a book— any book—and, unlike me, he'd read it through even if he didn't like it. Because if he thought you bought the book—the trick, to keep him in the habit of reading, was to make him think you did—he didn't want to be wasting good money, as he called it." Finally finished *Gargantua*, he said in a phone call a few days before he died. "I started it I don't know how many times in my life. The new translation you gave me worked. It was slow-going, though, so I'm not moving on to Book Two. Next up is *Bleak House*. Another novel you shouldn't go through life not having read. I better get to it soon because you also shouldn't go through life not having read *Moby Dick*, *War and Peace*, *Brothers Karamazov*, Dante's *Inferno*—why is it always 'Dante's *Inferno*' and not, for instance, 'Tolstoy's *War and Peace*'?—*Ulysses* and *The Golden Bowl*, and how much time does a guy my age have left? Those seven ought to do it. You've read them all?" and he said "Yeah, and *War and Peace* twice," though he'd never read *Bleak House* and *The Golden Bowl*, and had only read half of the *Inferno*, and last year, for the third time, couldn't get through *Don Quixote*, which Dan had read several times, and the *Karamazov* he'd read when he was around eighteen was abridged he learned more than forty years later when he took some of the books from his mother's library after she died. "And what are you talking about? You've plenty of time to read them, and they all read fairly fast, so add *The Magic Mountain* to your list. By the time you're done with those we should be able to come up with a few more big ones that neither of us has read, and we'll have a two-man book club." Still distributing food to the homeless twice a week. "Gets me out of the house for a few hours, which is good for my marriage, plus short walks and long runs and swimming in the indoor pool in town. And of course reading the *Times* through every day, everything but the ads and TV listings." "What about your writing project?" Stu said. "Started the book yet?" "Which one? I had so many I wanted to do and a few I even did a little fiddling around with." "*Our Gang*. The one about our old Brooklyn neighborhood and all the friends you left there when we moved to Manhattan. What they did with their lives the last sixty-some years, those still living, and whatever you could dig up about the ones who died. You said it'd be twice as easy to write than the novels you had ideas for, since you'd be using your reporting skills." "I dropped it along with the others, though that one came as close as any to being written." "Why? It was a great idea, and it'd really give you something to do the next few years. And if you put yourself down solely as a writer on your Schedule C form, and maybe Melody as your researcher and typist, you can take off all the expenses for the book, travel and otherwise—tell them one old Brooklyn pal you wanted to interview now lived in Paris." "No, I found out I'm no book writer. When I first retired I might have been able to do one. Now, anything that smacks of that kind of labor would cut into the comfortable inertia rut I've finally achieved after fifty-five years of nothing but working. But what about you? We've only talked of me," and Stu said "Same as always. We're fine, with occasional major setbacks and lots of minor frustrations, but nothing that doesn't end or we can't live with. And just five more years and three months and I'll be retired too."

Phone. "Will someone answer it?" he yells from his work table in the bedroom. "I'm busy." Nobody picks up the phone. He jumps out of his chair and grabs the phone on the fifth or sixth ring and says hello. "Uncle Stu?" "Say, how's it going? What's up?" "Nothing good, I'm afraid. I've very bad news to tell you, which I don't want to but it has to come from someone." "It's your dad." He goes through the house after, shouting "Janice, you around?" Then remembers she was driven someplace by the woman who takes care of her a few hours today; the woman knocked on his door an hour ago and told him through it they were leaving. His daughter's not home either. A friend probably picked her up by car. He has to speak to someone about it. He's supposed to call his sisters and tell them, but doesn't feel ready for that yet. He dials Dan's number. Dan answers and Stu says "Something impossibly sad's happened and Janice isn't home and you're the only other person I feel I can talk to about this right now. Manny called and said there was some kind of accident— a tree or a root sticking out or something. Or it could have been a heart attack or stroke. He said a lot but I forget most of it or have it all mixed up—but that you died a few hours ago on a park path and I feel like I'll go crazy if it's true." "It isn't. You hear me; my voice? I'm alive as you are, although nine years older but in much better condition, so maybe only a couple of years closer to the grave than you. Relax. Don't worry. And certainly don't go crazy. No event should cause that except perhaps the loss of one of your children, and then you can't go crazy, for you have to be stable enough to take care of your wife and other daughter because of their despair over it." "You're right, and I'm so glad," and he hangs up. Oh my God, he thinks, I forgot to say goodbye. He calls back and says "I'm sorry, I hung up without saying goodbye, but I guess it showed how happy I was that you were okay."

How many years ago? 1969, so almost 33. Dan and Melody had rented a house for the summer in Old Lyme, Connecticut. No, they bought it a few years before with Melody's older sister and brother-in-law. They'd arranged, the two couples, where each occupied the house every other week in the summer. One weekend a summer Stu and his folks were invited up. He loved going. Broke his routine and got him out of the hot city. Long walks on the beach, brief swims in the Sound, sailing with Dan and his kids on their Sunfish, evening barbecues. Dan would buy two enormous steaks—an inch and a half thick and more than enough to feed five to seven adults and a slew of kids and have some left over for lunch the next day—and cook them on a charcoal grill with corn in their husks and potatoes and what else over the briquets?—a pineapple sliced in half and wrapped in aluminum foil. There'd be fresh tomatoes and cole slaw made from cabbage and carrots they bought at a nearby farm. Cheese and crab dip and drinks before, usually gin and tonics. A couple of those, maybe three, and plenty of good red wine with dinner and a spinach or leafy green salad in a huge wooden bowl and pies that Melody made; whatever fruit or berry was in season. It was always dark by the time they sat down to eat, all of them around a long picnic table behind the house. The steaks cooked just right—medium rare and charred on the outside—and if you wanted more you just went to the steak platter and sliced some. Usually, friends of Melody and Dan's would be over with their kids. All the children would make up a play that day and rehearse it and perform it for the adults that night by candlelight. Then he'd walk his father to the bedroom his parents shared—first a long stint on the toilet where Stu would hold him straight so he wouldn't fall off the seat—and say to him when he got him into bed "A great day, huh? Different than the city." His father would say something like "It's always a treat to be here with my kids and grandkids. Dan's a terrific guy. Very generous, almost to a fault. What these dinners must cost him, not that I'm complaining, for they're delicious. But I'll be honest; he's nothing like me. Intellectual—he knows and talks so well about so many things, most of them over my head, though he doesn't mean to—and throws money around like it's confetti. Though he has no interest in money—that's the funny thing—but I hear his job pays a bundle. And his wife's very nice and so attentive to me. You should get a job like his and find someone like her, though Jewish. And the air's so fresh here, the nights nice and cool. It was wonderful sitting outside today under the big shade tree in front. Your mother loves it up here also, I can tell. Dan was smart. Well, when wasn't he smart, but especially now with real estate. The Dobbs Ferry house, which I thought he paid way too much for, but it turns out he made a terrific deal. Then this place when the price was low, and now, he says, these beach homes have shot up sky high. I should've bought something like this thirty years ago when you kids were still kids, but on Long Island in a community easier to get to and closer to our background. Long Beach, which we liked, or a town like that. Could've got one dirt cheap and it would've paid off twice over just in our not packing you kids off to camp every summer. Now it doesn't pay, and who's got the money? I'm old and sick and your mother's not getting any younger, so just coming here with you for a couple of nights every summer is enough for us. Though it would've been a nice thing to leave to you kids. But there were so many of you then, I thought, and we weren't finished, so how would you ever have divided it up?" "We would have. We all got along. And now we're down to four, unfortunately, and Dan has his own summer place and wouldn't have liked Long Island and Natalie seems to have settled in LA, so it would have been easy: just Harriet and me. But what the hell, and I used to love summer camp and so did all your other kids who went," and his father said "Good, because it set us back plenty."

Phone. Answers it and gets the news. Screams "Oh no, I can't believe it," and turns to Janice and says "Dan died; my brother Dan. They say he must have tripped during a run in a park and somehow got stabbed by his own broken ribs—his lung. It's too ridiculous; the reason's too farfetched. It can't be true, right? But it's what Manny just told me." Next day the police and doctors decide Dan got hit by a falling tree, tried to get up but he'd broken too many essential bones for standing so he just lay there, probably hoping for someone to come along, lost a lot of blood, then about an hour later a man walking his dogs found him still breathing but unconscious and his body very cold.

Earlier that winter. They'd talked about walking through St. John the Divine together. Stu had done it with his kids and alone and with his wife before they were married. She had an apartment on Riverside Drive a few blocks from the cathedral. Once when he and Dan were on the phone—this was a number of years ago—Stu said, when Dan asked what he'd been doing in the city, "Not much. Some writing today, maybe four hours of it—you know me, can't leave my typewriter home. And late this afternoon I wanted to get out of the apartment by myself, didn't know where I wanted to go, just started walking through the Columbia campus and ended up inside St. John the Divine. It's an interesting place to walk around. Huge, with monuments and memorials to everything: poets, firemen. An organist was rehearsing somewhere above for a concert or Sunday service—classical music, very powerful, Bach and Buxtehude toccatas, I think... not your typical schmaltzy churchy stuff. I sat and listened for about an hour. Reminded me of Paris when the same thing happened more than thirty years ago in a much smaller cathedral... well, every cathedral in the world's supposed to be smaller than Divine now, what with its expansion." "You know, I've always wanted to go in there. We should meet and do it one day and then go to the Hungarian Pastry Shop across the street, which I have been to, with you and your girls." Two months ago, during Stu's winter break, they arranged to go to the cathedral, walked around inside, sat up front a while—"Very nice," Dan said, "and so peaceful for such a big busy place, but, unfortunately, no music," and Stu said "What do you mean?" and Dan said "One of the times you were here you said you heard an organ recital and it reminded you of a cathedral in Paris," and Stu said "Right, I forgot. Buxtehude, Bach, or at least I thought so, but why do I think I can recognize Buxtehude? What a phony I can be," and Dan said "Why? You know a lot about music, so don't be so hard on yourself"—and then went to the pastry shop for coffee and cake. Stu suggested Dan take out food from the restaurant next door. "You love authentic Chinese food and this place is tops." So they sat in the restaurant and waited while the food was prepared. Dan refused a complimentary tea: "The old Riner trait we inherited from Mom: weak or too small a bladder; I'd have to pee halfway through the drive home and I forgot my emergency jar." After about fifteen minutes, when Stu saw Dan check his watch again, he said he felt lousy he'd suggested the takeout idea—"Now you'll probably get caught in rush-hour traffic," and Dan said "No big deal. It's been worth it, believe me, finally seeing you after so long. And the food's got to be fresh and good as you say if it takes this long to prepare." Their father, when Stu was a boy—Dan was already out of the house, in the army, then college—one Sunday a month would order out from a neighborhood Chinese-American restaurant chow mein and chop suey and fried rice and egg drop soup and always asked, or had Stu ask, if he was the one picking up the order, and which would embarrass him, for several extra bags of the dried noodles that came with the soup. Stu didn't like any of it except the fried rice. Too gooey, with vegetables in it like cooked celery and onions. When Dan was working in Washington the first time, he took Stu and several other people to a Peking restaurant downtown. Jowses, or however they're spelled—Stu was impressed when Dan asked for them by name, one order steamed, the other fried—moo shu pork with pancakes, Peking duck, a dish with "Mongolian pot" in it, whole rockfish—"Two of you should eat the cheek meat. Go on, it's under the slit in the cheek— sweetest meat in the fish." "What do I do with this?" Stu said after Dan dropped a pancake on everyone's plate and opened and spread it out with his chopsticks, and Dan said "First a little of that hoisin sauce there, smear it around. Next one of these scallion slivers, then the moo shu—serving spoonful at the most or it gets sloppy—and roll it up this way and eat it with your hands." Japanese beer made with rice. It was good. Stu said "Can I?" and Dan said "Sure; helps wash the food down," and he had another and then a third. This was in '54 or '55. He'd driven down with his brother, Jay and Natalie. He and Jay stayed at Dan's, Natalie with his new girlfriend, Zee, who became his first wife. "She's so sweet," Natalie said. "I was still in bed this morning when she hands me a glass of freshly squeezed orange juice and says 'How do you like your eggs?'" A bright, articulate, pretty woman. Long black hair, long body, couple of inches taller than Dan, gorgeous smile. Very natural, big generous spirit, a backslapper and joke teller. Dan was more serious, liked to laugh but not to joke. If he joked, his jokes fell flat. "I can't tell them— can barely remember them—so why do I even try? To mortify myself, obviously." They married that fall. "I knew he'd marry a goy," their father said. "He never went out with a Jewish girl in his life. I don't know what he has against them. They're the nicest, most beautiful girls in the world and can be the smartest—look at your mother—and make the best wives.

Now he's started something I'm convinced his brothers will follow, since you two emulate everything he does." Wedding was held under a huge tent on her parents' woodsy property in Wilton, Connecticut. She knew a number of Slavic languages, translated documents for a government agency. After the ceremony she changed into a Polish peasant dress and played the balalaika and sang Slavic folk songs and read an epithalamium in Russian and English she wrote for the wedding. A Russian band played kazakski music and Dan said to Stu and Jay "Come on, let's dance," and they crossed their arms and tried to kick from a squatting position and fell over one after the other. "I can do it when I'm not drinking champagne," Dan said, "but I don't know about my brothers." They had a son several months later. About a year and a half after that Zee said she wanted to spend a week with her parents—Dan told their mother this and she told Stu and Jay—that they hadn't seen their one grandchild enough, and took the train and called a few days later saying she wasn't coming home and wanted a divorce. "What did your folks tell you about me?" "Nothing. They like you. I just don't want to be married to you any longer. It's clear to me the marriage will never work." "But it's been working. It's been wonderful, as good as it ever was. There's nothing I can see that's gone bad. I love you. You've said you love me. There was that marriage poem all about your love. And we love our son. It'll be terrible for him if we split up." "It'll be worse if we stay together and fight." "I could never fight with you. I love you too much and I'm not the fighting type. Please come home and I'll forget we ever spoke about this. Or I won't forget if you don't want me to. We'll talk about it as much as you want, and with anyone else—a friend, a therapist; you choose one and I'll pay for it—but please come home, please. This will kill me, losing you and Isaac both." "You won't lose him. I'm not stealing him. You'll see him as much as you like." She never came back. He granted her the divorce without a fuss, said he'd give her whatever she asked for—the house, car, half his salary, all their savings. She said she only wanted a small amount of money for Isaac every month and, later on, his college tuition and expenses. She moved to New Mexico the following year. Dan flew out two to three times a year to see Isaac for a few days. He also saw him whenever she came East to see her parents, and had him two weeks every summer for about fifteen years. Isaac's now 44, looks just like Dan, Harriet said. She saw him at the memorial for Dan, organized by a few of his former colleagues in TV. Stu didn't go, and there was no funeral. Dan was cremated and his ashes were scattered in the Hudson. That's what he said he wanted, Melody said on the phone. He'd sailed on it numerous times and he loved the view of it from their front porch when the trees were bare and he thought scattering them in the river was the best way of not leaving anything behind. Anything physical, she said. The crematory service was private—something else he said he wanted, she said: just her and their children and spouses and Isaac if he could get to New York for it. Took less than fifteen minutes. A few short poems chosen and read by the children—Dan didn't read poetry, she said, and he specifically didn't want anything religious at the service—and some hugging, and that was it. Stu wouldn't have gone to the service if he had been invited, for the same reason he didn't go to the memorial: he knew he wouldn't have been able to hold up during it and didn't want to break down in front of everyone. Also, the memorial meant driving in with Janice and getting back that night, since he had classes the next day. "The resemblance between Isaac and Dan was uncanny," Harriet said, "even spooky. I almost jumped when I first saw him, for a moment thinking it was Dan, even though he's thirty years younger. I suppose I was just flashing back to what Dan looked like then. But also, Dan looked fifteen years younger than he was, and Isaac looked his age. And their build; the same. And height— relatively short: five-six or five-seven, Dan was, am I right?" and Stu said "He liked to say 'five-six and a half,' or 'bordering on five-seven.'" "Isaac's around that too, maybe an inch taller. But the face: same pug nose, curly light hair and lots of it—Dan never really grayed and you can bet he didn't dye it. High cheeks—you know Dan's; great bone structure there—one I'd love to have—and small ears and mouth. And the blue eyes, the only one in the family to have them. They're supposed to have come from Mom's mother or father—which?" and he said "Grandma Hannah." "Ah, to have those eyes—what I would have given. My lackluster brown eyes, for one thing. But even his voice. Gravelly. You were smart not to come. Lots of people getting up and speaking, some of them endlessly. One man—a journalist friend who covered the Korean War with Dan—crying throughout, but he went on till he'd read his whole, what I'd call, speech. Altogether, more than two hours of history and memory, few of them saying anything I didn't know, so for sure nothing you didn't. His capture by the Communist Chinese. One speaker gave the name of the boat Dan was captured on, so that was new. Years in the Chinese prison and Dan coming out thirty pounds underweight." "Eighteen months in captivity, and two or three prisons. They moved him around." "He said years. His work at PBS, or then it was NET. And CBS, INS, UPS." "UP. United Press." "Sailing across the Atlantic when he was seventy on a boat that was about the size and had the comfort of one of those terrifying river rafts that people pay to put themselves on to risk their lives. And there were three of them on it but only two berths, since someone always had to be on watch. Here's something I didn't know. That the boat, during a storm near the Azores, almost capsized and would have sunk." "Dan never mentioned that." "This speaker wasn't on it, but that's what he said Dan told him, and we both know Dan never exaggerated or embellished a story or lied. He probably didn't want to worry us, almost losing a second brother in the Atlantic, especially since he wanted one day to make the same crossing coming back, not that we ever could have stopped him. His war correspondent days in Korea and, five years before that, an army paratrooper in Japan. He certainly was a gutsy man. What I didn't like about the memorial were these monitors around the room continually changing photos of him. Dan on a boat, Dan finishing a marathon, Dan after he was released from prison and crossing some Chinese bridge to freedom. Around eight monitors, each the size of a large TV screen, so wherever you looked you saw him. I will say it was an impressive crowd, even distinguished looking—quite a number of television news executives were there, I was told—and everyone well dressed. After it was over there was a table of crudités and other hors d'oeuvres and an open bar, which everyone flocked to—something you'd expect from a room mostly filled with ex-newsmen, although by that time and after so many eulogies I think we all needed a drink. All in all, an event well done but extremely sad," and Stu said "I knew it'd be, which is why I didn't go. And the long drive and all those hours there. It gets hard on Janice's back and legs, never getting out of the wheelchair except to sit on the john. And we'd have to drive right back—not even be alone with you for a half hour—so you can see..." And she said "I know, and it's what I told everyone who asked for you. Believe me, you made the right move and nobody would say no. And I told you everything that went on, so it's like you were there."

Phone rings. He's writing and doesn't want to answer it. Nobody picks up, the answering machine will. Phone continues ringing. His wife either misplaced her portable phone or can't reach it and his daughter's either napping or out with friends. Answering machine goes on. His older daughter's voice on the machine gives their number and says "Please leave a message." "It's Manny," the caller says. "Uncle Stu, if you're there, pick up. If not, please call me. It's about Dad. I'm at his house." Stu lunges for the phone. "Manny," he says, "what's wrong?"

3

He'd never told Dan this. Thought several times to but then thought better. Made Isaac swear not to tell Dan or Zee about it. "Oh, on second thought, you can tell her," after Isaac swore he'd never tell either, "but not Dan. You do, he won't let me take you anywhere for the next few years. I know him. He's a one-serious-mistake-and-you're-crossed-off-the-guardian-list guy. In fact, Zee probably shouldn't know either. Since she has rights over you, she could stop me from seeing you too, though I don't think she would. I think she'd be a lot more relaxed and forgiving about it than your dad, which is no criticism of him, you understand. His reaction to what happened today would just be showing his concern for you. Because let's face it, we did a very stupid thing. Me a hundred times stupider than you because I'm the adult who was supposed to be looking out for you. But on third thought, let's play it safe. It came so close to being a total

STEPHEN DIXON

tragedy that I now think she definitely shouldn't know too, or not till you're around sixteen, okay?" He told Isaac this while they were drying Isaac's clothes over a fire Stu had made in a stone fireplace in a lean-to in a state park. Isaac had a blanket around him and was wearing Stu's coat. Stu kept a blanket and heavy sweater in his old VW Bus in case it broke down and he started to freeze while waiting for help. It should be explained that Isaac and Zee had come East to visit her folks and that Stu had rented a room in a town ten miles away to work on a novel for six months, and had driven over to take Isaac out for a few hours. He never finished the novel. Did write three one-act plays which he liked at the time but were never produced, though he tried, and today doesn't know where they are. He supposed if he searched through the file cabinets in his school office he'd find them. But to get back. They'd hiked through woods in this state park and came to a lake. Isaac was around—he calculates—this was the winter of '68, Isaac's now 44, so he was ten. Lake was frozen over, Without saying anything to Stu, Isaac started out on the ice. "Say, what're you doing?" Stu said. "Get back here. There might be a crack in the ice." "No, it's solid; look. At least two inches thick." "An inch at the most, and what the heck do you know about ice? You're from New Mexico." "I come to Connecticut every winter for a week. I'll be careful, I promise." "I'd rather you didn't, but all right, you can go out a little," because he didn't want him telling Dan and Zee how Uncle Stu had kept him from having fun by being too careful. And he wanted him to have fun, and so far he didn't think Isaac was having a good time with him. Not much talk and not much to do till

44

they got to the lake. And it's what he'd do if he were Isaac's age, Stu thought: go out on the ice far as he could so long as it was safe. And Isaac was smart; he'd know when it wasn't safe. So he let him continue out on the ice. "Go slower," Stu yelled, and Isaac went slower. He slid intentionally. "Don't slide or jump," Stu yelled, having walked about thirty feet out and tested the ice with his shoe several times to see how solid it was. Seemed very solid. "No extra blows or pressure on the ice, please. That alone could start it cracking. Little steps instead of big. You see a crack or hole—you see even a trace of water through the ice, and a crack or hole of any size, and you have to be honest with me or I'll never take you out again—you head straight back, but slowly, you hear?" "I hear. I'm all right." Isaac went a few more steps and slipped and fell and started laughing while he sat on the ice. "You see, Uncle Stu? Didn't even make a small crack. It must be three inches where I am, not two. It's been way below freezing the last month, my grandpa said, never going over twenty. But boy, it's cold on my fanny," and he stood up. "Okay, you convinced me," Stu said. "But only stay out there another minute and then very carefully walk back the same way you came." Isaac walked a little farther out—"Baby steps from now on," Stu yelled, "just baby steps"—and when Isaac went a few more feet, "That's far enough. Long enough too, much more than a minute I just don't trust it." "Why? I want to get to the middle." "No, it's fine where you are, almost in the middle, so now come back." "You come out here then," and Stu said "Your weight and mine in the same place might break the ice. Besides, I'd be scared for myself so far out, so why I let you do it I don't know. Look, do me a

STEPHEN DIXON

favor—" and Isaac said "But it's all right, and everything looks beautiful from out here. Really, you should come out, Uncle Stu." Suddenly he disappeared. Went down, ice went up, there was a big splash, then a hole of about three feet across and he was gone. "Oh God, no," Stu screamed, and started to run to the hole, saw a hand pop up, stopped and walked when he heard ice cracking around him, hand disappear, then a hand trying to grab the edge of the ice, both hands grabbing it now, then Isaac's face half over the ice, hair drenched, cap gone, teeth chattering, looking scared as he tried to claw his way onto the ice, then both hands sliding back into the water and his head disappearing and then his hands shooting straight out of the water and his head popping up again. "Stay up, stay up," Stu was yelling as he walked fast as he could without having the ice crack. "Don't yell or say anything. Save your strength; I'm coming." He was about twenty feet away when he heard ice cracking from several places around him. He got down on his belly and started pushing himself to the hole. "Stay up, stay put, don't go down. Hold onto the ice, try to hold it." Isaac grabbed the edge of the ice with one hand just as Stu reached him. He grabbed that hand and pulled him up a little and then put one and then his other hand under Isaac's arms and edged backwards and started pulling him out. "A little more, little more, push!" Stu said, and Isaac was out of the water. "Now we got to be careful. I'm going to move backwards while dragging you, so try to make yourself light and don't try to stand. I'll do all the work." "I can't move," Isaac said. "I can't do anything. I'm so cold. My feet feel gone. I'm sorry for what I did, Uncle Stu, I'm sorry," and he said "Shut up, just let me get you to land. And it's okay, it's okay, you'll be fine." He took Isaac's coat off, put his own coat on him and, both on their bellies, dragged Isaac and Isaac's coat for about twenty feet till he couldn't see water through the ice as he could near the hole. "Now you can stand. No, let's be extra safe and go another ten feet," and dragged him about twenty feet more and stood up and pulled Isaac up and held him up and said "Good, but now we shouldn't walk too close together. I'd carry you, but then we'd really be too much weight. We got to get you to a warm spot, though. There's a lean-to with some fireplaces over there, so you have to start walking to where I'm pointing—that way." Isaac shook his head and Stu said "Walk, I said. You'll be fine once you get started and it'll help get the blood flowing in your legs again." "I meant the car. If you get it warm I can sit in it." "You're right; what a dope I am. Now try walking. I'll follow about ten feet behind." Isaac tried walking, fell. "Then crawl, but get there some way." Isaac crawled to land, Stu behind him with Isaac's coat. "Too slow, too slow," after Isaac had crawled about forty feet, and he picked him up, tested the ice, it seemed solid, and carried him to the car, turned the engine on, got all of Isaac's clothes off, wrapped him in a blanket and a couple of towels and put his socks and shoes on Isaac's feet, drove around the park to get the car heated up faster, left Isaac in the car with the engine running and got a fire going in a lean-to fireplace and started drying Isaac's shoes and clothes. Later Isaac came out wearing Stu's coat and the blanket and sat beside him close to the fire. "I'm hungry," and Stu said "We'll get something after. First your clothes and shoes, because this sweater isn't doing it for me and my feet are freezing with only a towel around them. But you're not too cold?" and Isaac said "It's warmer here than your car. Your heater doesn't work too well when you're not driving." When the clothes and shoes were dry and Isaac said every part of his body felt normal again, they went to a coffee shop for sandwiches and soup and coffee and then to the grandparents' house. "Remember," Stu said in the car, "not a word of it or we'll both be up shit's creek. Sorry for the bad language, I'm supposed to be a better influence on you, and your father would be the first one to tell me, but you know what I mean." "So, have fun with Stu?" Zee said when they were all in the living room having drinks and cheese and crackers, and Isaac said "Yeah, a lot," and looked at Stu and Stu looked back blankly, the only signal he could think to give him not to say anything or give anything away by looking at him right after he answers. "Why, what happened?" she said and Stu said "What do you mean? We went to a state park, Crispin Park or something, named after an American Revolution patriot, I think. About fifteen miles from here, inland, and then drove around a little and went for a bite. A nice clean simple place on the road between the park and here. An Italian name but good wholesome American food. New England clam chowder about the best I've ever had. No corn starch; the real thing," though he hadn't had it—Isaac had had chicken noodle soup—but had seen it listed on the blackboard. "Delmoni's, that's the name of the place." "I know it," she said. "It is quite good for lunch. Been around forever. But you guys still look like you're hiding something. Come on, out with it," and Stu said "Out with what? What could we be hiding?" and Isaac said "Yeah, what could be wrong? We had fun. We made a fire in an outside fireplace in the park. Or inside, but in an outside inside place. What's it called again, Uncle Stu?" and he said "You mean a lean-to?" "Lean-to, that's it. We also slid on the lake ice there, but only near the beach. Nobody else was around. I could yell like a maniac if I wanted while I slid and nobody would hear." "You did yell like one," Stu said, "and I can't vouch that nobody but I heard you." "I did, that's true. It was great. Made me want to buy ice skates so I could skate for real, but that'd be silly for just one or two weeks a year." "Okay," she said, "nothing happened. You had fun. Good. That's why we come here and to see Dyed and Babushka. But the two of you, your looks to each other—I'm curious what they mean." "What looks?" Stu said. "Leave the young men alone," her mother said. "Nothing went amiss and Stuart did you a great service by taking Isaac for the afternoon and allowing you to see friends. Isaac for certain had more fun with him than if he had been left with Dad and me." Stu for the last twenty years had wanted to tell Dan what happened that day. Isaac was recently divorced from his second wife, had a child, had never finished high school, had had many different jobs and done lots of interesting and adventurous things. Drove from Cairo to Capetown in a Land Rover with a girlfriend. Lived in Mongolia in a mud hut for a year. Later snuck into Tibet and was caught by the Chinese after a month at a forbidden Buddhist monastery and put under house arrest. Was a fire warden living alone for months in an observation tower for several summers and also a firefighter dropped from airplanes into forests in Western states. Owned a sawmill in Alaska, trained dolphins in San Diego, set up and led camera safaris in Kenya, was the official White House photographer for a while and was now an acupuncturist and Chinese herbal doctor in Hawaii. And Stu had prepared several times how he was going to tell Dan about the near drowning. "I never told you this because I thought you'd be furious at me. Now that Isaac's twenty... thirty... forty..." but never did it. Let it come from Isaac, he thought. Or Dan might think it silly that Stu hadn't brought it up before. And maybe Isaac had told Dan long ago but neither of them had said anything to Stu about it. Well, Isaac he only spoke to on the phone about once every five years. And it was possible Dan had forgot to tell Stu what Isaac had told him or hadn't thought it important enough to talk about anymore. Or Dan might not have wanted Stu to think he was reprimanding him or accusing him of having done anything wrong. He was sure Isaac had told Zee by now. In fact, long before now. She might even have squeezed it out of him the same day as the accident after Stu had left her parents' house. Stu had meant to ask Isaac that about ten years ago but forgot to next time he spoke to him. If she did know, she probably never told Dan. Out of consideration for Stu—Isaac would have told her that Stu didn't want Dan, out of all people, to know. And because she wouldn't have wanted Dan to think she'd been somewhat reckless with their son, leaving him with Stu, who knew nothing about taking care of kids that age— especially one who could be as free-spirited and strong-willed as Isaac—while she went off with friends for a few hours. Also, if she knew, she probably never told her parents, who were now dead, because she didn't want to worry them.

4

His younger daughter comes into the bedroom and says "Phone call for you." He's working at his work table and says "Darn, I'm right in the middle of something. That's why I turned the ringer off." "Next time tell us to tell callers you're busy and you'll call back," and he says "Next time I will, thanks," and gets up and picks up the phone receiver and says hello. "Uncle Stu, it's Manny." Years ago when Stu was around seven he went into Dan's room and stuck out his tongue at him. Okay, he was a kid and the youngest of four boys in the family and did things like that. Dan was in bed talking to another brother, Newton, in the bed across from his. It must have been Sunday morning. That's the morning everyone but their mother stayed in bed two to three hours longer and sometimes till noon. Now he thinks he also said something like this to Dan, and he chose Dan over Newton to say it to because he was a cross-country runner for his high school team and had won several big races—"You think you're so fast? Try and catch me," and got into a runner's stance by the door. "Why waste my time chasing you? I'll just stop you before you start," and got out of bed and when Stu bolted down the long hallway between their bedrooms (he shared his with Jay), Dan threw a pillow at him. It hit his back, he tripped and was thrown forward and split his head open against the edge of his bedroom door. "Jesus, what the hell you do?" Dan yelled, and then "Newt, get some towels; get the folks; he's bleeding like a stuck pig," and took his pajama top off and held it against Stu's head and then held a bath towel to it because the shirt was soaked with blood, and then another towel when the first one was soaked. "I know how to use a tourniquet," Dan said to their mother, "but how do you stop a scalp wound with one? Oh damn, see what happens when you start roughhousing, you nitwit," holding Stu's head in his lap. "Don't talk to him that way," she said; "he could go into shock." Her brother, a doctor, was called and drove down from Washington Heights. By the time he got there, ice cubes wrapped in dish towels had been applied to the gash and their mother pressed sterile gauze to it till the bleeding stopped. Uncle Ben wanted to stitch up the wound while Stu was lying on the hallway floor. "No needles," Stu screamed, "I don't want any in my head." "It'll be much better for you in the long run," Uncle Ben said. "The cut will close quicker, your head will heal faster, less chance of an infection, and the stitches won't leave as big a scar as you'll get if I don't put any in. You want to be handsome for the pretty girls later, don't you, and I'll freeze it with ice first so it won't hurt," but Stu kept screaming

"No, I don't want to, and the bleeding's stopped, so leave it alone." "Don't be such a chicken," Dan said. "If it does hurt any it'll only be for a second or two at a time, like pricking your finger or a little worse." "No, I said no," and Uncle Ben said he couldn't force it on him—"the needle might slip, and all this aggravation will only make him start bleeding again"—so Stu's head was never stitched. About ten years later, while Stu was combing his hair, Dan pointed to the scar and said "That where your head split open that time? Scar must be an inch and a half long. But it was some gash, I remember. The back hallway was flooded with your blood. You should have let Uncle Ben suture it as he wanted." "I know, but I was afraid of needles then. It's not as long as it used to be, though—maybe because my head's grown larger. If I really comb my hair carefully, I can get it to look like part of the hair's part, if maybe a bit wider." About thirty years later Dan stared at Stu's head on the side the scar was on and said "I've just realized. You've lost so much hair in front that your scalp's finally met your scar. Seems much smaller than I remember it. Then it was around the size of my pinky. What'd I do to give it to you... I know something." "It wasn't your fault. I was acting like a brat, baiting you, possibly even spit at you, so, all in good fun—nothing malicious—you threw a pillow at me and I tripped and hit the side of a door. I'd probably only have the most miniscule of scars now if I'd listened to you then." "Why, what'd I say?" "To let Uncle Ben, who drove down to take care of me—he was always doing that for us—to stitch it up." "Easy for me to say, but I can see why you would have been scared of a needle if that was it. Who wants someone sewing up his head with real thread and also without anesthetizing the area, which I'm sure was the case. We should have taken you straight to Roosevelt and had it done there. They would have numbed the scalp or if necessary put you out, and you wouldn't have felt a thing. I wonder if Dad was trying to save money by not taking you to a hospital. It'd be just like him. What a character he was."

5

"Dad, telephone, it's Uncle Dan." "Stu?" Dan says. "Mom's taken a turn for the worst. If you want to see her you should come now. We're not taking her to the hospital this time. The doctor's been here and said she's not coming out of it and that if we keep her comfortable it'll be better for her and all of us if she dies here." He makes arrangements for someone to look after Janice and take the kids to school tomorrow and pick them up. On the train, a few seats in front of him, he sees someone he knows. The fellow points to the empty seat next to Stu and mouths he'll move to it. When he comes over, Stu, still standing, says "Listen, I'd love to talk, but I got word today my mother's dying, which is why I'm going to New York, so I just want to ride alone." "Sure thing; I understand. Never lost a parent myself, but I know it can't be easy." "This is my second," and the guy says "I'm sorry. I guess it's what we have to expect—the kids of the parents. Good luck, and see you under better circumstances," and goes back to his seat. The train's on time; the guy he knows must have got off earlier. He subways uptown, runs to her building several blocks away hoping she's still alive. He's carrying an overnight bag and two books and it's tough running with them. He stops a block from her building, pants, thinks no, you got to run; you don't want to miss her by just a minute, and runs the rest of the way. He has a set of her apartment keys and lets himself in. "Dan, hello, it's Stu," he says, going to the back. "Rosalie, or whoever, don't be frightened; it's Eleanor's son, Stuart." She's still in a coma. Only the woman who looks after her weekends is there. "Your brother left an hour ago. He thought you'd be here sooner, but he was here all night so needed to get home and some sleep, and knew you were coming. If anything changes—the doctor said she can go on like this another day—you're to call him, not the doctor." He sits beside his mother for a few hours. She seems peaceful, breathes lightly. He says her name and "Mom?" and "Mommy?" a few times but she doesn't respond. Someone calls asking for her and he says "She's sleeping now and I'll tell her you called." Then she starts choking and he holds her up and pats her back to get the phlegm up and lots of liquid spills out of her mouth and nose and her eyes quickly open and close and she dies. He rests her back on the bed, exchanges looks with Rosalie. "That's it," she says. "I've seen it before and that's how it always goes." He calls Dan a few minutes later from the phone on the night table. Melody answers and says Dan's sleeping. "Mom died and he wanted me to call him." "Of course; I'm so sorry, Stu," and gets Dan. "Melody told me," Dan says.

"When did it happen?" "About ten minutes ago. She was all right till she suddenly got agitated, and then it was pretty quick." "You're absolutely sure of it? Did you check her heart and breath?" "All of it and so did Rosalie. There's no sign of life. Rosalie says she's seen three of the elderly women she's taken care of die like this. They start choking, have to bring up phlegm, remain in a coma but open their eyes, and then the eyes close, or once one's didn't, but the body goes limp and they're dead." "You'll have to call the Fire Department and EMS. It's the law in New York, the doctor said. I left the numbers by the kitchen phone. No, wait for me. If there's no traffic, I'll be there in forty minutes. I don't want them storming in and taking over the place and maybe breaking a couple of her bones while they go through the routine of trying to revive her." Dan gets there, puts his ear to her mouth and nose, feels her chest, listens to it, checks her pulse. "She's still warm but not alive. Any movement you see in her torso is just gas." He calls the Fire Department and EMS. When he gets off the phone, Stu says "I'm so sorry for her. What a miserable last ten years she's had." "And before that with Dad and his illness and Deborah's, taking care of them both at one time for a few years. What a women, huh? We were lucky," and they start crying and hug each other. "Very nice, very nice," Rosalie says. "It's good to get it out. But remember, you got to call your sisters. They phoned a lot last night," and Dan says "Right," and calls them, one in Connecticut and the other in California. "All right if I go now?" Rosalie asks Dan. "Nothing more for me to do, and it's been a long night." "Would you mind just cleaning up the apartment a little first? I want it to look neat." She does and gets her things together and Dan takes her address so he can send her a check for their appreciation for the way she looked after their mother the last few years. Rosalie leaves, comes back and says "There's a whole troop of firemen at the door. Six of them, two with what look like breathing and resuscitation equipment." "We got a report of a death here?" the lead fireman says, and Dan says "Our mother, about an hour ago in her sleep." "We have to make attempts to resuscitate before we can confirm she's dead." "Believe me, she's dead. You don't have to work on her." "Still, it's the city, so no matter how long you say she's been dead, we got to try," and puts his hand on Dan's shoulder to move him aside. Each of them is over six feet and young and looks strong. Dan's short, slimly built, but he pushes the man's hand off and says "Nobody's touching her. I said she's dead. If you can't verify it without working on her, we'll wait for EMS or someone from the city's coroner's office to examine her." "You a doctor?" "No, but I know when someone's dead. I've been in the army. I also covered a couple of wars as a reporter. I saw enough to know what's dead or not. And that woman who was here? She's not a nurse but she's taken care of plenty of elderly people before they died, and she checked and double-checked to make sure my mother was dead." "That still doesn't make either of you experts. Please, with all due respect, sir, let us get by or we'll have to get a cop in here." "You can go if you promise only to look at her. No banging her chest or sticking a tube down her throat or a breathing mask on her. Even if there was a slight chance you could bring her back, which there isn't, we wouldn't want you to and neither would she. She's suffered enough."

"Okay," the fireman says, "just let us see her." "One of you should be enough." "Okay, you win; I'll do it," and Dan steps away from the door. The fireman goes into the back room, which used to be what the family called the breakfast room but for the last five years has been their mother's bedroom, her bedroom upstairs in this duplex being too hard for her to climb to. The fireman listens to her chest, puts his ear over her mouth. "Mind if I feel her forehead and hands and check for pulse?" and Dan says "No, go ahead." The fireman does. "Okay, I'm satisfied. But someone dies at home with no doctor present, EMS has to look at her too." EMS comes a few minutes later. The fireman says to them "She's finished; I checked. But do your job," and one EMS person picks up her hand, holds it a few seconds, lets it down gently, nods to the fireman and writes out a report and says "Who do I give this to?" and Dan says "I'll take it." Firemen and EMS leave. Soon after that a doctor from the coroner's office comes, examines her, gives the death certification to Dan. Two police officers are already there, ask Stu to briefly describe her death, talk to the doctor, one of them says to Dan "Let's see the death paper," looks it over and says "Fine. You can contact the funeral home anytime you want to pick up the body." Stu calls the number on a funeral home business card Dan gives him. Harriet comes. "Sorry I'm late. I got stuck in traffic on the Merritt and then couldn't find a garage that wasn't filled. I know I should've been here to stay with you last night," she says to Dan, "but I was too upset. Mom in back?" Then several nieces and nephews and their spouses. They all sit or stand in the back room till the funeral people come, ask them to leave, spend about a half hour in there, wheel her out in a sack on a gurney to the hearse outside. "Everything's already taken care of," Dan says to Harriet and Stu when they go back inside. "Funeral arrangements. Mom wouldn't have wanted anything formal in a funeral home or synagogue. She wasn't agnostic but I know she would have disliked having a rabbi give a big spiel over her when he didn't know her from Adam, so I thought we'd do it ourselves at the gravesite. I'll write something up. A short summary of her life and what I know we all felt. And anyone else can write something or speak extemporaneously about her. And a simple coffin. I've already selected one. Did all this weeks ago, without telling her, of course. Pine; no hardware on it. Simplest and least expensive they had. What's the sense of paying through the nose for one we're only going to see for twenty minutes, and she also hated anything garish or wasteful, so I'm sure she would have approved." "Mom was afraid of worms," Harriet says; "all bugs." "Maybe we should have her cremated," Stu says. "I recall her once saying that's what she wanted." "When?" Dan says. "Never to me. She said she wanted to be buried between Dad and Deborah—that she had saved that spot. Anyway, it's all been paid for and arranged, not that we couldn't change it. The funeral home's been told not to alter her body—not even makeup—in any way. All they're to do is keep her in a cool room till Tuesday and put her in the clothes Melody and I chose and gave them last week." "I wish you would've let me pick out the outfit," Harriet says. "She had certain ones she liked." "You're right, maybe I acted too hastily," Dan says. "If you want, get whatever outfit you want out of her closet and I'll bring it to the funeral home. But you know, the coffin's not going to be opened once she's in it, so I don't see the point of getting worked up about what she wears." "No open coffin?" Harriet says. "We can't," Dan says. "She's going straight to the cemetery from the funeral home and you're not allowed to open it there and you wouldn't want to." "But I want to see her once more. I didn't have enough time to say goodbye to her here. I want to be alone with her a few minutes." "Then see her today or tomorrow. Even if we had some sort of gathering at the funeral home before we went to the cemetery, an open coffin I definitely remember Mom saying she found tasteless and macabre." "I don't remember her saying anything like that," Harriet says. "But all right. I am going to the home the day of the funeral and ask them to open the box for me before she goes to the cemetery. Natalie will be here then and we'll go together, because she'll probably want to see Mom a last time too. And about the outfit? I'm sure the one you chose was good. Which one was it?" and Dan says "I forget. Melody will know. And you'll see when you go to the funeral home Tuesday. So that's about it. We'll all drive to the cemetery and meet the hearse there. If either of you thinks what I have in mind is too secular and wants to read a prayer at the gravesite— I know I don't—the funeral home or cemetery will have one of those little prayer books for the dead." "I'm almost sure Mom would like a prayer or two said for her," Harriet says. "Didn't she used to say them herself on Friday nights?" and Stu says "Only during the time Dan was captured by the Chinese and also for a few years before Deborah died. And yahrzeit for her parents. I remember the handkerchief or dishtowel over her head, her hands covering her eyes, and the candles and telling us not to blow them out." "She didn't do them for Dad, though," Dan says, "and she hasn't lit those Shabbat candles for more than thirty years. But you want to do it, Harriet, get the book at the funeral home when you go, or come with your own prayers." "I think I will." "So, anything either of you feel I left out? Because the kids are going to wonder what's taking us so long, and I'm sure they all want to go home." "No. Sounds good to me," Stu says. "I have no objections or anything else to add," Harriet says. "A very simple unritualized ceremony," Dan says, "or as much as we can make it one. And just the family, since all her siblings and their spouses are dead except for Uncle Abe, and he's too out of it to come." "There's Aunt Millie, Uncle Lester's wife," Harriet says. "But she's in Arizona and was always a recluse and kept her distance from the family, so I doubt she'd even be concerned Mom died." "Did Mom have any friends left?" Stu says. "Just Margaret on the block," Dan says. "She's been Mom's only friend for years." "Of course, how could I forget? Once a week or so the two of them having drinks and cheese and crackers here. Mom always looked forward to it. So she should be invited; I could drive her." "Not possible," Dan says. "She's in a hospice uptown dying from cancer, her son told me the other day. She could even be dead by now, though Harry, his name is, would have called me. I told him to because I wanted to go to the funeral." "I'm sorry," Stu says; "what a nice lady. Then it's only us like you say, and maybe a few cousins." "There's only one Mom would want there," Dan says; "Eliot," and Stu says "Eliot and Penny then. I'll call them. Harriet will give me their number, unless you want to call them, Harriet," and she says "Fine. And Rosalie should be invited too, and Dolly and Mariah, the weekday women," and Dan says "I've got their numbers. They might have a problem finding the time to come—the agency will probably assign them to other patients by then—but it's worth a call. I'll do it. So, my dear sister and brother, it's been a trying few days but now it's over and we all know what we have to do. I don't know what I mean by that. Just that it's been rough on us all, and for Mom's sake, since the last two months have been hell for her, I'm glad it's over." Stu and Janice had sublet their New York apartment, so he spends the night here, collects lots of photographs of his parents and grandparents and early ones of all the children from the bottom drawers of the breakfront in the foyer and the night table by her bed and puts them in his overnight bag, and next morning trains back to Baltimore. He and his family drive in that afternoon and stay at a hotel, since Janice and the girls don't want to sleep in his mother's apartment, and go to the funeral the next day. Dan speaks at it: "We lay to rest a dear and kind and loving mother, an adoring and generous grandmother, a beautiful, gracious, energetic woman with a sharp wit, an outspoken mind, an abundant curiosity, a great intelligence and, when she wasn't being maudlin and depressed, and God knows she had every reason to be—losing three children, taking care of her ailing husband for ten years and her youngest daughter for more than twenty, plus many other difficult things—my own imprisonment in China, for instance, and Dad's in Sing Sing—a rich sense of humor and zest for life. That's it for me. Anyone else want to speak?" No one does, so they bury her.

6

He's heading to the kitchen for a snack, passes Dan's photo on the fireplace mantel, stops and goes back to look at it. He put it there a few days after Dan died three months ago, the only photo he could find of him as an adult. It was taken at Stu and Janice's wedding twenty years ago. The ceremony and reception were held in their one-bedroom apartment in New York. Natalie shot a roll of film with her camera and a friend of his and Janice was given their camera and two rolls of film to take photos, but none of the friend's came out. "I may have put the film in wrong," the friend said. "Both rolls?" Stu said, trying not to show his anger. "You said you were a good photographer and knew cameras, because these pictures were very important to us." "I am a good photographer and I do know cameras, especially one as uncomplicated as yours. So now I'm thinking there was something wrong with your camera or you gave me film that had been exposed." Only half the photos Natalie took came out, and one was this one of Dan, or actually, Dan and Stu. Dan's behind him, squeezing Stu's shoulder, and they're both smiling. Stu cried during the ceremony. Dan might have too. He was standing next to Stu, had given him the rings when the rabbi asked him to, but Stu's eyes were teary from the time the ceremony started till a little after he and Janice were pronounced married. He looks a bit teary though very happy in the photo, so it must have been taken soon after the ceremony. Stu had gone through all his own photos looking for one of Dan. Then through Janice's, and she had about ten times as many as he, in a large cardboard box, most in the envelopes they came back in from the film developer, but they were all of her and them and their daughters and her parents and friends and of gardens and flowers and Russian churches and some just of cupolas and many of the cats she's had. Then he remembered the wedding photos and thought maybe out of the twelve or so that came out there was one with Dan in it. He asked Janice "What happened to our wedding photos—I haven't seen them in years?" and she said "They're where they've always been, or since we moved here—in an album on the desk in my studio, no doubt hidden under a pile of things. Why, you looking for one of Dan?" and he said "Yeah, I can't find any except kid shots with all the brothers and sisters but me, for some reason. Even one where he's holding Deborah, though looking afraid he's going to drop her, a week or two after she was born." "I know there's one of him in the wedding bunch; he's patting your back." He got the album and pulled out the photo and stood it up against Janice's jewelry box on their dresser, thinking he'd look at it more because the clock and phone were there. The box has no jewelry in it, but she keeps it there because the kids bought it for her. Her jewelry, what she has left of it—most was stolen when the house was broken into last summer while they were in Maine—she keeps in a lower dresser drawer so she can reach it from her wheelchair. But he kept finding the photo on the floor. That probably had something to do with his younger daughter fiddling with it while she was on the phone or she or someone else walking by it so fast that it was swept off the dresser. So he put it on the mantel. Nobody touches the mantel much except the cleaning woman, who comes every other Thursday and cleans it about once every two months. And when she dusts the mantel and everything on it—he's seen her—she puts everything back where it was. So he passes the photo a lot, sometimes stops to look at it, and sometimes several times a day. One night when he was drinking and thinking of Dan and feeling very sad, he turned the living room light off, lit a candle on either side of the photo and put his elbows on the mantel and got so close to the flames while staring at the photo but especially Dan that his face start-ed to burn and he had to jump away. He also broke down after a while and then blew the candles out and turned the lights back on. Stu was six inches taller than Dan, and though the photo's only from their waists up, the difference in their height shows. They look like brothers in it, and much closer in age. Almost the same nose: Dan's is smaller—he had the smallest in the family other than for their mother—and more pugged. Same high cheek-bones—also their mother's—and strong chin with a dimple in it: all four brothers did, which they got from their father. They both have more hair in the photo. Dan's started to recede, it seemed, when he was around sixty, but just a small patch in back and a bit at the temples. Stu's started receding when he was fifteen, but it was slow and he still had some hair on top in the photo—he doesn't now. Their hair is brown in it. Stu's is all gray now, in some places—sideburns and right above the ears—white. Dan's was brown when he died, with gray flecks. Stu and Jay's hair— Jay was three years older and two inches taller than Stu—must have come from their father, who was bald like Stu but around Dan's height. Dan and Newton's hairline—Newt was fourteen months younger than Dan and a half-inch taller—must have come from their mother's side, since two of her three brothers and her father had lost none of their hair, and all were considered tall. Jay's hair started receding when he was thirteen and went quicker than Stu's, so had he lived—he was on a ship that disappeared in the Atlantic when he was twenty-seven and at the end of a year-long round-the-world trip—he probably would have been balder than Stu. Newt, who died at nineteen—murdered in Turkey in a botched robbery while he was on shore leave—had thick kinky hair—the only kinky-haired redheaded person in the family and which had to have come from some distant Polish forebear. Had he lived, there was a good chance he would have continued to have the same hairline as Dan's. My brother, he thinks, staring at the photo. That was some day, the wedding, eh? Everyone there but Jay, Newt, Deborah and Dad. Food was good; half of it made by Janice and him, the rest from Zabar's. Great wine and champagne. A friend of Janice— a concert pianist—played before the ceremony began: Ravel,

Debussy, Satie. She was French. And when they walked down the aisle—Dan was already in front with Janice's parents and her best friend—the first prelude of Bach's *Well-Tempered Clavier*. Simple ceremony; two thin wedding bands. A rabbi, to please Janice's father, but nothing about the Jewish faith, and Stu had told him beforehand he wasn't going to step on any glass. Coldest January 10th in New York on record, the *Times* said the next day. After, Stu walked Dan and Melody to their car parked in a spot that someone had previously dug out of a three-foot-high pile of snow. Snow from a few days ago. It would have been too cold to snow that day, or that's what he'd heard. Temperature now around zero or two or three below. Their apartment building and the parking spot were on Riverside Drive, so maybe five to ten degrees colder down there, with the river and wind. As Dan was about to get into the car he said "That was the nicest wedding I've ever been to. I can't imagine it being surpassed in any way: food, drink, elegance, restraint, simplicity, all-around good feelings, genuine good taste. Even the rabbi, and I usually don't like those guys and how they speak and what they say, was okay. You know I'm an emotional guy but cover it up most of the time and sometimes I might even seem hard—I don't show my real feelings very much, I'm saying—but I'm so damn happy for you both. So happy I can't tell you how much," and he started to cry. "What happened, he had too much to drink?" and Melody said "No, if that were so, I wouldn't let him drive," and then she started crying. "Jesus, both of you; it's not that bad. You lost a brother but gained a sister-in-law. All right, stupid joke. Get out of here already, and watch out for black ice." He stayed in the street to wave them off. "Go home, it's freezing cold," Dan said, getting in the car. The car wouldn't start. Dan and he pushed it out of the parking spot while Melody sat behind the wheel. They pushed it along Riverside Drive for about fifteen minutes till the engine started, and then Dan got behind the wheel, rolled down the window and said "Toot toot," and drove off. Stu went back to the apartment. A few people were left whom he'd promised to drive home to the West Seventies and Sixties. "Give me ten minutes to thaw out," he said, and was helping Janice clean up the place when Dan called on the house phone downstairs. The car had stalled three blocks away. "Melody's with me, and she's so cold that I don't want her going out again till the car's started and warm. I'd call a garage but it might be hours before they come on a night like this. You mind helping me out again, but this time you driving and just I push?" "Oh no you don't. I'm warmed up, even had a shot of cognac and put on dry socks, so you drive and I push. —Okay, folks," he said to the people he was going to drive home, "you'll have to wait a while longer. Family comes first. Anybody want to help out in pushing my brother's car, be my guest," and the only man said "Wish I could, but my heart," and one of the women said "I'm really not dressed for it, especially the shoes." Dan and he jogged to the car, Dan got behind the wheel and Stu pushed. He slipped a few times, got wet and thought "So what? It's for my brother. It's invigorating and good for a laugh too. "What did I do at the end of my one and only wedding? Pushed my brother's car for an hour when it was ten below and I was getting soaked. What did you?"' Car finally started. Stu got in, they stayed parked with the motor going for about five minutes, and drove back to the apartment building. Stu got Melody, and Dan said to him through a crack in the window "I'm so sorry I had to put you through all this. I think we got it going for good, though. You're a great brother. I've never told you; I probably never will again. Ah, maybe I will when I'm much older and so addled that I forgot I already told you it once. And I still think it was the most beautiful and moving wedding I've ever been to." "Janice planned the whole thing," Stu said. "Whoever did it, and I'm sure you had a hand in it too, it was the best. Goodnight," and they drove off, Melody waving and blowing kisses to Stu. The people he was going to drive home had left. "They called our car service," Janice said. "You'd done more than enough on your wedding day, they said, and we still had the place to clean up. They also apologized for not being able to help you push Dan's car and hoped you understood why they couldn't." "It's all right. I'm glad I did it alone."

7

Stu was making Janice breakfast. He put a flame under the tea kettle, spooned vegetable powder into a tall mug of diluted cranberry juice—quarter juice, three-quarters warm water—mixed it around with a fork till the powder had dissolved, and went to the back and handed her the mug and put her morning pills into her mouth three at a time. While she drank the juice—it was fairly thick from the powder, so she drank it slowly—he put a flame under her soup (it was always the same breakfast, though the soup, fruit, bread and spread might change), put a slice of kamut bread into the toaster (she was on a wheat-free diet), and sliced half a banana onto the plate the toast would go on. Toast popped. The soup seemed ready—she didn't like it too hot—and he poured it into a Styrofoam mug and also poured some of the now boiled water into a taller Styrofoam mug that had a kukicha teabag in it. He got the bread knife from the dish rack by the sink to spread butter on the toast, looked around for the butter dish but had forgotten to take it out of the refrigerator when he took out the bread and juice. He hadn't grabbed a regular knife because the only knife in the silverware cup in the dish rack was the bread one and he thought he could just as easily spread with that, and the paring knife he used for the banana wasn't a good one to spread with. Holding the bread knife in his right hand, he opened the refrigerator to get the butter. But it'll be too hard to spread—it's better when it's been out for ten to fifteen minutes— so he should use the hummus he made yesterday and which Janice likes on her toast as much as the butter. He was holding the door open with the hand that held the bread knife and look- ing inside the refrigerator for the container of hummus when somehow the tip of the blade got caught in the top side shelf and snapped out of it before he could push the door back far enough to release it, and went into the side of his neck. Oh no, he thought, because he felt blood and knew if the knife had pierced the neck artery he could be dead in minutes. He felt his neck and it wasn't shooting out blood, just leaking it, so the knife must have only nicked the skin. He put the knife down, wiped the blood off his neck with a paper towel. There wasn't much and he touched the cut with his finger and it didn't seem long or deep. He wiped the cut again and there was almost no blood now. Thank God, he thought. He found the hummus behind a bowl in the refrigerator, spread some on the toast with the bread knife, cut the toast in half and brought the soup and plate of food to her. "You're not going to believe this but a minute ago I came as close to killing myself as I think I ever have," and she put her hands to her mouth and said "Oh my gosh." "It's all right, I'm fine, just a nick in the neck with a bread knife," and he showed her where, "but it was close." "How'd it happen?" and he said "Let me get you set up first." He put the food down, opened a folding chair and put it next to her, put the food on it and turned on the radio, which was on the sink, to the public radio station. "Maybe today I'll just listen to my tape player. Joseph Frank's Dostoevsky bio *The Years of Ordeal*, fifty to fifty-nine. It's quite interesting." "Good, you have something you like," and got her tape player from her studio and set it on the floor beside the folding chair. "My tea, and could you turn off the radio? If I try to reach it from here I'll probably knock it over." He shut the radio off and got her tea. "So," he said, "the tale of the neck and the bread knife. The tip of the blade got caught in the inside of the refrigerator door. I don't know how—I know I was holding the knife but looking the other way into the refrigerator for your hummus—and it sprung out before I could pull it out and went into my neck. Fortunately—" and she said "Put something on it." "I will. But you can imagine. Two months after a tree falls on Dan, me getting killed this way. Is it the carotid artery?" and she said "Yes, on both sides of the neck." "Not only what it would have done to you and the kids, but my sisters: their surviving brothers gone within two months of each other in freak accidents." He looked in the mirror. Bleeding had stopped. "I don't know what prevented the knife from going in deeper. It certainly had the force, after springing out of the door, to plunge all the way in." She put her hands over her mouth again. "Please stop. Look at the good side of it: that nothing worse happened," and he said "I'm sorry. And you're right; I will." He put rubbing alcohol on a wad of toilet paper and left the room. "My phone," and he said "Damn, forgot," and got the portable phone off the dresser and put it on the folding chair. Back in the kitchen, he looked at the bread knife on the counter. What would he have done if it had punctured the carotid artery? Blood would have been everywhere, and a lot of it, fast. Right after it happened could he have dialed 9-1-1 or yelled for Anita to? Even if she did, would they have got here in time to save him? They're at the fire station about three miles away. Suppose the ambulance or emergency crew there were out on another call? If they were and no backup team from another fire station was able to get here by now, he'd probably already be dead. Would he have been able to put a dish towel around his neck—the only kind of cloth towel in the kitchen? Or maybe there's a bath towel in the washer waiting to be washed and he could have got that out. Would he even have had the strength to do that—open the washer, pull the towel out—or pull any absorbent material out and wrap it around his neck? If he did, or if Anita had brought him a towel, would that have been able to stop the bleeding? Doubts it. Only a tourniquet could and where would he have put the tourniquet or instructed Anita to, if he could, and would she have been able to do it? Would she instead have been so horrified by all the blood and the sight of him getting weaker—dying in front of her—that she couldn't do anything but call someone or run outside to yell for help? It would have been too late for neighbors to come and none of them are doctors. And Janice was in back, and if Anita had wheeled her to the kitchen, what could she have done to help him?

Would he have been strong enough to get back there himself? Why would he have wanted to other than, when it first happened, to wake Anita up and tell them—just the sight of him would tell them—to get help. Could he have got in the car and driven to the hospital emergency entrance about five minutes away? No. If the carotid artery was hit he was sure he wouldn't have been able to do anything to help himself from the start. Was his accident in any way related to Dan's? Doesn't see how. Just coincidence, two accidents, and if he'd died, two deaths coming very close to each other. His poor wife, if it had happened. Not just losing him, but who'd take care of her after? His daughters; the older one was away at college and would have to hear of it over the phone. His sisters. Both would think are they also doomed to die in an accident or in some freakish way? First Newton '46, stabbed to death on a Turkish street, killers never caught. Then Jay, fourteen years later, on a freighter that went down with no survivors—all that was found were a couple of life preservers—probably hit by an iceberg or somehow split apart because of faulty construction or capsized in a storm. Six years later—though she had the disease since she was four—Deborah, from a rare cancer, von Recklinghausen's, which was almost always benign and not a killer. Their father in '72 from multiple disorders and complications—diabetes, Parkinson's, heart trouble, little strokes, and late in life—this was practically unheard of, doctors said—showing early signs of the same hereditary disease Deborah had but four years after she died of it. The remaining children in the family were told to get annual body scannings for it from then on, but after the first year or two none did. And just general deterioration from old age for their mother in '97—she did have emphysema for twenty years and when she was 80 she stopped smoking and in six months was rid of it—and five years after she died, Dan. He was running, tree snapped at the base in a windstorm and crushed him. Got to be more careful, Stu thought, but how careful can he be to avoid accidents like the knife one? Bread knife to butter with? What was he thinking? Thought it'd be simpler to use it than to get a butter or dinner knife out of the silverware drawer. One spread over a single slice of toast, that was all he wanted from it. But he should have thought a bread knife wouldn't spread butter well. And more careful when he drives. Don't go over the speed limit anymore or not by more than five to ten miles. That sort of thing. Not try to make the light when it's turning red. He washed the bread knife, put it back in the silverware cup in the dish rack, point down, which he did with every knife with a pointed tip. He felt the cut on his neck. It was wet, had bled since he last touched it, or maybe that was the rubbing alcohol he'd put on it. No, that would have evaporated almost instantly. He wiped the blood off with his handkerchief and thought that should probably be the end of the bleeding, for there was even less of it than the last time he touched it. He reboiled the water in the kettle, poured some into a Pyrex measuring cup and took it to his wife; she usually wanted a second mugful. "More?" and she said "Thanks." She held the mug out and he was about to pour but then said "Put it on the chair. I don't want to burn you." "Smart move," she said, "I don't blame you after what happened. Let me see it." He poured the water and turned around so she could see the cut.

"I'd put antibiotic cream on it and a Band-Aid." "Antibiotic cream okay. A Band-Aid will look silly on my neck. People will think I'm hiding a hickey you gave me." "Do it," and he said "It'll be fine without it and probably without the cream too. But you know what? It scared the living daylights out of me when it went in," and she said "I can see why. It's a bad cut." "It's not. But for a moment I thought I was a goner and that my life was going to rush right out of me while I lay on the floor." "You fell? You didn't tell me." "No. That if it had pierced the carotid I would have in seconds, no doubt, collapsed to the floor. Anyway, it's over, so let's forget it. I just have to be more careful with sharp knives from now on." He went back to the kitchen and got the bread knife and opened the refrigerator and wanted to reproduce the way the knife got stuck in the door, but couldn't find a place where it could have got caught. Just somewhere here, in the top shelf of the door, and then before he could do anything about it the knife, buckling under the pressure and something to do with his realizing it was stuck and perhaps overcorrecting the situation by pushing the door too far back, sprung out of wherever it was into his neck. Okay, enough; forget about it as you said.

8

Phone rings and one of Dan's kids answers it. "It's Stu. Could you get your dad, please?" Dan picks up and says "Stu?" and he says "I'm afraid it's happened. Dad died a half-hour ago. I'd have called sooner but it took me a while to get myself together to dial you. I'm okay now, I think. I'll call Mom if you want, and the others. But maybe it'd be better, and truthfully, cheaper, with Natalie in California—I doubt I even have that many coins—if it came from you. I also won't be very good on the phone, do you mind?" "Of course not. How was it?" and he says "You mean Dad's going or me staying here overnight?" "Both. How'd he die, in his sleep?" and he says "He was fine, if you can call it that, state he was in all night—never getting out of his coma, sleeping peacefully till an hour ago. Then, he was still in the coma but making noise, having trouble breathing, stuff coming out of his nose—fluid. I tried comforting him—you know, those glycerol swabs for his lips, because they were dry, and patted his face with a damp rag because he was sweating. But he became more agitated, though never opened his eyes. Moaned, seemed to be in pain, thrashed around. I thought he'd rip off the oxygen mask and pull out the tubes in him, so I buzzed the nurse's station and a nurse came and quickly summoned doctors, who shooed me out of the room. Twenty minutes later—I didn't know if to call you then, but also wanted to stick around in case they wanted to speak to me—they came out and told me he'd died. They said he went naturally. All his vital signs were down to almost nothing and no breathing on his own, and since we signed that 'don't resuscitate form'..." "It's okay, you did what you could. I'll call Mom. Then, as I want to drive right down and take her to the hospital, could you call Harriet and tell her to call Natalie? I wish I'd been there instead of you, to give you a break after two nights straight, but you said you could do it." "I'm all right; just tired. I did manage to sleep in the chair in Dad's room a couple of hours. Not well, and maybe not sleep— Anyway, I don't want to hold you up, but we did the right thing by not having them resuscitate him if he stopped breathing and taking all his life support off, right?" and Dan says "Those machines only take you so far and he probably would have got even more distressed. And look, I'll call Harriet; you've done more than your share. Go and rest, and I'll see you soon." "It was fine, really. I'm the only one with no family, kids, and no real job and who lives in the city. And I brought some books and a notepad with me and actually got some work done." Dan comes to the hospital with their mother. Then Harriet and her husband and aunts and uncles.

Dan calls the funeral home to pick up the body, and he and Stu go there to make the final arrangements and choose a casket. The woman who leads them down to the basement says "Let's start with the first one; some very nice ones there." "Excuse me," Dan says, "but we know how this goes—we did it for our sister six years ago—so I want you to take us to the last room where the least expensive coffins are and point out the cheapest one. We'll no doubt buy it but I want to make sure it isn't made out of plywood." It's plain unvarnished pine. "This one okay with you?" Dan says, and Stu says "Anything you want; I'm not against economizing," and Dan tells the woman "Now remember, or maybe you can just remind them upstairs, because they tried to sell us everything under the sun last time: no hardware on it. If this is the only one you have of this model, then strip the hardware, because I know everything here costs extra. And no embalming or makeup or recorded music and electric candelabra around the coffin in the chapel, and the smallest chapel you have. We want it simple and unelaborate and as low-cost as we can get. The hearse to the cemetery I guess we're stuck with, and maybe one limo—that okay with you, Stu, for Mom?" and he says "She'll feel better in it than just a car." "Either my brother or I will come back later with a suit of our father's and that's what you put him in and close the coffin and nail it up." "Mom might want a last look," and Dan says "I've talked to her about it. She doesn't want the body shown nor a hired sitter by the coffin to read prayers for him overnight. As for a rabbi," he says to the woman, "my sister will get one from her synagogue." "Got it," she says. "If those are your instructions, they'll be followed to the letter."

Dan writes out a check in the office and Stu says "We should all contribute to it." "Don't worry, I'm getting it back from Mom. They put money away for it, just as they have enough cemetery plots for all of us if we want. But think I'm going to waste good time and dough on that crap? No ceremony or chapel for me. I'm going straight to the incinerator." "I think it's what I'll probably do too." Then Dan says "Let's have lunch; you must be starved. I know I am." "But Mom..." and Dan says "She'll be fine. Her sisters and Harriet will look after her much better than us, and she seems to be taking it okay—deep down it must be a relief." At lunch Dan says "He was quite the character, our father. But normal for his generation and financially strapped background. No shoes in the summer to save on the leather? He had to succeed. Worked all the time. Money and his practice and cronies were everything to him. Didn't spend much time with his family. Came home for dinner, ate, smoked a cigar and read the papers and his dental journals, and later turned the radio on in his room to semiclassical music and got ready for bed. Wasn't there when we might have needed him, but that put us on our own and made us more independent or reliant on one another. A lousy dentist, though great at extractions and making plates, who ruined half my teeth by neglecting them or working on them halfheartedly. Even saving on x-rays and Novocain when I had painful toothaches and needed drilling. I'm sure he did that with you too, since he certainly didn't improve on his lax habits with us and innate stinginess. Jesus, he was cheap. Those shoes he wore of everybody else's. And pocketfuls of individual toilet paper pieces he took from subway stalls and used for his nose. A fool sometimes too. Getting into trouble. Going to prison when Mom warned him what he was doing was wrong and he'd get caught, and leaving her stranded. Late at night she used to tell me how destitute we were and that what she was earning at Macy's and from the tenants was barely enough to keep us going, which scared the hell out of me but I knew it'd hurt her worse if I showed it. So I'd say, patting her back, 'Don't worry, we'll pull through,' and Newton and I worked as delivery boys and such after school, and those two summers Dad was gone. She could have sold the building, but they weren't going for much then and where would we have lived? But, all that said, he was affectionate to us and good to his sister and folks, so that was something. A better son and brother than anything else. Also, an occasional philanderer, according to Mom," and Stu says "Dad? I never heard that." "Oh yeah. Maybe at times even trading expensive dental work for nooky, though I'm sure he got more than his work was worth and possibly something like a new outfit for Mom thrown in, if the woman worked in the Garment Center, since he took pride in getting the better of any deal. She should have divorced him when I was a boy. I told her to then—Newt and I did—if he was making her so unhappy and doing such dumb things, but she always smiled at us as if saying 'What did we know?' We wanted her to hook up with someone who didn't mind that she had seven kids and who'd treat her the way she deserved. But I loved the old guy; we all did. And he never raised his hand once to any of us, far as I know, compared to the horror stories I've heard from friends. He was, as Grandpa Sam used to say—Mom's dad; you probably don't remember him," and Stu says "Sure I do. He was the only grandparent still alive when I was born. His stories about white cavalry horses and leading a charge against the Cossacks," and Dan says "That was Leibush, his *lantsman* who they took in and who worked in Grandpa Sam's bar and grill. 'A diamond in the rough,' he used to call him, and once to me 'They broke the mold when they made your dad.' God knows why he wanted to have children. And so many of them. An even dozen, he told Mom when they got married, and had to settle for only seven. And then what he went through with Newt and Jay's deaths. That took its toll. He never talked about it but he sure showed it whenever their names came up. Face would flush and eyes fill with tears. With Deborah, because he was so sick at the time too and we were expecting it, not as much. It's true he was a much better father when it was just me and Newton and Harriet, though he always preferred the boys over the girls, another thing I found pretty awful about him. Openly saying it in front of them sometimes. Jesus, I used to get angry at him for that. But when Jay came along and in quick succession you, Natalie and Deborah—even dozen be damned, he packed it in with fatherhood and only went through a few of the motions, like demanding we kiss his cheek when we said goodnight. And those bad jokes of his told over and over. 'If I had a nickel'—when I'd ask him for one and then no doubt when you did too, but by then it must have been a dime—'I'd build a fence around it.' And the one about the glazier—I forget." "When we were standing between him and something he wanted to see. 'Was your father a glazier?'" "Yes, but what did it mean?" and Stu says "That we weren't made of glass. That our father,

because he wasn't a glazier, couldn't have made us out of it."
"I never understood it and he said it dozens of times. Now that
I do, it wasn't a bad joke for Dad." "How do you think Mom will
hold up?" and Dan says "She's relatively healthy, outside of her
smoking and drinking, so she'll be okay for the time being. And
with Dad gone, she can start living again. There's something to
be said about someone dying who's been chronically ill for years,
for what it'll no longer take out of the people who looked after
him. I know Harriet and I weren't able to help out much. So if it
weren't for Mom and you we'd have had to put him in a depressing nursing home, and he wouldn't have lasted long there. He
was too sociable and happy-go-lucky a guy to be cooped up in
one, with family and what relatives and friends are left visiting a
few hours a day. He needed to be home and have Mom around
to see to him and you up the block popping in to give him his
shots and exercise him and take him to the park and so forth, and
the rest of us coming when we could." "Well, thanks for coming
down when you did and for always being there when we needed
you," and Dan says "What I did was nothing. I'm not ashamed
of it, though. I did what I was able to and knew Mom and you
were handling things just fine. So thanks."

9

Phone rings. He's too busy with schoolwork to get up to answer it. Anyway, during the day, nine times out of ten it's for Janice. Rings twice more and stops. Minute later she raps on the bedroom door with something—probably her reacher. "Yes?" "It's for you; phone. You didn't hear me yelling?" "No, and damn, I'm very busy." "It's Manny. Want me to tell him to call back, though it sounded important." "He probably wants advice where to send his stories. He's begun writing them again, Dan said, and that he might call. Okay," and she says "And keep your door open," and he gets up and gets the receiver off the dresser and says "Manny; what's up?" "It's Dad. Something terrible's happened." "He's not dead, is he?" and Manny says "I'm sorry, Uncle Stu; he is." "Oh no, oh my God." Later—days—he thinks every time something like this happens—someone tells him such bad news—he always says "Oh no, oh my God," and in that order.

Weeks later. He wants to call Dan to tell him of a good review his new book's getting in Sunday's *Washington Post*. He'd say something like "I don't know why I think it's important enough to call you, but here I am calling you. It might be the only paper that reviews it. I'm not kidding. None of the prepub review services did, partly because it's such a small and not-well-known publisher, but mostly because they sent it to them too late—but it's a beaut. It was read to me over the phone by the publisher's publicity director who's also the proofreader and head of marketing. Actually, she only called to say I was getting a good review in the *Post* this Sunday and I asked her to read it to me." He always called Dan first with good news. Not so with the birth of his children; called him third. First Janice's parents, then his mother. This time he even went to the phone on the dresser to dial Dan. Didn't lift the receiver, just put his hand on it and stopped himself and said "What're you doing? You crazy?" He'd just finished speaking to the publicist and telling Janice about the review, and then, back in the bedroom, thought of calling him. Dan always liked it when Stu told him something good that had happened to him or one of the kids. He'd only started calling Dan to tell him of a good review—he never got many reviews of any kind for his books—after Dan had called him a few years back and said "Why didn't you tell me?" and Stu said "What?" and Dan said "the *Times* review today. It would have given me something to look forward to this week." "It was only an in-brief and not even a long one, so I didn't think it a big deal." "It was short, smart, well written and favorable and made the reader think why didn't the editors give it a whole page, the reviewer seemed to get so much out of it and obviously had lots more to say. But the point is, I don't always read the in-brief page and might have missed it if Manny, who reads every word in the book section, hadn't told me of it when I called him today. From now on, let me know beforehand. You don't have to tell me of the bad ones, unless you want to talk about where the reviewers went wrong. But our family, we've gone through so much, we can use all the good news we can lay our hands on."

Months later. He'd like to call Dan about the last few rough days. Janice's medical setbacks, lots of work at home and school and the van breaking down again, and Dan was usually the person he told these things. Money problems also, but Stu never told him that because he knew Dan would want to give him money or a loan that as far as he was concerned Stu never had to pay back. Stu once said "Don't things like this happen to you and your family?"—this was last year. "Or maybe they do and you don't like griping about them as I seem to," and Dan said "No, everything's been running smoothly lately. The health of all of us, girls' spouses included and even our cat, has been good for years now and car and house problems negligible. My marriage has never been better, I don't know why. Maybe it's just my age and that I've slowed down some and am less of a tyrant and grouch and appreciate Melody much more than I used to but as I always should have, and also that I've more time to relax. Retirement's been good. We have money. Not a lot but enough to help out the kids if they need, and you too if it came to that, and when Mom's building's sold we'll all be in much better shape. I love seeing my kids and grandkids, which we do about once a week. And reading, running, occasionally fishing, having a good dinner, seeing a couple of people, but only a couple and only for drinks. Speaking to you. Never feeling pressured or rattled by anything anymore. Going to New Mexico twice a year to visit Isaac and his daughter. And something I put right at the top of my greatest pleasures' list: fresh coffee and solitude and quietness every morning while I read the *Times* in my easy chair. I honestly have no serious complaints and can say the last few years have been the best of my life. Although the first three with Zee and then Isaac in Washington were good and possibly even a little better because of my relative youth and a terrific job with brilliant colleagues and that she was the first love of my life and he my first child. But I feel—physically, emotionally, you name it—and I opened myself up here a lot more than I normally do, didn't I?—great."

Years before. Stu was around ten. Day or so after a heavy snowstorm in New York. Some snow might have still been falling. Seems to remember that. Or new snow falling on old. He and his friends Billy and Smitty were in front of his building, hiding behind or inside two snow forts they'd made. It was evening, very few cars coming down the street. When one did— clanky chains on the tires then—they'd pop up and throw snowballs at it. The aim was to smack the snowballs against the windows on the passenger's side. Once, the car stopped and driver got out and yelled something like "You stupid kids. What're you trying to do, get me killed? Use your goddamn brains," and then drove off. If he'd made a move to them they would have run. A man walked up the block wearing a derby.

Stu had only seen derbies in movies. The man was around fifty and as he was about to pass them—they were standing in the street behind their forts—Stu held up a snowball and made a gesture to his friends as if to throw it at the man and they nodded Do it, do it, and he threw it at the derby, wanting to knock it off as he'd seen boys do in movies. He really thought he could do it. He had good aim, was a good pitcher, and the snowball was the size of a baseball and packed tight. He hit the man in the back. "What the hell!" the man said, and started for them but slipped on the sidewalk and fell and began screaming. Stu and his friends ran up the block. About ten minutes later they came down the other side of the street and hunched behind a tall pile of shoveled snow to see how the man was doing. Dan was with him. Someone must have seen the man on the ground and rang Stu's bell, the first one on the roster, or Dan or someone in the family had heard the man screaming or seen him in front of the building from one of their second-story bedroom windows. Dan was just in a long-sleeved shirt and dress pants and was on one knee talking to the man. He must have seen Stu behind the snow because he yelled "Stu, get over here. I can use you." He came over with his friends, hoping the man wouldn't recognize him. "There's the rascal that thrown the snowball at me. I known it was him because he was the only of the three that had it in his hand when I passed them. You nitwit. You should've known better than to throw at anybody in this slippery weather." "Oh boy, are you in for some trouble," Dan said, and Stu said "I didn't mean it. I was throwing at the number 29 above our front door and by mistake he got in the way." "You was aiming for this, don't tell me," the man said, taking off his derby and swatting the snow off it. "I wasn't, for honest. I'm sorry, really sorry." "Mom's called for an ambulance," Dan said. "He's broken or sprained a leg and can't stand. You and your friends help me sit him up on Flo's stoop where I've put some newspapers," referring to the building next door which had a stoop to the second floor. Their building did when his parents bought it, but they renovated it where it now had steps down to the areaway. They tried moving the man to the stoop but he said it was too painful. "Let me sit where I am." "Go in for a couple of warm blankets," Dan said to Stu. "I don't want him freezing to death also." "What about you? You must be cold," and Dan said "Good idea; my parka. I might be out here a while." Ambulance came and the man was put on a gurney. Dan told the doctor he'd like to go along to make sure the man got set up okay and that the hospital knew his family was taking care of all the bills. Stu went inside, asked his mother if he could skip dinner tonight. "No, you have to eat. It's enough we lost one person at the table because of you." After dinner he did his homework and then waited in the dark at his parents' bedroom window for Dan to come home. It was around nine by now, a school day tomorrow unless school was called off because of the snow, which almost never happened, so he'd have to go to bed soon. Then he saw a cab pull up and Dan get out. He went downstairs and asked how the man was and Dan said "Not good. He broke a kneecap. You know how serious that is? It can never be fixed. He'll walk with a limp the rest of his life." "It *was* an accident, believe me." "Accident my eye. Like he said, you saw his derby and tried to knock it off. I did plead with the guy not to sue us.

Gave him a real sob story. That though we own the building, it brings in zero after expenses and our living in the first two stories of it because of the seven kids. And that my father lost his dental license years ago and was now a textile salesman and not doing well at it. He said because we're taking care of all his medical expenses and that I came to the hospital with him, he won't sue. That wasn't my intention, in taking him there, but I'm glad it helped. We were lucky you threw your snowball at such an understanding man. 'Boys will be boys,' he said when I left him, and even smiled about it. When I first spoke to him out front, I thought he was going to take us to the cleaners. He didn't want to overpenalize you, he said; that it seemed you felt guilty and remorseful enough. I don't feel as generous to you as that. You want to throw at one another, fine, break your heads for all I care, but to an old guy because he was wearing a funny hat? You knew the sidewalks were slippery and that old guys aren't so agile on their feet." "I forgot." "You forgot what, both? But if he can forgive you, I suppose I can too. I don't know about Dad, though, when he sees what it's going to cost. The insurance company's only going to cover so much. But okay, I lectured you enough, and I'm hungry. Did anything I say sink in at least?" "Yes. Everything. If you can tell Dad that and that it was sort of an accident, even if my snowball was the main cause of it, it'd help," and Dan said "We'll see." Stu, for about a year, worried he'd see the man limping up the street. And that when the man saw him he wouldn't be as generous anymore and would say something like "See this bum leg? That's all your doing and it's for life. I shouldn't have been so nice in not suing your family."

Dan had said the man lived two blocks away in a rooming house much like Flo's, but Stu never saw him again. His father just called him a stupid fool that night and didn't give him his allowance for two weeks, and that was the end of it.

10

Brother of a neighbor dies. Stu reads it in the *Sun*: long obituary with a photo. At first he got startled because he thought it was Peter, the brothers look so much alike. He'd met him at a party Peter and Terry gave when one of their sons graduated high school. Talked a while with him, mostly about what he did. Stockbroker. Stu wanted to know about it, not to invest but how it works. "How does one invest? How does the investor know when to pull out? What percentage of the profits does the broker make? Or am I showing my ignorance, besides maybe impertinence, and it's a straight fee from the start based on how much is invested? How much insider trading really goes on? What exactly is insider trading? Is it wise for anyone to invest who isn't a stockbroker?" Questions like that. And "Do you like what you're doing?" "You betcha. I love all the people I deal with, clients and coworkers, in good times and bad. Sometimes I even

get a terrific rush from it—something akin to prolonged ecstasy,
I can say with a little exaggeration—when the market's going to
hell and then suddenly rallies when you never expected it to and
we make a big killing just before the closing bell. It's the best job
in the world—and I'm not referring to the money—and I'm the
luckiest SOB there is to be working at it. What do you do?" Peter
and Terry lived up the hill from Stu. He and Janice have had
them down for drinks a couple of times, and once when they
threw a party for their immediate neighborhood: a dead-end
street (Bollington) that serves six houses up a fairly steep hill.
Stu's house is at the foot of it, thirty feet from the main road and
about 200 feet from the first house up the hill. The other houses are worth around three times as much as his and are at least
twice as large. Stu's jokingly called the area Bollington Heights
and his house the former quarters for the people who worked in
the other houses. William, the brother, was 42, the youngest son
and one of seven children, just like Stu. Stu didn't know Peter
was one of seven till he read the obituary. Same ratio also: four
boys and three girls. One day he thinks he'll ask him or Terry
what order the boys and girls went; his was two brothers, sister,
two brothers, two sisters. William's the first child in his family
to die. Stu's the last brother left in his family. William's mother
survives him; Stu's died five years ago. Father died in '89; Stu's
in '72. Father was the majority leader in the state assembly for
six years and the lieutenant governor for four. Peter had never
mentioned that. He thinks of going up the hill and offering his
condolences to him. And after that to say something like "Your
first sibling to die. I've lost four. Of course, I'm about ten years

older than you—more like fifteen." Peter would probably ask how old he is and then give his own age. "But three of them pretty early in my life, and the fourth, my dear oldest brother, just eight months ago. First one when I was ten; second, fourteen years later, both of them brothers. And the third, my youngest sister— I've two other sisters; you and I both come from families of seven children, and same ratio of boys to girls—six years after my clos- est-in-age brother, and at the time my closest sibling too." He won't say any of that. And condolences he'll give some other way than going up the hill. He goes into the kitchen and looks out at Peter's house. Two cars in the driveway and one on the street out front. Usually around this time—late morning, weekday—no cars there. Two of their three boys are away at college and the third lives in another state. And Peter and Terry—lawyers— leave separately very early—six-thirty, seven; Stu's seen their cars come down the hill when he's gone out for a run or to the end of his driveway for his newspapers. So, relatives, maybe friends, to be with them. Their boys could be home now too because of their uncle. Possibly more cars parked near the garage, which he can't see from this window. Actually, it might be a good time to go up. All those people; he wouldn't have to stay long or say much. Just his and Janice's condolences and if there's any- thing they can do. But why would he want to go up? It'd be pre- sumptuous. They're not good friends. They're good neighbors. Peter—though usually one of his sons, on his or Terry's orders— had mowed their weeds in back of the house and along the road when Stu and his family were in Maine for the summer, but with- out being asked to. Just doing what good neighbors do, Peter and

Terry have said, and they wouldn't let Stu pay their sons when he offered. Every Christmastime they leave a poinsettia plant by their door. Because of that, Stu and Janice started giving them in return a box of candy from a very good Baltimore chocolatier, as it calls itself. But outside of having them over for drinks and that party and their having Janice and Stu over about three times in the nine years they've been in this house, there hasn't been much between them but pleasant and sometimes jocular talk for a few minutes when he meets one or both of them at the neighborhood market or in the local Y or when Peter and Terry drive down the hill alone or together (not when they're heading for work; then they just wave) and see Stu by his mailbox or near the end of his driveway or pushing Janice in her wheelchair outside, and they almost always stop to talk for a minute or two from their car. And there used to be an annual Bollington Heights party a week or so before Christmas another neighbor-couple gave just for the adults and that's when they'd talk for a while if they happened to be sitting or standing next to each other, but the people who gave it moved away two years ago. Those parties, in fact, are what made Janice want to give their party for the immediate neighborhood "to keep the tradition going," she said, and because they all got along so well together, but where the couples could bring their kids if they wanted. He goes in back to speak to her. "You know who died? Peter O'Lochlin's brother, William. A very lively guy. You remember him." "No, I don't, and I'm so sorry. Which one was he? Peter has several brothers and I think we've met them all," and he says "He had three. This one sat down next to us at their son's graduation party last June and we spoke to him a long time. Outside, on the patio. A stockbroker. I kept asking him questions about it. It was interesting because he was so candid. Here," and shows her the photo and she says "Oh yes; what a shame. Such a nice fellow, and so young. How old does it say? I don't have my glasses," and he says "Forty-two. Youngest son and maybe even the youngest child. Died two days ago. Just collapsed and never made it to the hospital." "Nobody told us," and he says "Well, we're not exactly their closest friends." "But we saw Louisa yesterday and they're very close. She must have known." "Maybe she had something else on her mind. Or didn't have the time; she was on her way to Graul's before it closed. Or she didn't want to upset me because of Dan. But awful, isn't it? And of a heart attack. Now they'll all, the brothers and sisters— seven of them including William; strange, huh?—have to be worried it could happen to them too. I was thinking of going up, saying something to Peter. Some cars are by his house now, so I wouldn't be the only one there." "Fine, if you want, but what do you plan to say?" "You know, that I'm very sorry—we both are— sorry and saddened, and also something related to my own loss of Dan, but which I think could help. That I've gone through it recently. Or what I've gone through. Because some people don't realize, I was thinking of saying—not the person going through it, but friends and colleagues, let's say—that losing a sibling you've known and loved all your life can be worse than losing a parent, but of course not worse than losing a child. That the pain over it eventually lessens and sadness and so on, but they never recede entirely and he should know that and that any grief he's feeling is natural and probably good. That it helps you get through the worst period, right after you find out and for weeks, or for however long, later. The pain never went away with Jay—not by a long shot. That one was the worst because we were so close. It still comes back to me—he does, like on his birthday and in my dreams or he just comes into my head—and I get all weepy over it, and it's been more than forty years. Losing Deborah was also very tough, though we knew it'd happen and even thought she'd die sooner because she'd been sick so long. My folks didn't think she'd survive her first operation when she was five. So what was also heartbreaking was that her disease and fighting it and all those operations and her continuing deterioration till there was just about no bone or muscle left in her neck and she couldn't keep her head erect without a brace, was almost her whole life. Newton's death—well, I was ten, so it was different. I didn't know how to react. I mean, I was sad, but more so for my parents and Dan, who was only fourteen months older and as close to him then as I was to Jay. I don't know. Does one say things like that—bring in his own experiences—to someone who just lost a brother I'm sure he was close with, because you could see at that party how tight their family was? Maybe I should think some more about it before I say anything," and she says "It's true; you wouldn't want to say anything you didn't feel absolutely safe with." "Truth is, I wouldn't know what to say. I never do in such situations. Maybe just standing there with a long face and saying how sorry we are and that there's really nothing else to say are all I should do. Of course, inwardly I'd be sad for my loss of Dan too, and underneath that, for my other brothers and Deborah, though maybe not. Dan right now's enough." "I'm sure

your just going up and offering your condolences will be
appreciated, if they're seeing visitors." "Those cars I mentioned,
so I assume they are. Funeral's day after tomorrow. Different
than the Muslims and Jews, which are 'bury them fast.' Which is
better? Giving you time to adjust that someone you loved is
going to be buried or getting the body out of the way so you can
start recovering from the death and burial?" "Maybe you should
just go to the funeral and speak to Peter after if there's a time
and place to there. That would also give you time to think of
what you want to say." "Then I'd have to say something to all
the brothers and sisters. And the mother. Do you remember her?
Attractive woman, white-haired. Smoked a lot, like my mother
until she was forced to stop, and also like Mom she didn't seem
to be aware she was blowing smoke on people. Look, probably
the best thing to do is what I first thought and that's to go up
now when other people are there and express our condolences
and come right back," and she says "That should be enough, for
Peter and you." "So you don't think I'd be going too far with even
that? Okay, I'm on my way, but I should put on better clothes."
He changes into corduroy pants and a dress shirt and shoes
instead of sneakers and his coat and starts up the hill. No, he
thinks when he's halfway there, he's just doing it to get a good
cry over Dan. Actually, not just for that. Also to give his condolences. But he can give them when he next sees Peter in his car,
if he stops and rolls down his window to talk, or when Peter's
starting or walking off one of his weekend runs. Or just a
condolence card. And not one he puts in Peter's mailbox but
sends through the mail. He doesn't like those cards, nor to spend

two-fifty or so on one, but other people seem to think they serve a purpose, or just a note. "Dear Peter," he could say. "Janice and I are deeply sorry over the loss of your brother and want to express our condolences. I've thought of things to say but there are really no comforting words when one loses a close brother. Any brother or sibling. I lost my brother Dan eight months ago and am still in a state of—" Doesn't sound right. Just a condolence card, then, with a note he'd write on it that Janice and he learned of his brother's death in the newspaper today and want to say how sorry they are over his deep loss and his family's. "If there's anything we can do for you, please let us know. Again, we are deeply sorry." Something like that. He goes down the hill, hoping nobody in Peter's house saw him standing there. When he gets home Janice says "How is he?" and he says "I got halfway there and turned around." "Maybe this is the solution. At the end of the regular death notice for William—" and he says "Oh, there was one? I only saw the long article with the photo." "Same page. It says that friends can pay their respects between three and five tomorrow at the Loyola School chapel, which is where Peter's sons went and it's right near here. Would you like to go? I'll go with you," and he says "No, I'd never be able to get through it and it'd look so peculiar, my breaking down in front of them. I'll just send a condolence card I'll get at the drugstore and speak to Peter about his brother sometime after."

11

He called Dan and said "I'm only calling to tell you something that might interest you that happened today. Of course, also to hear how you are. But that, later, for I don't want to lose what I called to say, unless everything with you's not okay," and Dan said "No, we're fine. What?" "I was going through my top dresser drawer to throw out all the useless papers and single socks and so on, and came across Dad's old business card," and Dan said "Which one? His dental office or the one he used after he lost his license and sold textiles for what was the company called... Lakeside?" and he said "Brookhaven. On Seventh Avenue and 38th." "And a third card. In fact, four," and Stu said "This one was for his 40th Street dental office—his last," and Dan said "That's what I was getting to. First the Delancey Street office, which he had from 1919 till we moved to the West Side in '37 and he set up his practice there. Then Brookhaven, if you're right, and it sounds right—Brookfield or Brookhaven," and he said "Take my word. Haven. I worked in the Garment Center almost all through high school, putting away dough for college, if I got into a good one, because you know I never would have got it from him. Pushing those dollies through the streets for coat and suit houses, and I used to stop in on him there." "I never did. Was at college and the army and my early reporter jobs and then covering the Korean War and the Chinese grabbing me, and by the time I was released he'd got back his license and opened the 40th Street office. I even think my imprisonment and all the press it got helped him convince the State licensing board to return his license, since he was supposedly suffering so much over me. Maybe he was, but you know what a finagler Dad was. What'd I miss about the textile place?" and he said "It was just a small cluttered office behind a big fancy front, with a few other salesmen and lots of cigar smoke. 'This is my son,' he always said when I came by. 'This is my son.' He said he didn't need anything but a place to leave his briefcase of swatches overnight and to put his orders through before he went home, since he was pounding the pavement all day selling. Must have been hard on him. He was already fifty when he started the job and never in good shape. He did pretty well for someone who went to dental school straight out of high school and whose only other job when he got out of prison was working in a war factory for a year." "I worked alongside him one summer separating and stacking army patches for uniforms. He got me the job," and Stu said "He got me all my Garment Center jobs. He liked to see his kids working. Gave him satisfaction he'd done something right with us and also helped cut down on his expenses. Anyway, I found this business card for his 40th Street office and it brought back a lot. For sure the dental office smells. And just climbing the long flight up to it and sitting on the torn Naugahyde couch or one of the torn chairs in the waiting room, waiting for him to finish up with a patient so we could take the subway home." "What was the address again?" and Stu said "I got it right here. Two hundred West, N.Y. 18, N.Y. Office hours, it says, 9 a.m. to 6:30 p.m. and by appointment. So he put in a good day, and six days a week too, till his Parkinson's forced him to quit." "Yeah, but how many of those hours were spent kibbitzing with his cronies who always seemed to be around? He didn't do well there, not like the ones on Delancey and West 75th. The building and office were too shabby, so mostly he got walk-in trade, extractions for five to ten dollars, fillings for patients who didn't know better or wanted them dirt cheap and, for less money than I bet any dentist in the city charged, the occasional bridge or plate. I didn't see him there much because after the Chinese released me I went to work for INS in Washington before joining the CBS bureau. I know I never went to him for my teeth then. I hate saying this, and I never let him know it, but except for plates, bridges and extractions, he was a lousy dentist." "I know; we talked about it once. But he might have been that way only to his kids. Mom said he didn't want to inflict pain on us, so he didn't drill too deep." "If that was the case, why didn't he give me Novocain when I needed it last time I went to him? Don't tell me he wanted to spare me the pain of the needle. No, he wanted to save the two bucks the Novocain cost, I'm sorry to say. Worse than Dad, though, was the Chinese dentist who pulled my tooth in prison. In my cell, also without anesthetic, and the tooth was abscessed. I knew enough from Dad that you wait till the abscess abates before pulling the tooth out. But this dentist said he can take it out now or a month from now, when he'd be back. And next time he might also not have anesthetic and sulfur to bring the swelling down first, and by that time the infection might go to my brain. So I had no choice and longed for Dad's hit-or-miss dentistry, because I forgot to say when I had a cavity Dad never took an x-ray. I gripped the arms of the chair a guard brought into the cell for the extraction and without knowing it tore one off. Literally, I thought I'd die when he grabbed the tooth with the forceps and started pulling. A little guy too, shorter and slimmer than me. He didn't have Dad's wrists for extractions, either, which Dad was always so proud of." "I never heard that story," and Dan said "I wrote about it for INS when they holed me up in a Hong Kong hotel for a week to write a series of articles on my capture, but the editors toned down the extraction part because they thought it too grisly." "I remember the articles but not the tooth. Also your stay in Hong Kong, which disappointed us because we were eager to see you, but Dad kept saying that professionally it was a good move. For a week or so the headline of it bannered across the entire top of the *Journal-American*'s front page," and Dan said "And most of the other Hearst papers. But the card you found. Phone number start with Bryant something?" and Stu read from the card "'Bryant 9-2170. If no answer, call,' and it gives our old Endicott-2 number. 'Dr. Morton Feingelt,' and under it just the word 'dentist.'"

"Not 'dental surgeon' or 'D.D.S.'? I thought all his dental cards said one or the other on them. But now I remember even a fourth, or what are we on, fifth business card of Dad's. Technically, Mom's too, since they were supposed to be partners. 'Mortel Corp.,' a combination of their names, with our home address and phone number. That was during Dad's textile days and sometime after." "I remember it, but what business were they in?" and Dan said "Just Dad: monkey business. Hanky-panky business. No business. Selling, making and buying nothing. It was a tax dodge, a fraud, which Mom must have given him hell for, involving and possibly inveigling her, if he got her to sign papers, in another of his schemes. The card gave this fake company a look of legitimacy, as did the stationery with letterheads. I could just see his defense. 'Of course we were running a business out of our apartment; why else would we have had the cards printed?' What a hoot, your old man. For here he was, trying, through all his connections, to get his license back, while at the same time risking getting flagged by IRS and going to prison again." "I liked it, though, the company name linking them together as if they truly were a team," and Dan said "When you look at it that way, it might have been the most romantic thing Dad ever did in their marriage. So we don't come from a family of romantics, on the male side at least. Crybabies, maybe. Dad, you, occasionally me when nobody's looking, and I forget about Newton and Jay, but probably them too if they had lived."

12

Soon after Dan died Stu started making tea his first drink in the morning after coffee. Or tea first, then miso soup and then he'd make coffee. All before he woke Janice up, which usually was 8:30. Actually, first drink he'd have when he got in the kitchen in the morning was a glass of water with several vitamin pills. Then tea, miso soup and coffee. At first he didn't like tea so soon after waking up. But he remembered Dan telling him "At your age, maybe at any age, coffee's too strong and harsh to take that early on an empty stomach. Think of it. You wake up, wash and shave, do some exercises you say, and then pour down your throat—okay, not 'pour'; too hot for that, since I think you drink it black like everyone else in the family." "Not Dad. He had it with cream or milk and two teaspoons of sugar." "I meant everybody alive, though of the deceased, Jay and Mom definitely only drank it black. And maybe Dad's way, coffee so early's okay.

But tea's better for the stomach lining, and you want it for it's medicinal properties too. So green tea over any other, and after that, any uncaffeinated herbal tea. Then, your stomach warm and relaxed and unattacked and you're a few articles into the newspaper—I'm assuming you read the paper with your morning coffee," and Stu said "The *Sun*, fairly quickly because there's rarely anything in it, after a peak at the lead stories and obits in the *Times.*" "Anyway, then you can have your coffee." "But I like miso soup after I finish my first mug of coffee, so I'd probably want it after my first mug of tea," and Dan said "Change the order then: tea, soup, coffee," and that's what he's been doing since a little after Dan died three months ago: water, tea, soup, coffee, all before he got Janice up. But since he's now drinking two hot beverages, he also reads a few articles in the *Times* with the coffee and maybe an op-ed piece and interesting obituary. Also, a few weeks after Dan died, Stu was driving to the Y. It's only five minutes away and he tried to get there every day for around twenty minutes in the fitness center, pulling this and pushing that, and then fifteen minutes in the free weight room using the dumbbells and weights. While driving there he thought why doesn't he ever do what Dan did at his Y and swim? He'd never been in the pool. Never even walked through the door in the shower room, the only men's entrance to the pool, to look at it, which he'd overheard from Y members was beautiful, especially after its remodeling. He swam in his workout shorts that day and liked it. Dan had urged him to swim, long as he belonged to the Y, but he told him the only time he swam was in Maine in the summer. The water was warm—too warm, some men in the locker room said—but ideal for him. Cool water was good for lakes, rivers, oceans. *Cold* he never went into. Swam ten minutes and then got bored with it, not tired. Now he swims ten to fifteen minutes every day and works out before only around ten minutes each in the fitness center and free weight room. Dan said he never used his Y's fitness center and free weight room. "I just want to stay in shape and maintain my wind. Heart and lungs over physical strength. Besides, bulging muscles would look ludicrous or just out of place on an older guy like me." Running and swimming were the only exercises he did and a little stretching before he swam and ran. Every other day he alternated half-to-one-mile swims with ten-to-fourteen-mile runs. "Most I've ever done," Stu told him on the phone, "was twelve miles in Central Park when I was living a few doors from it. I was with Tina then. She came out to the park with me and I said 'I'm going around the park loop once, if I can make it. Dan said it's six miles almost exactly, which'd be twice as far as I've ever run.' She said she'd wait for me on a bench by the road, read a book, and she cheered me when I set off. I don't know how long it took me; probably two to three times what it'd take you. There were a couple of really steep hills. When I completed the loop, exhausted and slowly approaching her, she yelled 'Go for another six; do it, Stu. Go beyond yourself for once, and here's your big chance. I'm also engrossed in my book and don't want to stop reading.' I thought what does she mean? I've gone beyond myself lots, in my writing. I didn't feel like going another step, but I wanted her to admire me—see what a sap I can be?—so I ran past her and she stood on the bench and waved and cheered me on again—'Yea, team. Go, my sweetie; go, go, go.' I knew when I was out of sight I could just walk around, stop for a coffee someplace, and then circle around her and get back on the loop road and run the last five hundred feet and say to her 'Look at me; barely a sweat. Who could've imagined, and in better time than my first loop.'" "Nah, no cheating in running. Do what you can and live with it," and Stu said "I know; was only kidding. And I made it with plenty of sweat, but it took half an hour longer than the first time. Though I know you'd love to turn me into a fellow marathon runner and where we could start out together at the annual New York City race before you fly away miles ahead of me, that was the last time I'll run so far. Wasn't fun and I actually thought I'd drop." A few weeks before Dan died he said on the phone "We're looking for a new car and I think it'll be one of the hybrids. Fifty-plus miles to a gallon and they're much better for the air." Stu said "But they're new designs with a radically different fuel system or something, so all the kinks might not have been worked out of them yet. And they're small and I hear quite expensive," and Dan said "So what do we need? One lean woman and a short guy and sometimes a couple of infant grandkids in tow. And no sales tax because buying those cars is part of the government's energy-efficient program, so there's two grand right there. You also can end up saving five thousand dollars on gas for the lifetime of the car if the one you drive now averages twenty-five miles a gallon, as ours does. To me it seems the most practical and environmentally sensible and ultimately the most economical car to buy. Will Melody and I be alive six years from now to begin reaping the monetary gains

from owning such a car? We'll see, though there's more chance
she will, being much younger than I." A month after Dan died
Stu thought maybe he should buy a hybrid like Dan was going
to. But do they really need two cars? Only when the modified van
breaks down, which it does a lot, but then he rents a car for
around thirty dollars a day, and the van's usually fixed in two
days. They will have to get a second car when Anita needs to
drive and is still living at home. The van was rebuilt so low that
its undercarriage is vulnerable to damage when it's driven too
fast over speed bumps and potholes, that he doesn't want her
driving it. And if she drives it to high school, let's say, what
would he use? After she goes off to college he'd use the van
for Janice and to take things to the dump and the hybrid all the
other times. He priced out the hybrids. Both models have a base
sticker price of more than twenty thousand, and because they
were so new on the market, the few used ones were almost as
high. He thought: If they had to have only one car and no longer
needed the van because Janice wasn't in a wheelchair anymore,
small and expensive as the hybrid was, he'd buy it for all the
reasons Dan gave and because they drove so well too. What
could he have been thinking, though, wasting his time going to
car dealers and pricing and test-driving them? They were talking on the phone about the *New Yorker* and Dan said "But I have
to admit, the articles have gotten better with the new editor; not
so Hollywood gossipy and glamour-puss anymore. But it really
ticks me off when those unattached subscription cards fall out of
its pages during my walk from the mailbox to the house. What
I've begun to do is put those postage-free cards into the mailbox

and send them back to the magazine unsigned. My hope is that if they get enough of these they'll think about discontinuing the policy." "I doubt it'll make a dent," Stu said, "but here's to you for trying. I also hate those cards when I'm sitting in my easy chair reading the magazine and they fall out and I have to pick them up off the floor." "If the two of us send the cards back each week, maybe we could make a dent," and Stu said "I'll see. Because you're my brother and it means so much to you, probably." After Dan died Stu started putting these cards in his mailbox. Then he thought the mailman would get suspicious, all these blank subscription cards to the same magazine once a week, so he put one or two in it twice a week and also dropped them in public mailboxes. Then he began writing on some of the cards: "Clean up your act, will ya? Fasten these stupid cards to the magazine so I don't have to pick them up when they fall out on my walk from my mailbox to the house. Yes, I'm a subscriber!" This never happened to him; the cards only fell out when he was sitting in his easy chair and opened the magazine. Another time: "I'm 86-years-old and have been reading your magazine for 60 years and been a subscriber for more than 40, now mostly for the entertainment and book reviews and of course the cartoons. But I must protest that these subscription cards of yours are always spilling out of the pages, forcing me to bend over and pick them up and possibly one day breaking a hip doing it. Please stop sticking the cards loose into the magazine, a plea from a frail old man." Another: "Surely you're aware of the expression 'preaching to the choir.' Well that's me, a longtime subscriber, so I don't need your subscription reminders in my copy of the *New Yorker* every week." Another: "Is there a way for you to leave out the unfastened subscription notices to subscribers? If not, then don't stick them in any of the copies you print or I'm canceling my five-year subscription and I've four years left on it." Another: "Pleez cease putting free-fall subscription cards in your magazine. You don't, then as V.P. of FAMOLSC (Free All Magazine Of Loose Subscription Cards) I will urge our sizable membership to return unmarked all their NYer cards to you at your expense, and not only the loose but the attached." Another: "I am sick of the litter your unattached subscription notices create and hope the deluge of them you get from me will signal to you how I and many readers of your magazine feel." He continued to mail the cards for a month and then decided it was a futile activity and he was only doing it because Dan had, and stopped. Before Dan died, when Stu ran, and he ran every day for a mile or two, he did it without stopping unless he got a leg cramp or whatever that pain in his side is called—stitching, he thinks Dan said—and then he'd walk a little or stand still a few seconds before resuming his run. But Dan had said he often stopped his run if something was interesting to look at. He'd told Stu that at a cottage Janice and he had rented in Maine, the summer after they'd met, so twenty-three years ago. Dan had interviewed a marine biologist sixty miles south of them for a PBS documentary he was writing and producing on whales. After, he drove up to see them and next day drove back to the Portland airport to return the car and fly home. Early that morning before Janice was up, Dan asked Stu if he'd like to join him for a run. "Are you kidding? You'll be going at a good clip for an hour; I could never keep up." "So I'll slow down and cut my run in half. It'll give us some more time to talk." "Me? Talk and run at the same time? No, go. I don't want to spoil your fun. I'll do my twenty-minute slog while you're gone." Dan asked which route did he think was the best to take and Stu said "If you go left at our mailbox, it's a hilly mile and a half to Naskeag Point. At this hour you might see some lobster boats pulling up traps. Though you can also, a mile down Naskeag Road, go right at Back Road. You get to see shore and saltwater farms and sailboats, and it circles around to Naskeag Road, which you take a right at to get back here. Total distance, maybe three and a half miles. Or go right at our mailbox and run to town and back, a total of around eight miles. That should do it for you, though there's a long steep hill on that one too," "Good," Dan said, "I'll decide which way to go when I get to the mailbox." He did warmup exercises—not much; he said they were mostly a waste of time on him: sitting on the floor with his legs straight out and touching both feet for a minute. Then standing on one foot while holding up the other leg by its knee for about fifteen seconds and repeating it with the other leg. After, he said "Last chance," and Stu said "No thanks, I know my limits," and Dan said "I should pee first, but I'll do it off the road," and left. Janice came downstairs an hour later and said "Where's Dan? He didn't leave yet, I hope," and Stu said "Went for a run. He should be back soon." An hour later when she was going back upstairs where she worked and Stu was typing in the living room, she said "He's not back yet? Should we be worried? Maybe he got hit by a car, or something with his heart," and Stu said "Or a moose ran over him. He's all right, don't worry, and he has to be back soon because his flight's at three." Dan came back an hour later and Stu said "Where you been? Running a marathon?" and Dan said "If I were and only stopped to pee once, I would've been back fifteen minutes ago. Nah, I ran about twenty miles, a lot more than I thought I would. First to town and then to the point and then coming back I thought I might be missing something—your scenic route—so I took Back Road. When I got to your mailbox I felt so good and the temperature was still perfect for running, that I ran to town again. Reason it took so long is that I stopped several times to look at the boats and old houses and wildflowers along the roads. Also to pick blueberries and eat them, and I found a wild raspberry bush so had to have those too. If I just push to finish when I'm not racing, running becomes too much like a chore." Stu stops once or twice now during his runs, though of course they're much shorter than Dan's. He usually runs the same route. Down his driveway, left on the street that goes past his house, down to the end of it about half a mile, left at the road there for about quarter of a mile to the market, then turns around and runs home. Sometimes he only goes to the end of the street and back. Not much to see. Same houses, a few cars passing. Weeds along the street that seem to change from month to month. A few yards with flowers and flowering bushes in them. About twice a year in spring, two ducks, male and female, looking for food in the stream that runs along his side of the street. And after a heavy rain, the stream widening and rising and rushing over rocks and branches and clumps of leaves. And one house about halfway down the street where the new minister of the church across the way from them lives with his wife and three boys. The youngest boy is often playing alone by the fence that separates the house from the stream and usually yells hi to him, and he almost always stops and says hello back and "How you doing today, Len?" for he once asked his name, and things like that. Dan never mentioned stopping to talk to people when he ran, and Stu can't say why but he doesn't think he did. Probably waved, though, and to runners going the opposite way or in the same direction as he passed them, he probably said hello.

13

The dream he has about Dan seems important. For one reason, it's the first he's had with him in it since he died six months ago. Dream started with Stu getting out of a chair and asking a woman in the chair next to his to save his place. She nodded— he didn't know her—and went back to talking to someone on the couch opposite them. Room was crowded. It was a party, much like the one in Greenwich Village that Stu had met Janice at. In fact, thinking about the setting, it was the same room and the dining room adjoining it was the same too. Most people standing, lots of laughter and muffled conversation, tinkling of glasses and silverware on plates and some cigarette smoke. He left the room, though he isn't sure where he was going. In the next scene he came back and saw a young man sitting in his chair. The man was talking to the people on the couch and didn't get up. "Excuse me," Stu said to him, "but I'm afraid this is my chair. I asked someone to save it, but she's gone. I told her I was going to the bathroom or for a drink and I'd only be gone, unless the bathroom was taken and the bar was crowded, for a few minutes." The man never looked at him, continued talking, so Stu said to the people on the couch and in the chair next to the man's "Excuse me, but you all heard what I said. I told this young man here that this is my chair. I'd asked someone to save it for me— a woman. She was wearing a dark dress, it could have been black, and a string of pearls or something around her neck, and she was in her early thirties, I'd say, and had a long blond braid down her back. But she's gone and I've no idea where she is. Anyway, she's not here to confirm that I told her this, and this man won't give back the chair when I swear it's mine. He ignores me. I don't want to fight over it. But I am feeling a little tired—I know I don't feel like standing and there aren't any empty places to sit in this room—so I just want my chair." "Good," the man said, looking up at him, "—fight." Stu grabbed him out of the chair and wrestled him to the floor. He held him down with his hand on his neck and said "Have you had enough? Do I get my chair back or do I have to bang your head against the ground?" He looked around to see what effect his actions were having on the others and saw Dan coming toward him through a crowd of people in the dining room. Nobody seemed to notice Dan but they parted in front of him as he walked. Stu thought "Oh no, he's going to scold me. 'At your age,' he's going to say, 'for a stinking chair you'd attack one of the guests and disrupt the party and make a total fool of yourself. When are you going to grow up?'" But Dan smiled at him as he walked, and Stu thought

"No, I know that smile; he's glad to see me." Then Stu thought he saw a pearl or stud in Dan's left earlobe, something Dan would never wear. But it was, some kind of tiny sparkling round jewel, which then came out of the lobe on its own and moved at the same pace as Dan but always a short distance in front of him till it darted to the right and disappeared. "My brother," Stu said, and went to him with his arms out. Just as he got close enough to hug him, Dan, still smiling, began to dissolve in different directions till he completely disappeared. "This always happens to me," Stu thought. "With my mother, with my brother Jay, with my sister, and father; everyone in my family who's dead. They never speak. They smile as they move toward me. Or they don't smile and just stand still. And when I get to where I can touch them, they disappear. It's so damn sad," and he started sobbing. Then he woke up and Janice stirred and said "What's wrong? Are you crying?" He didn't want to disturb her so he said "No, and it's nothing. Just a bad dream." "Do you want to talk about it?" and he said "Don't see how I could; I already forgot it. Go back to sleep." "Could you put something over my feet? Even with the blanket on them, they're cold." He got up and put a towel over her feet and got back in bed.

14

Stu's parents were married in October, '26, and Dan was born eight months later. "Your father was thrilled the first one was a boy. He wanted a dozen children, all boys—seriously. That was way too many for me. Six, all right, and evenly split—that I could manage. He loved you boys. I loved my boys also. Something went wrong with the girls, though. Not Deborah. She got sick too young for anything but her illness to go wrong with her. If she was difficult at times, who could blame her? But the older two? I treated all my children equally, favored none of them, so why didn't they turn out as nice as my sons?" "What are you talking about?" Stu said. "They're every bit as good as the boys and always were. What do you have against them? Dad, we know. He didn't get along with women as well as he did with men. And he was old-fashioned on the subject too. Girls you have to support and give dowries to and pay for their weddings and so forth, while boys take care of themselves and get jobs early and help support their old parents later on. So, sons over daughters, unfortunately, which I always felt guilty about." "I had nothing against my girls. It's how *they* acted, not me. Though maybe I'm wrong. I probably am, as I am about most things, you and Dan must think." "We don't. Where'd you get that idea?" "And let's face it. Your father, much as he adored his boys, was an absent father from the start. You're not surprised to hear that. Well, you shouldn't be. Absent even before Dan was born, if that's possible. He dropped me off in front of the hospital with your Aunt Bella and then drove to his office downtown and told me to call him when I had the baby. When I was wheeled back to my room, without Dan—he was premature, and unusually small for even a little less than eight-month newborn, so was in an incubator in another room—" "Oh, that 'premature' line is what you like to say to show he wasn't conceived before the marriage," and she said "It's true. I was a virgin when I married and remained one, so to speak, in that I never knew another man, unlike your father with women. I was very attractive then— you've seen the photos; not like the old hag I am today—so I had plenty of opportunities, but knew it wasn't something I'd feel good about after, so didn't. Dan was conceived—I know this for a fact but won't go into details because I know you'll make light of it—on my wedding night. And I carried small and was natu- rally slender, that right up till the time I went into the hospital people didn't know I was pregnant unless I told them. But with the hospital room, when I got back to it without Dan, your father was sleeping on my bed. He could sleep anywhere. He even thought to close the door and had to be shaken to wake up." "So you had a private room?" "With all of you. I insisted. One reason—it's not looked on favorably today but wasn't even frowned on then—was that I smoked and didn't want a woman in the next bed telling me she was allergic and to put out the cigarette. The truth is, I smoked with all my kids till I was wheeled into the delivery room. People said later Dan and Newton were short because I smoked during my entire pregnancy with them. But look at you, and Jay was tall too. It didn't affect any of my children's health either, as you now read it does. Only one of you became seriously ill and she was my last baby and I'm sure it had as much to do with the stress I was going through over your father's trial the months before I had her. But with Dan and Newton, those were the best years of our marriage. We were relatively happy, I was young and healthy and your dad was making lots of money legitimately from his practice, and taking care of two infants with a little help wasn't hard at all. After that, everything went to pot and I should have divorced him before I conceived you or even Jay. I hope I didn't say something wrong just now. But once I knew the sort of man I was married to—he had a happy-go-lucky attitude and good sense of humor, which for the most part I liked, but otherwise we were vastly differ-ent—and what he was doing to wreck the family, I never should have had more children with him."

As far as Stu knew, nothing much of consequence happened to Dan till he was in high school. Sure, as the family story goes, hit by a car when he was twelve while playing in the street, but somersaulted over a few times, stood up, laughed, and not a mark

on him except grease stains on his arms and face. When he was
nine, rode his bike into the rear of a moving trolley car, and
again, not a bruise, but bike was smashed. Nearly drowned in a
lake when he was five because he couldn't swim, but twenty
minutes later jumped off the dock again and dog-paddled out to
the float where the big kids were. Family first lived on Ocean
Avenue across from Prospect Park. Photo, the family favorite, of
the first four kids, all dressed alike though Harriet in a short
skirt that matched the boys' shorts, their hair parted and combed,
standing in a row in front of their apartment building, youngest,
Jay, to oldest, Dan, who towered over Newton. "Dr. Barish, the
pediatrician for all of you," their mother said, "had a growth chart
for Dan that said he'd be six-two—the Jewish giant, he was
calling him. Always the tallest boy in his class—there were several taller girls—till he mysteriously stopped growing a year
before his bar mitzvah. The family moved to the West Side when
Dan was ten and Stu almost one. "Do you know the story?" Dan
said to Stu on the phone. "We were on our way back to Brooklyn
from the Peekskill bungalow colony we went to every summer
for two months, Dad coming up weekends. With five kids—Mom
was pregnant with Natalie at the time—and two women in help,
we had to make two trips. On the second trip, Dad got off the
West Side Highway and headed east. Mom said 'Where are you
going? This isn't the way.' 'It's a shortcut I found,' Dad said. He
drove down 75th Street, parked in front of a brownstone in the
middle of the block—there were plenty of parking spaces then—
and said, pointing to the building, 'So what do you think?' 'What
do I think what?' Mom said. 'We have to get home. I've lots of

work ahead of me and the kids start school day after tomorrow.' 'The building,' he said. 'Five stories. Sandstone, the facade's supposed to be. Large stoop but that should probably go so the main entrance is on the ground floor. I understand the last owner was a Russian count. So I'm saying, do you like it?' 'It's very nice,' she said. 'Looks like it needs lots of work though. But what are you really saying? You planning to buy it, move your office and us here? If you are, let's have a closer look at it some other time and then talk, but not now.' 'Too late,' he said. 'I bought it. We own the monster.' He got out of the car and clapped toward the building. 'You can come out now,' he said, and Newt, Harriet and Jay and the woman taking care of them came out from under the stoop. 'I've moved all our furniture and things here over the summer,' he told Mom. 'And many of the rooms have been cleaned up and painted. This is where we stay tonight. The Brooklyn apartment's already got new tenants in it. So now, what do you think?' 'This is the worst thing you could have done to me,' she said, and started crying. 'To do it on the sly. Without even asking if I wanted to move. Why?' and he said 'I thought it'd be a nice surprise. And with you pregnant, sparing you the headache of seeing buildings and deciding on one and then all the moving. So I was wrong. You want to blow up at someone over it, do it at me, because I'm always the fall guy for everything. But it was a great buy. The building's been on the market for five years and empty since the Crash. And the neighborhood's good, with plenty of fine shops on Columbus Avenue and the El there, and we're a half block from Central Park. And for the kids, close to the Natural History Museum and a good public school, so with all that we should consider ourselves lucky.' I don't do a half-bad imitation of Dad, do I. Anyway, he said, there was nothing to be gained from crying. Then he told the kids to go in. Not you; I don't even think you could walk yet. That we'd know which rooms were ours by whose clothes and stuff were in the closets. The big front room on the second floor is ours,' he told Mom. 'Of course, it'll have to be renovated.' That he was going to have his office on the ground floor in front when the stoop goes. The top three floors will be tenants, two apartments on each. He had it all figured out, had gone over it with an architect. 'We'll get income from the rents,' he said, then or another time. 'Also, save on all sorts of expenses because of my office and both owning and managing the building ourselves. Light bulbs, cleaning supplies, utilities, etcetera. We'll put them down as building expenses and practically get the apartment for free. Come on,' I remember him saying, 'dry your tears. It's the best possible deal and investment. We'll live here for the rest of our lives, and you and the kids, should anything happen to me, though nothing's going to, will always know you've a roof over your heads.'" The apartment: foyer, dining room, kitchen with an eating alcove, rear room they called the breakfast room—though it was where they ate dinner; breakfast they had there only on Sundays—leading to the narrow L-shaped backyard. Second floor: kids' bedroom and master bedroom, long hallway to an enormous living room, which none of the children were allowed to use, except to practice piano. Or even cross through—something to do with the valuable furniture and antiques and saving on the wear and tear of the expensive carpet—and two bedrooms connected by another long hallway, the back one first Dan and Newton's, and when they left home, Harriet's. Two staircases, one from the breakfast room and the other from the foyer. Four bathrooms, not counting the one in the waiting room, which they could only use during office hours if all the others were taken. Office had a separate entrance from the ground-floor public hallway and a door connecting the waiting room and apartment foyer. Their father bought the building mostly with money he'd made illegally. People would contact him for an abortion. He'd set it up with several abortionists he knew, all doctors, and get a cut of the fee. "The money rolled in for years," their mother said, "and I hated every cent of it. Dad had shoeboxes filled with thousands of dollars at home because he didn't want to bank it and risk catching the eye of the feds, as he called them. I told him I'd rather be destitute than to have money this way and that he'd get caught eventually and everything we have will disappear. The building, his dental license, and he'll wind up in prison and the kids and I on relief. We didn't, but for a few years we were very hard up." A woman died during one of these abortions, the doctor panicked and dismembered her and buried the pieces in paper bags on his summer estate. She was reported missing, traced to the doctor, he confessed and fingered their father as the middleman. "I told the cops nothing," their father said. "Tight-Lipped Mo, I was known as, even as a kid. You needed someone to keep a secret, you came to me. Teachers would squeeze my head between two of those wooden school passes and I still wouldn't squeal on a pal." More doctors got caught, newspapers called it the largest abortion mill in New York City history, their

father was tried and convicted along with a number of doctors—
two of them committed suicide after they were sentenced—and
sent to prison. "I did it standing on one foot," he liked to say.
"Because of my good behavior there—fixing teeth in their dental
clinic and making free bridges and plates for several prison offi-
cials—I even took care of the dental lab costs, which could run
into big money—I got my three-year term reduced to a little
more than a year and a half. Some of my best patients, when I
finally got my license back, came from connections I made in
prison. Doctors, lawyers, bank executives; very prominent people."
Their mother took out a second mortgage on the building and
got a job at Macy's. She had an interior decorator degree and
helped customers design their rooms and pick out furniture. The
family also lived frugally: no new clothes, sold the car and gave
up the summer bungalow rental and got rid of the housekeeper
they'd had for years. She came back, worked for nothing, saying
that way their mother could save on paying someone to look after
the younger children and that when their father was released and
making money again, she'd ask for her back wages. Dan and
Newton got after-school jobs. "We had to," Dan sad, "to help
Mom out. All of it but a buck or two went to her." He told
Stu a couple of times about seeing their father in prison. "Mom
wanted to change the last name of the kids. She was ashamed of
Dad's because of all the coverage he got in newspapers with the
abortion scandal and was concerned his name would hurt us in
the future. She sent me to Sing Sing to have him sign the
papers—powers of attorney I think they're called. She felt he'd
throw them in her face if she brought them there herself.

So I went by train, was frisked by guards at the prison entrance, wasn't allowed to touch Dad, not even shake his hand. He kept saying 'Rip those documents up and give them back to her to choke on, because I'm signing nothing.' I told him Mom said he had to and gave her reasons: better for the kids, etcetera. 'The hell with her,' he said. 'May she drown in a bathtub, for all I care. She's just getting even with me and for being born with what she thinks is an ugly Jewish name. She wants to go back to the nice not offensive *goyische* one her father, feeling he could do better in business, changed to when he came over, but I won't be part of any of it.' 'That's not the name she's chosen,' I told him. And that she'd keep his name, much as she hates it, though I didn't tell him that, but we'd have the new one. 'Fine.' 'Fine what?' he said. 'Fine,' I said, 'with an i-n-e. That's the name she chose for us.' And he said 'What kind of name's that? Sure, common enough and close to Feingelt, but also a million miles away. It's a dumb name, a no-name. "Everything's fine. The weather's dandy and fine. We're all fine, or we're all Fines, thank you, how's by you?" Why not "Finery"? Why not "Finest"? "New York's Finest"— why not that if she really wants a stupid name?' I told him his name was all right with me and that I didn't think it would hurt me later on. That I'd keep it but not when all my brothers and sisters have a different name. 'So convince them not to go along with the name change,' he said. I told him Newton I might have some luck with, but I can't with the others. They're underage. 'I'm underage too,' I said, 'but if you sign the papers I promise I'll change my name back to yours when I reach twenty-one, even if it'll be peculiar having a different name than the rest of them. Now, my sticking with Feingelt, would also hurt Mom.' And he said 'And it won't hurt me if you go with the change? But I won't put you on the spot. She's who I'd like to put on the spot. In one. Down a hole fifty feet deep, that kind of spot. Okay,' he said after a while, 'I'll sign, but only if you keep your promise to change it back. You do, I know all the kids, the way they look up to you, will follow.' Then he got a pen from a guard and signed and signed, one power of attorney for each kid. 'Now I'm to get somebody here who's a notary,' I told him. The guard in the room made a call and another guard came and notarized all the documents. 'There,' Dad said. 'And you're a good son. You did what your mother asked you to and were persuasive and patient about it to me too, which shows a lot. Too bad you had to do her dirty work, but that's the way she is.' Then he said 'It's not too long a trip for you from the city?' And I said 'Less than an hour.' And for the first time he said 'It must be awful seeing me in here.' I told him I found the whole thing interesting. 'What kid do I know has ever been inside a prison?' 'Good,' he said, 'I'm glad you're getting something out of it. My being here's also good for you in that I'm no longer hounding you to do your homework and helping more with the younger kids and so on.' 'You never hounded me about anything,' I said. And he said 'Then that I'm no longer giving you a poke or whack every now and then.' And I said 'You never did any of that either. I can't remember you ever hitting any of us.' 'That's because I never believed in it and could never touch one of you that way. My mother,' he said, 'I loved her and would do anything for her, but she used to beat the hell out of your Uncle Ted and chase him with a broom and even slapped me a few times for things I didn't do. My dad—a more peaceful and timid man never existed; he wouldn't slap a flea biting him. Then he said 'You know, all of a sudden I'm feeling a little reckless. Also because after signing those papers, what more do I got to lose? Even if we're not supposed to, I'm going to kiss your cheek when you leave, just like we'd do at home.' 'Don't,' I said. 'It's not worth the trouble you can get into.' 'You're probably right,' he said, 'but you at least know what I wanted to do.'" When Dan was twenty-one he told their father he was going to change his name back to Feingelt, just as he'd promised. "Dad said not to," Dan told Stu on the phone a few months ago when they were talking some more about the name change. "'Maybe,' he said, 'when you're all over twenty-one you can all think of doing it. But it'd be ridiculous, you with a different last name than them. It's ridiculous now,' he said, 'all you kids with a different last name than your folks, but that's what she brought on you.' I told him that by the time Deborah's twenty-one I'll be thirty-four and established with the name I have now, so I wouldn't want to change it back then. He said 'She'll never live that long, I'm sorry to say.' What a thing to say; I couldn't believe it. But I said 'Then Natalie and Stu—I'll be thirty to thirty-one when they reach legal age, so still too old to change my name.' So he said 'Okay, then I'm done, finished. Just live my whole life with all my kids with a gentile name. Nobody will know what you are, which to me, with what the Jews went through for thousands of years and the worst of it done just a few years ago, is a crime.' I told him Fine can be a Jewish name. 'There are plenty of Jewish Fines, if that matters.

Most people will think it's been shortened from a longer Jewish name, like Finkel or your own.' He said 'No, people will never know you're my kids. You'll do well in whatever you go into and I'll be proud of you for it, but I won't be able to boast you're my kid because nobody will believe it with the other name.' Then for the first time I said, I don't know why—it just shot out: 'So, like Mom said, you shouldn't have got in trouble and none of this would have happened.' And he said 'Shut your mouth; I never want you to talk to me like that, because I never talked that way to you,' and he turned away and I'm sure he was crying, but I couldn't see it. I never felt so bad for him, nor did I ever bring up the name change to him again or anything connected to it. But you know he never stopped cursing it and Mom for causing it to the end."

15

"One more thing before we hang up," Stu said, "and which I always wanted to ask you. Well, not always, but for a long time: What was I like to you as a kid? I'm curious how you saw me," and Dan said "I don't have much recollection of you then. You guys started coming, after Newton and Harriet, one after the other, it seemed. Too fast for me, and the apartment was getting too crowded and noisy, so I tried not to be around or have much to do with any of you. I don't know why Mom and Dad wanted so many, since Newton and I were more than enough to handle. We were always fighting, right from the time we were tots, they said. Once, I shot him in the face with my BB gun, something I'd never let my own kids have, and another time he broke my violin over my head. I was aiming for his chest with that gun and he for sure wanted to smash in my head. And we had plenty of fistfights where we both came out bloody. Only later, when we were in our early teens—so it wasn't for long, since he died shortly before he was twenty—we got close and did things like go camping together and pal around as friends. Harriet also had a temper and was kind of bratty, so maybe the folks thought they'd have better luck with the next batch. Anyway, you were what—fourth boy and fifth child, but nine years younger than I, so why would I bother with you? When you were one I was ten, and I always had lots of friends and interests—reading, sports, music and school. Mom would ask me to look after you at times when you were a baby and her helper wasn't around, but what did that take? I plopped you into the crib and let you play with your toys there or sleep or die of boredom, for all I cared. And when you started toddling I'd let you play in your playpen or a safe corner of the room. I certainly wasn't going to do anything for you but hand you your bottle and take it away when it was finished, and if you crapped in your pants, which I'm sure you did plenty, nobody ever showed me how to change you, not that I would have if I'd learned. When you were three and four and probably, like the rest of us had been, in nursery half the day, I was in my last year of grade school or my first in high. In a nutshell, you were a squirt to me, somebody small for other people to deal with and whom I had only the flimsiest irreducible connection to. Mom also asked me to read to you sometimes and I must have, but children's books were never something I liked even as a young boy. I was reading semi-adult fiction by the time I was seven—Conan Doyle, Verne, the lighter Dickens—and history and biographies and explorer books, so I no doubt read you the ones I was currently reading. You fell asleep a lot during it, which might have been Mom's objective. Newton was much more attentive to you. He used to wrestle with you on the floor, letting you get him in a leg scissor hold, where he'd scream in pain for you to stop. He always let you beat him and you seemed to believe you did. He also took you for walks in the park and to play catch—you and Jay—or show you how to throw a football or go to the carousel or zoo there. He was a good brother, I was an aloof one. It's too bad; I'm sure I missed out on something with the younger kids. When you were six or seven, I was dating girls, trying to kiss them, reading serious literature—D.H. Lawrence, all the great Russians, Hemingway, of course—and running cross country in high school, thinking about college, since by then I was sixteen and a senior. So again, I did practically nothing with you, only what I was asked, and that, indifferently and ineffectually, in part to lessen the chances of being asked again. When I was seventeen—this is beginning to sound like my favorite poem then—I was in college. Year later, I enlisted in the army and after that I rarely lived home for long. By then you'd gone from being a squirt to a shrimp. That's how I foolishly saw you, though I always thought of you as a good kid. What do you remember?" and Stu said "Nothing much clearly, but one instance stands out. You had an old Hudson—green, four doors, a large car with a small rear window and boxy shape, and a gray fabric, like flannel, for seat covers. You were driving up to see your friend Lev Hirsch, who had a house somewhere near where we used to rent a bungalow outside of Peekskill." "Pine Lake Park, a summer colony. We went there for around ten years. Number of the bungalow we always had was the reverse number of our 75th Street building. Actually, it was Lev's wife's family summer cottage up there that he and Dorothy, just married, used to go to in the winter." "And it had snowed overnight, you went to shovel the car out, and I said I'd help you. We had two shovels for the building, one for snow and the other an old coal shovel for when the building used to use coal. After we shoveled the car out, you said to me 'Want to come along?' I was thrilled because it was the first time you voluntarily asked me to go with you someplace, and also without Jay. So we got in the car and drove off—it had been parked on the park side of Central Park West—and it got about two blocks before it died and we had to push it back to the spot we'd dug it out of." "I was recently discharged from the army and soon on my way to Syracuse under the G.I. Bill, and if I'm not mistaken that Hudson drove its last two blocks that day. Look, I'm sorry I was such a lousy brother. I knew at the time—I knew for years, because I can remember thinking this plenty—that you and Jay wanted to be with me more than I wanted to be with you, unfortunately, but that's the way I was. Nephews, nieces, little brothers and sisters— it's terrible, but kids meant nothing to me till I had my own."

16

"Dan, Dan, it's the goddamn van again—no, I didn't mean for that to sound poetic or, rather, rhymic—but it's beginning to be where I don't know where to turn or what to do." This is what he'd like to call Dan about. Dan was the one he always called when the brakes of the van went again or he got another flat, second in a month, six to seven in half a year, no explanation for most of them because the mechanics only found a puncture once and the tires were good or new, and he couldn't put the spare on and drive to a service station to get the tire fixed because in the conversion of the van the jack plugs were removed. He felt stupid complaining about these things to anyone but Janice and Dan. The last time he called him about it, he said "You can't believe what happened today," and Dan said "The van," and Stu said "The brakes again. I don't know what the solution is. Every time I get them fixed, they work for a month or two and then I step on the brake pedal and there's little to nothing there. So I bring it back to the place that fixed them, get the front brakes fixed again, then the rear brakes, then the whole system replaced—back and front brakes and master cylinder and power booster and something to do with the suspension system and I'm out three thousand. The van's good for a few months this time and then one of the brakes goes, usually the rear, putting the entire braking function on the front ones, so they go quickly because it's too much for them. By now I've had the entire brake and suspension systems replaced, so it's not costing me anything anymore other than renting a car while the van's once again being looked into and fixed. It's also the worry of it—when will the brakes go again? With me alone in the van? When I'm with Janice or one of the kids? For sure not with either of them driving, since the van's so dangerous I'd never let them take the wheel. Will the brakes go entirely when I'm going seventy miles an hour and suddenly have to stop?" "I don't know what to tell you anymore," Dan said. "It's awful; it shouldn't happen. Most cars made today are maintenance-free or close to it for fifty thousand miles, and after you get the thing troubling you replaced, another fifty thousand. We both know it all has to do, and probably most of the flats you've had too, with something in the van's conversion. But you need this modified van to get Janice around, so it's a terrible predicament. You've brought the van to a Dodge dealership, right?" and Stu said "Twice, two different ones, and both said they wouldn't touch the brakes because they'd been altered in the conversion. The conversion people, when I told them this, said that wasn't true, the brake system's the same as in the original van. That's why I brought it to a brake specialist, and they keep fixing it because of the warranty on the job, but it never lasts for long." "And the company you bought the van from," Dan said, "—I know they're in Arizona and you had it shipped from there to your home when they were done modifying it, but they must have a service representative near you who could look at it," and he said "I did that too— one in the DC area and another, which I only called, in Pennsylvania, right over the Maryland line. Both fix everything in the conversion but the brakes; for that they send the van to a brake specialist near them, so it'd be the same thing I did without the long trip." "Now I remember you telling me that. Damn, I wish there was something I could do to help. Like wave a magic wand under your brake system and all around the van so you won't have any more problems with it, or not for a couple of years. Maybe you'll just have to give up on it and buy a new one, but from another company," and Stu said "They go for forty-five thousand now—the one we have was thirty-four—so I don't see how we can afford it." "Buy it on time, which I realize, with the interest, will shoot up the cost a lot, but you can't drive a vehicle you know is unsafe. I'll loan you whatever you can't come up with if you want to pay it in full," and Stu said "Thanks, that's very generous of you. Really; very. I'll talk it over with Janice, and if for now we decide no, I'll still keep your offer in mind. You're probably right about a new van. But the price of one, when I still feel, if the brakes worked, that we got a few years left on the one we have, makes me want to stick with it till I've exhausted every possibility of getting the brakes permanently fixed. You've been a big help, though. Not just your advice, but for me to have someone other than Janice to complain to about it," and Dan said "Always think of me for that. I've lots of free time and years of reporting prepared me for being a good listener, and if I have a similar complaint with something of mine, I'll call you," and Stu said "Yeah, and I'm sure I'll be a great help." He picks up the phone and starts to dial Dan's number. *Oh, this is crazy,* and puts it down.

17

"I don't know if I ever told you this," Stu said to Janice, and started telling her, when she said "You did, a number of times. What especially made you bring it up today?" and he said "Just came to me when I was slipping my belt off my soiled jeans to put on my clean ones." "Something I never asked was did you ever speak to him about it?" and he said "Too sensitive an issue to; better to keep it to myself. He might think I've been carrying a grudge over it all these years," and she said "Not if you preface it right. Just say you've always thought it too sensitive a memory to talk about with him, and you hold no grudge over it, but that you're both past sixty now, and you wonder what he'll make of it. Maybe nothing, you can say. Maybe, you can also say, you have the entire experience wrong and you've just been imagining it or it's one of those memories that someone else had and which you adopted as your own," and he said "I can't be wrong on it. He did it several times to Jay and me. Took off his belt.

Or stormed into our room holding or brandishing the belt and whacked us on the buttocks and back with it. Did it till we cried or pretended to cry, which only took a few whacks, and then said things like 'Don't ever talk back to Mom again, you hear?' Or 'You give Mom' or 'Pola,' the woman who worked for us for years, 'that kind of crap again, you'll get more of this from me.'" "God, how that must have frightened you. He's such an even-tempered man now, it's hard to imagine he was ever that rough. Maybe the army had something to do with it; you said he was in it for two years and went through some rugged training." "It could have been," Stu said, "but this also happened before the army. But most of it during and a little after, you're right. I remember his paratrooper boots—the sound of them as he stomped up the back stairs—so the latest he did it was forty-six, a little after he was discharged but still wearing those boots, because any time after that Jay would have been too old and big to get beaten like that. As for being mild-mannered—he is now, but then, and years before, he could be a scary tough guy some-times." "But the point is, he's changed, so you should talk to him about it if you want. He might just laugh at it now or say he's thought of it too and regretted having done it but never wanted to bring it up because he didn't want to relive it for you. Or he was too ashamed. I'd think it'd be a relief to him that it was finally in the open where you could discuss it and that you hold no grudge and never did. Am I right about that?" and he said yes. "I thought so; you're not the grudge-holding kind, and same for Dan. The two of you could even joke about what an imp you might have been then, though of course you didn't deserve such punishment, and what a henchman he was for your mother.

Actually, you wouldn't want to mention even that. But it was so long ago that you both would be able to talk about it easily, I'd think, almost as if it had never happened." So one of the next few times he was on the phone with Dan—he'd stopped himself in two other phone conversations, but then thought it was something he should do to get it over with and in the open between them, so do it now—he said "I was talking to Janice about this very old memory of mine. Not a pleasant one for either of us— you or me—but one I haven't thought about for around fifty years and which suddenly popped into my noggin the other day and she suggested I bring it up with you," and Dan said "So? Go ahead," and he said "Truth is, I don't much like talking about it. And remember, I've no animosity or anything like that to you regarding this. In fact, I'm even trying here—in relating this to you—to determine if my memory's correct or even comes close to it." "Jesus, what the heck could it be? Sounds as if I'm in for it." "You're not, believe me," Stu said. "Okay: when Jay and I were kids—Jay eleven or twelve, let's say, and me three years younger. And maybe we were big brats at the time, stuck out our tongues to Pola or Mom or talked back to them. Maybe Mom wanted to discipline us for something not even as bad as the examples I gave and she didn't have the energy that day to do it herself, though this happened with you a few times, so that explanation doesn't work. And I can't see Jay or me ever sticking out our tongues to Mom. But you know, didn't clean up a mess we made, let's say, when she asked us to. So she, unfairly, I think, asked you to do the disciplining for her," and Dan said "Are you getting at the times I was a little hard on you guys?" and Stu said "More than a little hard. Now I remember. Your paratrooper boots. So it must have been when you were in the army or just out," and Dan said "After my discharge those boots were the only footwear I owned for a while. The shoes I'd left at home, Mom, as she had a habit of doing—cleaning out our closets without first warning us—threw all of them out, good ones too with shoetrees, and my feet hadn't outgrown them. Like Dad, she could be a real character at times." "They were something, those boots. I used to—we did, Jay and I—get petrified the second we heard you come into the house when we knew Mom was going to tell you of something bad we did, and stomping up the stairs in them. Though maybe the boots were from a later period than when what I'm talking about happened. For Jay would have been too old then, and so when you stomped upstairs in them, it was only to discipline me." "So what did I do," Dan said, "to either of you? I ran upstairs, with or without boots, and told you loud-mouths to treat Mom or Dad or even your kid sisters with more respect. Maybe shoved you, forced you to do fifty regulation pushups and ordered you not to leave your room for an hour, and that was it. Because Jay never mentioned to me anything worse I did before or after I was in the service, and you know how outspoken he was when he got older. It was hard for him to hold anything back." "Well, he might have to spare your feelings. But you'd take off your belt when you came into our room—by this time we were under the covers of the lower bunk of the dou-ble-decker to protect ourselves—and rip the covers off and sometimes pull up our shirts to hit us with the belt. I have to admit, for a couple of years it made me a little frightened of you." "Who'd blame you, if that is what I did, although I don't remember any of it except having paratrooper boots and the noise they made on the stairs. Not the front ones which were carpeted, but the back." "You did it, believe me, several times, but once it was over we seemed to forget it and resume whatever we were doing. Maybe because you held back on those whacks and so didn't hit us that hard. It was Mom's fault—a lot of it. She shouldn't have asked you to punish us. That wasn't your job and I'm sure you didn't want to do it. She should've just told you to talk to us because she wasn't getting through to us or because she didn't want to be bothered. Dad, he never disciplined any of the kids except maybe once a year or so when he exploded at one of us over something—I think usually me—and hit us over the head with a rolled-up Sunday *News* or *Mirror*. I used to say it was the Sunday *Times*, but that would've been impossible. Too big; he couldn't have wielded it. He could have with two hands, but that wasn't the way he swung it. I also remember him chasing me with it—I wasn't just going to stand there—till he trapped me in a corner, or I stopped because I thought he'd get a heart attack, and let him hit me on the head." "He never did that to me," and Stu said "Because you were his favorite, which you deserved to be. You looked out for the family more, took on lots of the responsibilities, and never gave them any lip, according to Mom and Dad. Or whatever the explanation. Why should I think I know? But there it is. Janice, as I said, thought it'd be a good idea to get it off my chest and that you were a big-enough guy to accept it. Not 'accept it'; that wasn't what she said. That you wouldn't take it wrongly or think I was saying it accusingly and that maybe you'd want to get it out too," and Dan said "I'm telling you, I still don't remember doing anything like that. Yelling at you; once throwing a pillow at you where you stumbled when it hit you and cracked your head, but I didn't intend to hurt you. I'll take your word on this belt business, though. I was young when I got out of the army and it could be I'd been trained too hard to be aggressive, because of the war still on and the invasion of Japan being planned, and some of it might have lasted a while," and Stu said "That's sort of what Janice thought too. But now I'm sure it had to be pre-paratrooper, when Jay was eleven at the most, so 1944, and it probably only happened once or twice," and Dan said "But didn't you say it went on for two years or more?" "It might have seemed like that, for some reason, but now it's becoming a mixed-up blur. Before the army, when you were done with para-trooper training, after the army—I just don't know anymore and it doesn't seem worth figuring out," and Dan said "Still, after this call I'm going to go back in my mind and see what I can dig up," and Stu said "If it hasn't come out by now, I doubt it ever will, but do what you want," and they started talking about something else. In their next phone conversation Stu asked if he'd had any luck remembering anything about what they'd talked about last time and Dan said "If you mean the belt beatings, I tried to but nothing came up. Again, I take your word on it and hope you'll accept my apology for what I did, and if you have a one-way track to Jay... no, that's stupid. But whether I did it or not, and I'm not, by saying this, trying to get out of it, I don't think I'll be spending anymore time thinking about it," and Stu said "I agree with you completely."

18

Dan said on the phone "I didn't tell you this story before?" and Stu said "I don't think so. Even if you did, I forget most stories and jokes told me, so I'm the perfect guy to hear them again." "Every other Sunday afternoon when Newt and I were kids Dad would drive us into the city from Ocean Avenue, where we lived then, to go to Loews Delancey. The theater manager was a patient of his and let us in for nothing. You remember Dad: he never paid for a theater seat if he could help it. He used to say 'If you don't know the manager or anyone at the stage door and someone hasn't slipped you a free pass, walk into the theater backwards so they think you're leaving.' I don't think he was kidding, either. And while we were there—always a double feature and a couple of shorts and a newsreel and no money for refreshments—who knew what Dad was doing. You once said Mom told you he had girlfriends, while to me she said he was too tight to spend a nickel on another woman, so couldn't have had any. I think he mostly went to his office nearby to work on someone's teeth and then met friends at the Café Geiger—this place on Second Avenue, I believe, where Yiddish actors and writers and impresarios had coffee and tea and schmoozed for hours. Dad liked those flamboyant types, with their ascots and astrakhan coat collars and hats, since he was a little like that himself, though not the clothes. He always picked us up at the theater an hour late and we'd have to wait in the lobby for him. After about ten times of this—don't ask what took me so long— I started bringing a book with me and Newton did too, but he didn't like to read as much as I, so the wait was harder for him. We were six and seven, seven and eight, eight and nine, for this went on for years. But one Sunday took the cake. Dad arrived his usual hour late, even though he always checked with the manager as to when the show broke, and we got in the car to go home. But he parked, after a few minutes, and said 'Wait here, I'll be back in a minute.' The car was warm for a while and then got very cold. We had no idea where he went. The minute turned into an hour and by now we were freezing our butts off, as it was around twenty degrees out. I couldn't take the cold anymore and told Newton 'Let's go in someplace where it's warm.' He said 'Dad will get mad if he doesn't find us in the car.' I said 'Mom will be madder if we freeze to death, so come on,' but he said 'You go and when Dad comes back I'll tell him where you are. I don't mind. My coat will keep me from freezing,' he said, 'and if you also loan me your sweater and I hug myself real tight.' 'You're crazy,' I told him, but I gave him my sweater and went into a coffee shop across the street and asked the counterman if I could stay there, that I was waiting for my father. I had a view of the car and was hoping Newton would leave it and join me. After half an hour, I went back because I was afraid he really would freeze to death. Good thing I did. His eyes were closed, body was cold; he looked as if he'd died peacefully, and his hands, even in thick mittens and in his coat pockets, felt frozen, as did his nose. 'Newton,' I said, 'get up.' He didn't move. Holy hell, I thought, he's dead and everyone will blame me, the older brother who let him die there, and I shook him hard and he still didn't move or open his eyes. I asked people on the sidewalk for help. 'Someone call an ambulance,' I said, 'my brother's freezing to death.' A man carried him to the coffee shop, the only place open. They covered him with coats and an ambulance came and he was worked on and then taken to the hospital. His eyes opened a little during all this, though he didn't respond when I called his name, and the doctor told me his body temperature had started climbing back to normal and he'd probably be all right. Also—something I was too stupid or paralyzed to think of doing till then—to call my mother and tell her what hospital Newton would be at. Meanwhile, where's Dad? I'd kept my eye out for him through the coffee shop window and was starting to worry about him. I called Mom and told her about Newton and that it was more than two hours since I last saw Dad. She said he'd called a few minutes ago and said everything was fine, the boys had enjoyed the show and he was about to stop in somewhere for Chinese take-out before heading home. 'That guy!' she said. Then she asked what hospital Newton was in and I said 'Oh my God,

I forget.' If you don't think this happened this way, think again. Put it in a short story and nobody will believe it. I asked the counterman what hospital the ambulance had come from and he said 'I thought they told you, because I wasn't the one who made the call.' He phoned around and found which hospital had sent the ambulance. Mom said she'd go straight to it and for me to wait for Dad and have him drive there. I waited in the coffee shop till the counterman said he had to close up. I then waited in the car. We're talking of almost three hours since Dad said he'd be back in a minute, and remember, he was probably in the immediate neighborhood somewhere. A cop came and asked why I was sitting there with no motor running; didn't I know how cold it was? So as not to get Dad in trouble, I told him my brother had got very sick in that coffee shop, had to be taken away in an ambulance and that my father had gone with him and told me to wait for my mother, who was coming by subway from Brooklyn to drive me and the car home. He said 'You can't stay in the car—I don't want any kid freezing to death on my beat,' and I said I'll wait in the coffee shop, which still had its lights on, and crossed the street and stood in front of it as if I was about to go in. Moment he was gone, I ran back to the car. Then Dad came, and good thing too, because I just had a light coat and no sweater. I told him what had happened and he looked shaken and said 'God almighty, I walk away for twenty minutes and the world falls apart under me.' I told him what the doctor had said about Newton and that he looked much better when they put him in the ambulance and he said 'Good, they were only being extra cautious then, taking him to the hospital.' In the car I said

'By the way, you were gone for a lot more than twenty minutes, almost three hours.' 'Not three hours, don't kid me,' he said. 'Then two,' I said, 'but a long time. Where were you? You were lucky I didn't freeze too,' and he said 'I had to look in on a patient whose tooth I extracted the other day. He was hemor- rhaging bad and the teabags I told him to apply to it weren't stopping the bleeding and he was too weak to come to the office.' 'Then you should have told him to go to a hospital,' I said, and he said 'I knew I could treat it myself and save him some money, for the guy's broke, and I did. But oh boy, am I in deep hot water with your mom. She's going to kill me for leaving you kids for even a few minutes in the car.' I told him, because I was starv- ing, that Mom said he was getting Chinese food, can I have some? and he said 'That's what also took time. The three places I went to said I'd have to wait half an hour, which was too long, I felt, what with you kids in the car, so I gave up on it.' Then I told him I'd stopped a policeman from giving the car a ticket. I was lying, of course, but I thought it'd make him feel better. He said 'A ticket? On Sunday?' and I said 'That's what I asked him, but he said we were in a no-parking zone for even a Sunday and that it would be a big fine too.' 'Ah, he was just ticket-happy,' Dad said, 'making up his quota at the end of the week. What'd you say to stop him?' and I gave the same story of how he had to go to the hospital with Newton and I was waiting for Mom, and he said 'Good, you're a smart kid, quick with the line, just like me. Because that's all I needed. Not only Newton in the hospital and what that's gonna cost, but a ticket on top of it.' So that was our Sunday at the movies." "And Newton? He came out all right?" "He stayed a few hours at the hospital, maybe some tests; nothing wrong. But a year later he admitted to me he faked being unconscious because he wanted to ride in the back of an ambulance and also so he'd have an excuse to miss school the next day and never to be dropped off at Loews Delancey again. I didn't believe him. But I told him if I'd known he hated that place so much we both could have said we didn't want to go anymore, and he said he thought I liked going there—gave me a chance to get out of the house and see lots of movies and also get in some reading while we waited for Dad. I think that was the last time we went there. In fact I know it. For shortly after, since Dad knew we no longer liked Loews Delancey because of that bad experience and maybe because he wanted to forget it too, the theater manager hooked him up with the manager of Loews State on Broadway, which had a first-run movie and stage show, and one Sunday a month we were dropped off there."

19

On the phone, another time, Dan said "When it gets this warm there's nothing I like better than sitting on the porch reading the op-ed articles in the *Times* and drinking iced coffee in a tall glass filled to the brim with ice." "Never liked iced coffee," Stu said. "Had it maybe twice and both times it tasted like old cold coffee and I didn't finish them." "I forgot to say that in addition to the porch and the shade its roof gives I like it even more if there's a breeze. Did you have your iced coffee with milk?" and he said "I don't like milk in coffee. Just black," and Dan said "Milk makes it taste almost like a coffee egg cream. You also have to add seltzer or club soda—seltzer's better because it's less gassy," and he said "I never heard of anyone doing that." "That's how you make good iced coffee. Cold espresso the best, but any strong black coffee will do, and the coffee refrigerated in a jar before you put it in the glass so the ice doesn't quickly melt. Try it next time. Regular milk, seltzer, cold espresso or strong coffee, lots of ice, in a tall glass. Cools me off faster than anything other than a gin and tonic with lots of lime and ice, which I like around six before dinner, the iced coffee during the day. But the gin and tonic only sometimes. Usually it's a kir or iced-cold ale or beer. I'm not much into the hard stuff anymore—no good on the stomach and who can say what liver damage all those martinis of the past did," and Stu said "I'm afraid I still like them, but vodka, and two the max. Though even on rocks, not a drink for a warm day. And sure, after you helped make Mom and all the other kids in the family lushes—Dad, nobody could influence—you quit," and Dan said "I wasn't that heavy a drinker, nor do I think I had that great an influence on any of you," "You had it—believe me you did, with booze and everything else. Books, ethics, journalism as a profession, way we should behave, authentic Chinese food early on, learning how to use chopsticks, going out with gentile girls—the rest. But we were talking about iced coffee. One of these days I'll try it your way. Can't do me any harm, so give me the right proportions." Dan died the following March and on a hot July afternoon about a year since they had that conversation, Stu made himself fresh coffee and then thought "Too warm for hot coffee. Try it iced. In Dan's name. No, that's silly. Just try it. You haven't had one for maybe thirty years." He made it the way Dan said he made his and even remembered the proportions: eighth milk, quarter seltzer, rest coffee and ice, and better yesterday's or the morning's coffee than fresh, though he didn't see why that would improve the taste and he could even see why it'd make it worse. That's right: Dan said the old coffee should be refrigerated in a closed jar for a few hours and preferably overnight, but no time for that. The ice he put in a tall glass half filled with fresh coffee did melt a little. He spooned out the melting cubes and tasted the coffee. It was cool enough where he didn't think it'd melt new ice and he put some more in, milk, seltzer—didn't get the proportions exactly the way Dan gave them and the milk was plain soy—mixed and drank it. It's good, he thought; tastes something like a coffee egg cream. He never had a coffee egg cream. Vanilla was the only flavor he liked in his sodas as a kid, so it tasted like what he thought a coffee egg cream would, though maybe he was only saying that because Dan did.

20

Doesn't know what to do with himself today. First anniversary of Dan's death. Monday; Dan died on a Sunday. There was a strong wind that day where he died. No doubt contributed to the tree falling on him. Strong wind today; March, winds. He called in sick today at work. Couldn't go in. Felt too depressed. There were several memorial candles on his fireplace mantel he'd bought for other members of his family and this morning he lit one for Dan and put it in front of the photo on the mantel of Dan and him at Stu's wedding. On the phone he told the administrative assistant at work that he wasn't feeling well; something with his stomach. "Probably a virus," she said. "Are you throwing up?" and he said "No, but I feel like it." "You didn't take the October flu shot the school gave out to all its employees?" and he said "I did, but I understand it doesn't cover all the flu strains, and this year there are about five. Could you please put a note on room

38's door—do it on both doors—saying my class is canceled and it'll be made up the Monday after the last day of classes, and also a note on my office door that office hours are canceled today too?" and she said "I'll get the work-study student to do it, and feel better." He sits and reads in the living room, but doesn't feel like reading. Not even the newspaper. No magazine either, and he has two he subscribes to he hasn't read. Nor sitting. Walks around inside the house and Janice says when he passes her study the third time "What are you doing? You're making me dizzy." "It's crazy, I know. Just getting off extra energy. I feel so restless today, but I can't do anything. I called in sick before though I'm not sick, except maybe in my head. It's Dan's first anniversary; his death," and she says "I know, but I didn't know if I should say anything. I can imagine how bad you feel, calling in sick, which means you have to make it up, right? Just what you wanted—another week of school. Why not go for a walk outside? Thermometer here says it's forty-five, which is probably close to what it is, so not that cold." "Good idea. I'm in a state where I can't even think up things to do." He puts on his muffler and jacket and cap and goes outside, thinking maybe a long walk for a half hour or so will help, and gets about two hundred feet from the house and starts back. Doesn't want to walk. Doesn't want to go anyplace. What is it? It's just an anniversary. The first, okay, but just an anniversary. Yet it seems to have some unexplainable hold on him. That's not it, but something. Something preventing him from acting normally. As if all he can do today is walk around and eat. And he's eaten plenty already. Too much before noon. It's usually tea, coffee and miso soup, and later on, around ten, a piece of toast and slice of cheese, either real or made of soy, with a smear of mustard on it, and he's had two sandwiches of fake bologna and real cheese and lettuce and mustard. Then several slices of soy cheese. Carrots and celery and cherry tomatoes and three mugs of coffee and two of tea and he didn't make the soup. Didn't feel like it. Wanted each time something solid and filling. Every fifteen minutes or so looking inside the refrigerator and half the time taking something out of it. Olives and another time a whole pickle. And crackers from the cupboard. Can't write. That's out of the question. Typewriter's set up on the dining room table and he wouldn't even sit down and take off the cover. He paces back and forth in the living room a few times and then in the kitchen opens a cupboard to get a can of peas to make vegetarian chopped liver. Janice says from her study "Why don't you go to the gym? You go almost every day, so go now and work off your excess energy there. Makes sense, doesn't it? Just don't stay too long, because I'll need you in about an hour. Relief comes at two." "Who today?" and she says "Doris. She and Valerie switched days." "I don't want to see anyone, I really don't. Not Doris, not Valerie, not Adelle. I wish no one was coming." "Thanks a lot." "You know what I mean. You wouldn't have to worry if no one came. I'm home; I'll look after you. But you're right. I should go, work it off. It'll do me good." He puts on his sneakers; gym shirt, shorts, towel and washrag are in the back of the van. He kisses Janice goodbye, gets in the van and starts it up and will wait a minute and a half till the engine's warm, but after a minute turns it off. It's ridiculous, he thinks. I don't want to exercise today. Face it: you don't want to do anything. I should just go to bed. He goes into the house and says from the kitchen "You all right? Need anything? Because I'd like to lie down for an hour, probably less." "I'm set for now," she says, "but I'll need you in less than an hour. What happened to the gym?" "Like the walk, I can't do it today. If you want me, just yell," and he goes into the bedroom, kicks off the sneakers and lies on the bed. Minute later, he thinks if I'm going to nap, turn the phone ringer off, and he turns it off and gets back on the bed. Three minutes later he sits up. I'll never be able to nap, he thinks. I don't feel like resting. I feel like moving. But moving to no place. But I can't do that all day. Think of something else to do. Write a letter. A letter, yes, good. He gets his typewriter, brings it to his work table in the bedroom, sits down, takes the cover off, puts paper in and thinks who do I owe a letter to? No one. I always answer my mail in a day. Maybe the mail today will bring a letter I can answer, but I've no one to write right now. Write Andy and say you're writing before his response to your last letter comes because it's that kind of day, you want to write someone about what's been troubling you, Dan's death, the first anniversary of, and so on. How you're unable to do anything today but write this letter, in fact. In fact you can't think of anyone else you'd be writing this to. But who am I kidding? he thinks after he types today's date on top and "Dear Andy." I don't want to write a letter, and he takes the paper out and puts the typewriter cover back on. So now what? Call Harriet or Natalie. Call both. Natalie's work number he hasn't had for years. When he asked for it once, in case he had to call her, he said, she said "It's better if I call out rather than people calling in. My supervisor gets angry if I receive too many personal calls. Now if you got e-mail or instant messaging, we could gab all day." He calls Harriet. "Yes?" and he says "Hi, it's Stu," and she says "Hold on; I'm with someone else but I'll tell her I'll call back," and he says "Don't bother; this isn't important. Just wanted to say hello. And of course you know what today is, though I don't want to keep you," and she says "Yes, it's sad, isn't it. But don't go away." Minute later she's back. "So?" and he says "I lit a candle. Me, the atheist—absolutely zero belief in God and the afterlife and anything connected to any religion except for the literature in it—candles. To remind me of Dan, as if I needed reminding." "I lit one too. You're referring to the yahrzeit kind, or is yours a regular dinner candle?" "Yahrzeit. I had to go to Pikesville, the Jewish part of Baltimore for them." "In New York, they're everywhere. And I believe in God, though I didn't light mine out of any religious conviction either. I light them for Mom and Deborah and Jay and Newton too." "And Dad?" and she says "Not Dad. I don't know why. Not because I can never remember if his birth date is August seventh or ninth and I also can't remember what day in May he died." "The tenth." "Five-ten; that's easy enough. I'll remember. I still don't think I'll ever light one for him because it'd be hypercritical to, seeing how hard he was on me my whole life. Dan was hard on me too, but it's different. He was my older brother by three years and felt he had to look after me and he died so tragically, yes?—while with Dad he just went at me every chance he could and it was more natural his death, diseases from old age and a different life expectancy. Maybe that's senseless. You can tell me." "No, do what you have to; who am I to say? And all our relationships to one another are different. But the rest of the family. Do you light candles on their birthdays or the anniversaries of their deaths?" "Mom and Deborah I do both. Jay and Newton only on their birthdays, since I'm not sure what exact day they died. Newton's I could have found out; for one thing, Dan knew. But now that he's gone, how? I should have asked him, but I thought he'd find out why and ridicule me. 'Candles? Shtetl stuff; greenhorn, dumb!'" "I don't think so. But there must be records somewhere about Newton," and she says "Do you have them? Do I? I asked Melody a month after Dan died for all the personal papers of our family—he was the recordskeeper and unofficial family historian, am I right?—but she said she threw them out. A month! She couldn't have called one of us first? To see if we wanted them or just to have a look at what was there? It made me a little mad, but out of respect for all she was going through, I held my tongue. Now I'm not so glad I did, because it still rankles me." "No, it was best. And for Dan—you doing both, birthday and death?" and she says "I didn't on his birthday, I'm sorry. Meant to, but I used my last memorial candle on Deborah two months before and forgot to replenish my supply. But in the future? Yes. Look, if you want to talk more, I told this woman—a client, so I have to be nice to her—I'd call back in five minutes. That it was a family emergency." "You'll have to think up one to give her if she asks," and she says "You can bet she will. Because she's paying me good money she thinks she can have her nose in everything I do. I bought her two of your books, by the way. It's good for business, yours and mine. She won't read them—she has no interest in it—but she loved them as gifts. I'll tell her you called and were very sad over Dan's anniversary today. That wouldn't be a lie. Then I'll call you after I get done with her."

"No, this is fine. Just felt like talking to someone about it. You know, I also light one for Deborah and Mom. For some reason those, before Dan, have been the only two." "Newton, I can understand; you hardly knew him, and I won't even go in to why you don't do Dad. But Jay? You were so close. How come?" "It was so long ago, maybe. But so was Deborah—and I only started this candle stuff when Mom died—so I'm not sure. As for Dad, I never think about the day he died till a couple of days after. And his birthday's in August when we're in Maine, and it'd seem odd to light one there," and she says "That's part of my problem too." After he hangs up he thinks he should have asked for Natalie's work number. She'd have it; those two are very tight. But that's okay; he really doesn't want to talk to anyone today. Tomorrow when he wakes up, the candle will have burned down completely. He'll feel different. He'll be able to teach, get out of the house, run, exercise at the Y, go to the store. Drive, read, write, talk to anyone—life. He wonders if next year on this date it'll be the same. Maybe if he hadn't lit a candle it wouldn't be this bad. He goes into the living room and sits in the easy chair and thinks he should put on some Bach. St. Matthew or St. John Passion or a sad cantata. I could listen to that, he thinks, but he doesn't want to get up now that he's sitting. He stares at the candle. His eyes get tired and he feels himself dozing off. He thinks I've exhausted myself with all this running around. Next thing he knows he's awakened by Janice's voice. She needs him to do something for her. He looks at his watch. Half hour's passed. Amazing. So fast. Felt like a minute. Maybe this is how he'll get rid of the day. Sit in this chair with the light off, stare at the candle, nap.

21

A man who works out in the Y Stu goes to has become something of a celebrity there. Seems to run in all the Maryland marathons and 6K and 10K races and always comes in first in his class, the sixty-and-older masters', though he's now in his early seventies. Stu knows this because of the newspaper clippings put up around the Y, the most recent one showing him crossing the finish line and a clock there giving his time, and scrawled in marker at the top of the page "Once again our champ's victorious." Stu's also been in the exercise and locker rooms when people the man didn't seem to know congratulated him for his time or standing in a recent marathon or race and said things like "How do you do it? Quite the achievement for an old geezer. Keep it up; you're doing a good job humiliating the rest of us," and the man laughed and said "As they say, you're only as old as your heart, lungs and legs." "Good genes too can't hurt," someone said, and he said

"Mine are awful. My folks died from heart disorders before they were fifty, as did my only brother, and my sister of a stroke when she was sixty. Health-wise, I'm the anomaly of my family." Today Stu sees him showering. His back's to him; short, slim, about as tall as Dan, strong leg muscles like Dan had, and when he turns around to spray the soap out of his backside, flat stomach, also like Dan. Only major difference, it seems, is the hair. Dan's was full, with a little balding at the temples and in back, and mostly brown, while this guy's as bald as Stu, with a couple of tufts on top, and like Stu, the sides white and gray. Stu's wanted to talk to him about Dan a few times but never felt right starting the conversation. Would seem too much like bragging, he thought when Dan was alive. "I've an older brother who, like you, is a terrific runner. Was first in his class in the country for a number of years in three different masters' categories: forties, fifties, and sixty and older." And once Dan died he didn't think he could talk about him without breaking up. Now, just the two of them in the shower room, more than a year after Dan died, he just blurts it out. "You're very much involved in running— marathons and races... seen you chugging up and down the hills here a number of times and also the newspaper clippings about you the Y hangs up," and the man, washing his chest, says "Those articles; it's embarrassing. I tell them not to, but so far haven't gotten them to stop." Stu adjusts the temperature of his shower and says "Of course, running's not all you do. You're a scientist of some sort," and the man says "Psychotherapist." "Oh? My mother-in-law was one. But I wanted to say, my oldest brother ran a lot too. And like you, he excelled at it," and the

man says "He run locally?" and Stu says "No, only in New York
and Boston—marathons. And Paris once, when he was on a business trip, but the Boston and New York ones many times."
"I never did either of those. I know I qualified for them, but those
races always seemed like a stampede. Now Paris—that'd be nice,
but no one's sending me there on business, so it'd take a good
deal of money and rearranging of time. But your brother's not
from around here, you're saying," and he says "Westchester, New
York. He died recently—well, more than a year ago, running. If
you can believe it—" and the man says "I'm very sorry. And he
wouldn't be the first runner to die of a coronary, running," and
Stu says "It wasn't that." The man's through showering
and starts drying himself; Stu finishes rinsing himself and turns
off his shower. "It wasn't a heart attack or stroke. He was running by himself when a tree fell and killed him." "My goodness.
In all my years of hearing of running accidents and deaths, that's
one I never heard of. A tree? And killed him? Unbelievable." "It
was very unusual and to me a great personal loss. Because... ah,
I don't want to go into it. But I was thinking," getting his towel
off the hook, "that you might have heard of him. He was fairly
well known—actually very well known as a masters' runner. Dan
Fine?" "Dan Fine? Daniel?" and Stu says "He never went by
'Daniel.' I don't remember anyone ever calling him that, though
I'm sure it happened. Nor on his byline—years ago he was a
reporter" and the man says "Nope, never heard of his death or
him as a runner." "Do you read the running magazines?" and the
man says "I get two of them; subscriptions, although I don't read
everything in them. Haven't the time." "He's been in the main

ones, *Running World* and *Runners Magazine*, if I have them right."
"He was in those, and not just his race time?" and Stu says
"Articles about him, with photos. One—I remember the photo-
copy of it on my mother's refrigerator door—talked about the
three different masters' categories he was the best in the country
at—forties, fifties and sixty and older. Also his training regimen,
which the article said was unlike any other serious runner's. Ate
an enormous bowl of buttered pasta the night before the race and
one energy bar the next morning with an extra strong double
espresso. Didn't warm up much either. Maybe stretched his legs
for a minute and twirled his arms a few times. Ran ten miles a
day for a month, then a couple of twenties with a skipped day in
between, and didn't run the day before the race." "Most of that
sounds close to what most long-distancers do prior to a race,
except for the warmups. That I'd think he'd have to do more of
before running or else he'd cramp up," and Stu says "All I know
is that the article called his regimen highly unorthodox, the food,
training and warmups. But his name still doesn't ring a bell? He
was about five-six, build like yours, which I guess is a runner's
build. Dan Fine?" "Dan Fine. Dan Fine." Closes his eyes and
seems to be thinking. "Nope, doesn't register." "Champion
master's runner in the U.S. for about six years each in all those
categories till some guy who just entered it—you know, forty,
forty-one, while Dan would be forty-six or -seven—would start
to beat him by a few minutes. Dan would always come in second
or third in those, never lower, till he qualified for the next
master's category and would start being number one again. He
was considered a phenomenon in the masters' running world,

I was told. My older sister also ran marathons and K-races. Not with Dan's success, by any means, but she always placed pretty high and had her drawerful of commemorative T-shirts and shelf full of trophies. She said that runners would stop her— not during the race but at the awards' ceremonies—and talk about him in almost worshipful terms. He rarely went to these events where he was awarded something. Too modest or busy to, so they mostly had to send him his trophies and shirts." They were now in the dressing room and Stu starts dressing. The man wraps a towel around his waist, sits on a bench and uses another towel to dry his calves and feet and between his toes. "You said your brother ran in the Boston and New York marathons?" "Not only in them, but he won, for his class, about ten of them. Not ten each, but an awful lot—three or four in each category," and the man says "Whatever the number, just that he won even once. I don't see how I could have missed that information. I follow those races; they're the big two. I also watch them on TV, but they never much focus on the masters' runners, so there's another reason it might have got by me." "I'm not making this up, you understand," and the man says "I wouldn't think so and I definitely wasn't suggesting it." "My wife and I once even watched part of the New York marathon from the street; Dan had told me around what time he'd run by the place I said we'd be watching it from. And when he ran past—we didn't yell at him; didn't want to distract him, and he wasn't looking around for us either. He just seemed to be concentrating on the race. But a few people in the crowd yelled things like 'Go, Dan!' and 'Yeh, Fine; show 'em where you live.' What I'm saying is that they recognized him, and that was just one little spot," and the man says "That happens, even here in the Baltimore races with me. Sometimes there's a program and they know your name from your number. But again, I'm terribly sorry about what happened to him, the tree. Such a freakish thing. When was it? Maybe you told me," and Stu says "A year ago. March. There may have been a small mention of it in the running magazines, if they have obituaries or news items like that." "They do. I didn't see one of him, but that doesn't mean it wasn't there. A tragedy. Were you close? Sounds like it, so even worse. Excuse me. I have to shave. It was nice talking to you," and Stu says "Same here." The man puts on flip-flops, reties the towel around him and goes over to the sinks with his shaving kit. Stu says goodbye when he leaves the locker room, and the man, face full of lather and neck shaved, waves his razor at Stu's mirror reflection and Stu waves back. He looks at the bulletin board in the entrance to see what the man's name is, but the last newspaper clipping of another race the man's won has been taken down.

22

Things he left out. For instance, only time he remembers yelling angrily at Dan. The lead up: nine months before Dan died they got a second phone line for Janice's and his daughters' computers. Before that, no one could call in if someone in the family—not he; he'll never use a computer—was on line. The second line was to be used only for the computers or if someone wanted to call out and the other phone was tied up. For the first few months with the new line they got a number of personal calls for a Sidney Forb on the phone that was beside his daughters' computer in the dining room. Then one to two calls a week for a while, and then nothing for a month. Then they started getting three to four tele-marketing calls a month for Forb on the computer phone. Then two to three a week and then at least one a day. To each he'd say or told Janice and his daughters to say "Mr. Forb doesn't have this number anymore, so please take it off your calling list," and the telemarketers were always polite about it and said they would. But one morning, when he was working in the dining room, and during a period when they were getting only one to two telemarketing calls a week for Forb, he answered three of them in an hour. "Jesus," he said to the third caller, "how come we're getting so many of these telemarketing calls today when we were down to almost none?" and the woman said "All I can tell you is you must be in our computer, or your phone number is, if Sidney Forb doesn't have the number any longer, so in all the other computers that dial you. Want me to remove it from ours?" and he said "Please, will you? It's a big nuisance." When the phone rang ten minutes later, he jumped up from the table and grabbed the phone receiver from the computer station and said "Listen, I've had it up to here with your goddamn calls every other minute to sell us something nobody here wants, and even if we were halfway interested in it, would never buy because it came from one of these calls. Just remove our phone number from your files, which I don't even know because we only use this line for our computers," and Dan said "Hey, hold it a second; what's the problem?" and Stu said "Oh gosh. Thought it was another telemarketer selling us another gravesite or whatever they were trying to sell this time," and Dan said "They've been annoying you? Same with us, but once you tell them to delete your name from their computer list, they're compelled by law to." "Doesn't seem to work. Cut one head off and two appear, or seems like. But I'll keep trying. You saw me in action, though, and probably my approach is wrong. Scares them off before they can punch the right delete key into the computer, or whatever they do.

As I said, it's our second line and I really don't know the number," and Dan said "Janice gave it to me as an emergency backup in case I couldn't get through. I never thought I'd need it. But your phone's been busy for two hours—I knew it couldn't be you because of how much you say you hate talking for more than a couple of minutes on it—so I thought I'd try this one," and he said "Janice is out with her caregiver and Anita's in school, so the phone must be off the hook—I'll check. But is there an emergency with someone?" and Dan said "She's out of danger now and has been moved from ICU to a private room, but Harriet was rushed to Lenox Hill late last night with a serious intestinal infection. I've just seen her. She's on IV and still a bit weak, so don't call her just yet; I'll keep you informed." "You know," Stu said a while later, "that was the first time I can remember ever yelling at you like that. Of course it wasn't you I was angry at but those poor guys who are paid to make those calls," and Dan said "You were very young, so you forget. But when you were three or four and a little late at putting even elementary words together, you used to get so frustrated at your inability to communicate, or maybe you thought it was our inability to understand you, that you'd scream stuff nobody could understand at everyone. More to me than anyone else, because at the time I thought your stammering attempts at speech and subsequent frustration were very funny. You once even beat my legs and chest with your fists, I was laughing so hard and you were so mad. I was what—you're eight years younger than me, right?" and Stu said "Nine years minus six days," and Dan said "So I was twelve or thirteen, old enough to know better, but on this matter

I didn't. Later, when you were able to speak comprehensible words and then put short sentences together but were still quite a stutterer, I didn't laugh anymore—I'd learned by then—and it's been smooth between us since, I'd say. Though I'm sure, over the years, each of us has been a pain in the ass sometimes, but not so much where we had to voice it," and Stu said "I don't remember being mad at you for anything or thinking you were a pain in the ass, even when you threw that pillow at me that made me fall and split my head open. At the time I felt I deserved it because I was being such a brat to you. And after all, it was just a pillow, so I knew it was an accident." "Damn," Dan said angrily, "just when I'd completely forgotten the incident, you had to bring it up. Only joking."

23

The time Jay said "You should see Dan do pushups with just his fingers and toes. He can do ten of them straight without stopping," and Stu said "Why should that be so tough?" and Jay said "Try it yourself," and Stu got on the floor, Jay told him how to do it, and he tried but couldn't raise himself. "So, he might be able to do one, two, but I don't think anyone can do ten of them without stopping. That'd seem impossible," and Jay said "I saw him, and I bet he can do it again, and more," and they went into Dan's bedroom—he was in bed, sitting against the headboard, reading—and Jay said "Stu doesn't think you can do ten pushups straight with just the tips of your fingers and toes," and Dan said "So he doesn't. What's it mean to me? And maybe I can't do them," and Jay said "But I saw you, and we'd like to see you prove it now," and Dan said "Why should I prove anything to you guys? Anyway, if I do it it's something I do for myself— for exercise—and nothing I want to show off or demonstrate.

You came in on me doing them. Next time knock, or say before
you get to the door, if it's open, that you want to come in, but
that's the only reason you saw it." "Please," Stu said, "I want to
see how it's done," and Jay said "He means he wants to see that
it can be done, since he told me he doesn't think anyone can do
it." "No I didn't. I said 'Maybe, at the most, he can do two, or
someone could,'" and Dan said "What's the difference what you
said. It'd just be grandstanding, doing ten," and Stu said "No it
wouldn't. We know you don't want to. I want to see how you can
do it so then I can try," and Dan got on the floor, said "Don't let
on to the folks I've been acting so stupid with you guys," and did
ten. "That's my limit for now. At school I've done twenty and
thirty straight, but there I wasn't wearing bulky pajamas." Years
later, when Stu was in very good shape, worked out at home
every day, pushups, situps, running in place, lifted barbells he
found on the street, was the best built boy of all his friends, "The
Rock," they called him, he still couldn't lift himself up like Dan
did, not even an inch off the ground. That's how strong Dan was,
though he never looked it. Thin, narrow shoulders, no real mus-
culature, meaning his muscles didn't bulge, except for his calves.
He was wiry, that's what; never weighed more than one-twenty,
he thinks he remembers Dan saying; maybe one-twenty-five. But
right till almost the end of his life he could do strong things. In
his thirties, helping Stu move from one apartment to another, he
carried an oak dresser with all the drawers in it down three
flights of stairs. Just lifted it with his hands on either end as if it
were an empty cardboard box. Refused Stu's offer to help, saying
"You bring down other things; I want to finish this fast because

I have to get out of here in an hour." Would hold a bentwood chair straight out by the top of its back for more than a minute, and Stu once caught him holding two other wooden chairs straight out, just testing his strength when he didn't think anyone was looking, Stu supposed. "How the hell you do that?" he said, after Dan, his back to him, put the chairs down and sat on one, and Dan said "Do what?" and Stu said "Those chairs, out like that, even for five seconds; even to get them up at the same time. I've got fifty pounds on you and big muscles to your flat flesh, but I tried a few times lifting just one the way you did and couldn't get it halfway up." "That's about all I could do with one," and Stu said "All right, we won't talk of it." And a photo Stu saw in Dan's apartment under a stack of books—he was looking through them, curious what Dan was reading—of Dan on a beach holding up two women, each seated on one of his arms and the three of them in bathing suits and smiling at the camera. Dan was in his twenties then, covering the Korean War for a news service, and the beach and women were Asiatic. Only the last few years of his life, after he hit seventy, did he begin to look and maybe even feel his age. He still ran, and a lot of those runs for long distances, "but at a slower pace and no marathons and big hills anymore," Dan said, "unless they're only going down. When I think of the running times I did from my forties to my sixties, I can't believe how much I've slowed down." A little loss of hair, his face sagging somewhat, body a bit thinner, loss of what tone he'd had. And he walked sometimes like an old man who wants to walk with the quick gait he had thirty years before, one foot falling behind, stumbling up a curb or step.

24

Another time. Dan and his girlfriend Zee surprised the family by driving up from Washington and stopping in. "Surprised" them because weeks before Dan had told their mother he wouldn't be able to get off work that long weekend. Doorbell rang and one of the kids went to it, Stu thinks it was Natalie, and yelled out "Hey, look who's here. Dan and Zee." After kisses and hugs their mother asked if they were staying for dinner—she could easily set two more places and she had enough food for a small army—and Dan said "Sorry, we're having it with Zee's folks in Connecticut later this afternoon." "But you'll have coffee and cake and talk a little before you leave," and he said "Sure, maybe even a sandwich. I'm a little hungry. You too, honey?" and Zee said "Just tea, thanks, if there's any and it's no bother." "Don't let her fool you," Dan said. "She's got a terrific appetite. She's just saving it for later." Stu got sad; didn't know why. Or he knew:

wanted the whole family to be together at dinner. Dan was in a Chinese prison the last two Thanksgivings and Christmases, and he didn't want to come in for the seders this year, partly because he couldn't stand any religious ritual or event. He in fact worked a double shift the first two days of Passover so another Jewish reporter could have off. They always held the holiday dinners around the long table in the dining room, which with leaves could fit fourteen people if they put two at each end. That seem right? Five at each side? Probably, because the dining room chairs were wide and had arms, four at the most with four chairs added from the breakfast room. So the table could fit twelve, and they always seemed to have that many for their holiday dinners. If they had more, a card table was set up in the dining room for the youngest kids, with chairs brought in from the kitchen alcove table and upstairs. So Stu was sad and disappointed, but it was silly to get that way over it and he knew that but couldn't help it. His eyes must have got a bit watery, or something in his face, because Dan said "Anything wrong?" and Stu said "No, nothing," and Dan said "What? That I'm not sticking around for the turkey feast? Look, Zee's family is much more traditionally involved in the holiday than ours. It's practically a religious fête with them, even if the holiday's supposed to be secular and nonsectarian and just down-home American and they profess to be a-religious—no churchgoing or anything like that, except for marriages. But more the case, her family's been celebrating it since its inception, and on both sides. Her parents are each ninth- or tenth-genera-tion Yankee. With us, what? Both Grandpa Sams and Grandmas Bessie and Hannah came over around 1890 and didn't know

Thanksgiving Day from a hole in the wall, if it was even a legal holiday then. And Mom and Dad didn't start celebrating it either till after Harriet was born. From what I remember—correct me if I'm wrong," he said to their parents—"in the early days we had veal chops and baked potatoes for Thanksgiving because they thought turkey and stuffing tasteless and too dry, and no candied yams and creamed onions and so on. Really, kid, I'm surprised you're taking it like this. The holiday shouldn't be that important anymore." "Well, it is to me. That's the kind of shlump I am. We have so few traditions in the family, I hate for one to disappear." "Look, understand that much as I'd like to stay for dinner, it's more important for Zee to have it at her home than for me to have it here." "So let her have it with her family and you have it with yours," and Dan said "Excuse me, but that's got to be one of your more ridiculous suggestions, and it's not even a nice one, making it in front of her. We're practically living together. Don't be shocked," he said to their parents. "We're also planning on getting married. Her folks will be my in-laws, is what I'm saying. So you see my reason?" and Stu said "You're right, it was a dumb suggestion and I was being unreasonable. I got too sentimental—a fault I have," and Dan said "It's only a fault if it's out-of-place sentimentality, which this was," and he rubbed Stu's hair and Stu smiled. "So, all's forgiven?" Dan said, and Stu nodded. "*Mazel tov*, if it's true about you two getting married," their mother said, and Zee said "We wanted to break it to you and Dr. Feingelt differently, but this happened." Their father didn't smile or say anything, although when Zee went over to kiss him, he let her. After Dan and Zee left, he said to their mother "Oh boy, are we in for it now. It wasn't enough he didn't want to go to dental school, which made the other boys not want to be dentists too. Now he's marrying a shiksa, which you'll see will also be what they do." A few weeks after the engagement was announced in the *Times* by Zee's parents, Dan called home and told his mother "Don't buy the new dress you were planning to for the wedding, because it's all off." Someone had clipped out a newspaper article of thirteen years before of their father's involvement in the abortion ring and being sentenced to prison, and sent it to Zee's parents anonymously. "This person must have had a deep-seated grudge against Dad to have saved the article for so long or gone to a library's or newspaper's morgue and cut it out. It was done neatly, too, with scissors, and on it it just said 'We thought you'd be interested in the kind of family your daughter's marrying into.'" Zee's mother called her and said "Is this disgusting story true?" and Zee said "It must be if it's in the newspaper and with a photo of Dr. Feingelt being led down a courthouse staircase by the police. Dan never mentioned a thing about it, which doesn't make me too happy either." "Their conversation," their mother told Jay and Stu, "must have gone something like that, Dan said. He told Zee there was a very good reason he hadn't told her of it. 'It was a notorious scandal tucked away deep in the family closet,' he said, nothing his parents wanted any of their kids to blab about to even their future spouses, 'but I now see,' he said, 'where both they and I were wrong.' 'So,' Zee said, 'wanting to give their kids a simple almost gentile surname to help them advance a little easier in life than the Jewish one would, wasn't, as you told me, why they changed your name when you were very young,' and he told her no and that he wasn't as young as he said he was when the name change took place. In fact, that he was the one who brought the legal papers for his father to sign. And that his father was dead set against the name change and still is. 'So you lied to me on a number of accounts,' Zee said, and he said he did but only for the reason he gave. As for his father, he told her, he cared less about people knowing what he'd done than that his kids no longer carried his name. And as far as his eighteen months in Sing Sing, he told her and this I wish he hadn't, for what did she do that she now deserved to know?— that Dad even joked about it at home and with his cronies. That unlike most of the men in prison, he did it 'standing on one foot,' as he was fond of saying." Zee broke off the engagement. Dan was sure her folks had convinced her to. "It was enough she was marrying a Jewboy," he told their mother, "but the son of a former jailbird and one involved in something as messy as an abortion scandal? By this time, I'm sorry, but I didn't care and told her everything. That the abortion ring was discovered when one of the women died on the doctor's table. That he panicked, and I think I got the sequence right, and to get rid of her after the bungled abortion he cut her up and put the pieces in garbage bags. But a small part of her got stuck in a kitchen drainpipe when he was washing her blood down it and a plumber found it and that led to an investigation and the doctor spilling his guts out on everyone in the ring so he could get a reduced term. I could be wrong about the facts how Dad got caught, but I didn't take any guff from her and said if she was calling the engagement off because of what Dad had done long ago and paid a heavy price for—prison, the family short of money for a few years, losing his dental license and his kids his last name—then the hell with her and her folks." Zee phoned him a few weeks later, said she'd been rash and asinine about the whole thing, and that if he still wanted to marry her, she very much wanted to marry him. Eventually her parents came around too, invited the folks out for dinner and said they still wanted to hold the wedding at their home.

25

Stu was twelve and already had a little mustache and about twenty hairs on his chin. His mother said "Don't you think you should start shaving? and he said "Why, I'm too young? I'll start when I get closer to my bar mitzvah or right after." "But you look like a gigolo with that thin mustache and a bum with that stubble on your chin." "What's a gigolo?" and she said "An unsavory male character you don't want to look like or be mistaken for. You want to know more, go to one of the dictionaries in the house," and she spelled the word. "Meantime, I'll speak to Dad. He'll help you clean up that sweet face." "If I shave once I'll soon have to do it every day—that's what I heard. I don't like that every shaver's face and neck and sometimes the lips get cut, and then when you go outside you have to have little pieces of toilet paper stuck to your skin. Once, Dan cut his lip with a razor and it bled for an hour, even when he kept putting that white stick that burns on it, which is supposed to stop the bleeding." She said she's sure for a year he won't have to shave more than once every few weeks, and by then he'll be used to it. "And if you use an electric razor, which Jay has, you won't get cut." His father told her he didn't have the time or patience to teach him how to shave, "and I didn't have to teach his brothers either. Jay was taught by Newton. Newton by Dan. And Dan, without asking me for it or anyone telling him he had to shave and how to do it, went into our medicine cabinet when he was twelve, got my razor and shaved all his first hairs off. Next day, with money he made after school, he bought his own razor and blades and shaving soap." Jay told Stu "Dad's got it all wrong. Dan taught me how to shave. It was his safety razor, a brand new blade in it, which cut me to ribbons the first time, which is why I inherited Dad's electric razor. Dad never liked using it anyway. Said it didn't shave as close." He got out the electric razor. "Plug it in the wall and slowly go over the hairs. Do it as fast as you would with a straight razor, nothing will come off. Oh. No washing the face beforehand and go against the grain," and Stu said "What's that?" and Jay said "Forget it, doesn't matter with so few hairs. Just shave what you see off." Stu started shaving and the razor kept pinching his face. And Jay had to unplug the razor once and with scissors cut the mustache hairs away from the blade part to get the razor off. "It's an early version of the electric razor," Jay said, "maybe an antique. It doesn't do that to me, though, but I never let my mustache get so long." The bathroom door was open and Dan walked past. "Jesus, don't use that thing," he said. "It'll take all day and won't even give a clean shave. So Jay had a bad experience with a safety razor? It was an imperfect blade, probably one out of a thousand, and it happened his first time, so go figure the odds of that. Be brave, use a regular razor," and got out his, put a new blade in from a cartridge that appealed to Stu, and instructed him how to shave. "Tomorrow, to celebrate the end of your peach-fuzz days, I'm getting you your own razor and brush and shaving soap in its own tub." Dan also taught him how to tie a bowtie when Stu was going out on a date. He got behind him in front of Stu and Jay's dresser mirror, tied the tie a few times to show him how it was done. Stu said "Leave it, it looks perfect," and Dan said "No, I want you to learn. I bet you tie it right the first time," and Stu almost did, with Dan tightening the two ends a little so they were straight. He also taught him how to drive and then drove him to the DC Motor Vehicle building for the written and road tests. Around that time he tried teaching him how to type with all his fingers, but Stu continued to use only three, and the right pinky sometimes for the cap-letter key. "I'm sure I'd still be three- to four-fingering it also," Dan said, "if I hadn't taken typing in high school. Most valuable course I ever took, including in college." When Stu was around fifty-five, Dan, seeing him with shaving nicks on his neck and cheek, said "You ought to change your razor. One you're using must be from another era," and suggested the kind he used. "And what do you lather up with—shaving cream, or are you still using shaving soap?" and Stu said "You remember; but neither. I lather my brush with whatever soap's in the soap dish." "No wonder your neck's so raw. Wash yourself with a mild soap and hot water first, then put on the shaving gel or shaving soap. After, splash lots of witch hazel on your face," and Stu said "That's what I think you told me when you first taught me how to shave, other than for the gel, which wasn't around then. But I stopped doing it a few years after." Month later he called Dan and said "Were you ever right about my shaving. I did everything you said—state-of-the-art razor, shaving soap, washing my face with hot water first, witch hazel as after-shave—and I haven't cut myself once since I started and the redness on my neck is gone." "Here's another tip. Don't automatically junk the blade after five or six shaves, or whatever's your max. Every so often I get one in the pack that works for fifteen to twenty shaves—one even went for an entire month—without losing its razor edge. I'm not sure why, though I know it's not a bonus the manufacturer throws in for buying the product, because once you know what one of their blades can do, you have to ask why all the others aren't as good." "Money," Stu said. "They'd sell fewer blades. That blade was a mistake, and I'm sure when they produce one and know it, they throw it out." "Maybe," Dan said, "or maybe they're unaware how good a blade they can make. Someone ought to write them and include one of these fifteen-to-twenty-shave blades. Because I'm retired and have twice as much time on my hands than I can use, I'll do it, and now that you have a stake in the matter, I'll inform you of the results." "Good. Fewer blades I change, the better. Seriously, though, since when do you have so much free time? What about your book projects—that 'our gang' one especially, looking up your childhood pals from Brooklyn and Pine Lake Park, to see what they've done and what's become of them?" and Dan said "Good ideas, that's what I'm best at, and refining other

people's work. But I'm no book guy—that's what I found out
in trying to write them. Articles—short ones and mostly about
running—okay. I haven't the eyes, interest and sustained concen-
tration anymore for the long haul, or never had, except for the
eyes," and Stu said "Really, what does it take? You sit down, you
stay there a couple of hours, page a day or two pages in three,
and in a year, minus a total of two weeks off for hangovers,
stomach flu, birthdays, travel and just not wanting to make it to
the desk that day—you'll have three hundred manuscript pages,
or three hundred in a year and a half, more than enough for most
any book." "Nah, you have to start that routine when you're much
younger. When you reach a certain age, or at least when I did,
all these once important and exciting things you looked forward
to doing when you retired seem silly and futile. Besides, most of
the 'our gang' are probably dead or ailing," and Stu said "So you
include them. You find out what they did before they got so sick
or died," and Dan said "Nobody's going to want such a book;
too depressing. Best for me now is just to read books. The only
writing I do, other than for the one or two running articles a
year, will be along the lines of my razor blade campaign and
maybe some local newspaper op-ed pieces to save the Hudson." A
year later Stu said to Dan on the phone "Something came to me
about the razor blade I was shaving with this morning. It goes
back a while ago to what you said about it. You told me, and you
were right, that every so often one blade in the blade package of
the kind we both use will give me twice as many good shaves as
the others. You said you'd write the company and tell them how
come all their blades aren't as good. Did you?" and Dan said

"That's not what I told you. I said I'd let them know about this anomaly of a blade and that I'd enclose, as an example, one of the good ones in the letter, and was there a reason for this blade to be so much better than the others—that I was curious. You understand, I didn't want to be accusing them of anything under-handed, but what I got back from them were programmed evasive answers. 'All our blades,' the consumer affairs spokes-woman of the company wrote, 'are made to produce the very best results that a blade can, and all of them are manufactured under the same exacting conditions. If one blade lasts longer than the other,' she said, 'it's because of a number of contributing factors: duration of facial hair growth, condition the shaver keeps the blade in'—you're supposed to clean and dry off the blade after each use, etcetera, and store the razor in a dry place. How hot my shaving lather is—'Warmer the better,' she said and type of shaving cream and gel. She said nothing about shaving soap—I suppose they don't make one—and recommended her company's brands for the best results. In other words, what I expected: corporate bushwah, which I didn't think worth passing on to you. She did, though, include with her letter a box of ten blades of the kind we use, which she might have thought was my reason for writing in the first place, plus a box of five of a more advanced blade for our razor that she claimed would give an even closer and smoother shave, and which they no doubt hope I'll start buying. It does give a little bit better shave, but I'm sticking with the old one because it's cheaper and you get one or two more shaves out of it. I should have divided the boxes up with you, since it was our conversation that got me to write the letter."

26

An incident. Stu was baby-sitting, his mother called it, his two younger sisters. They objected to the word; "He's not old enough to be a baby-sitter," Natalie said, "and we're not babies." "Still, I'm putting him in charge," their mother said. "So when it's time to go to bed—ten, we'll say?—and he tells you to, you go." Everyone else in the family was out or away. Folks at the annual Grand Street Boys gala, he thinks. Anyway, some function where they dressed up, but not in evening gown and tux. Dan in the army or at college. Newton in the navy, he thinks, and if so, then Dan was probably in the army, since they were in the service around the same time. Harriet, he thinks, went to a party or the last show of a movie downtown and was given permission to come home late. Jay, he thinks, was spending the night at his best friend's apartment up the street—no, he's sure of it. Remembers him leaving excitedly with a little valise—his first sleepover, though it wasn't called that yet. His two younger sisters were asleep, or at least in their room and quiet. Around eleven, Stu in his pajamas and lying in bed, his back up against two pillows (his and Jay's), reading a comic book and drinking soda out of a glass filled with ice to make the bottle of soda last longer. This was unusual, soda. His father objected to soft drinks in the home— "The number one cause of caries," he said—except for birthday parties for the kids and when he and Stu's mother gave a party. Tonight she said Stu could have a Pepsi, his favorite cola because the bottle was twelve ounces instead of Coke's seven, as a reward for baby-sitting and also because she knew, she said, how sad he was that Jay wasn't sleeping home. "That's not true," he said. "I'm happy I have the room alone for once. I can do what I want without being bossed around, and his loud snores keep me up." So he was in bed, a little frightened being alone in the apartment so late, really, for what could his sisters do to help him if anything bad happened, but glad he had a soda and a stack of comic books he'd traded with a friend that day, when he heard a noise downstairs. Thought he did, anyway, and stopped reading, held his breath so he could hear better, and heard the noise again, like a clicking and now what seemed like someone trying to shove a door in. The noises were coming from the front of the apartment. He got out of bed, listened at the door to the living room, which was right outside his room. Heard the same clicking and door-shoving and went to the front staircase above the foyer, even though his mother didn't want the younger kids going through the living room, and listened. Someone was trying to get in. Seemed the key wouldn't work. Pushing the door to make the key work? Pushing it to force it open or break it down. What to do? He was there to protect his sisters and the house. At least to protect his sisters. He was scared, had been a little when they went to bed and he was left alone. But got over it by reading one comic book after the other and drinking the soda. Now he was really scared. If it was Harriet or the folks, they wouldn't have any trouble getting in, and it couldn't be Jay because he'd never give up sleeping over at his friend's. So what to do? His gun. He ran to his room and got his cap pistol out of the night table he shared with Jay. He had no caps in it. Used up the ones that came with the gun and no store seemed to sell them. Someone had told him caps weren't allowed in New York anymore because kids were getting burned by them. But the gun still looked like a real one. Metal, with a barrel that spun. Had got the gun out because he thought it'd protect him. That the robber, if he got in, would maybe think it real and run. And it was definitely, he thought, someone trying to break in. Probably even knew Stu was alone with his sisters, so it'd be easy. And then he'd do something to Stu and maybe to his sisters before he robbed the place. Stu couldn't run and hide because then his sisters might get hurt by the man and he wouldn't be there to try and stop him. He walked slowly down the curved front stairs with his back sliding against the wall and the gun out, finger on the trigger. The robber was still fiddling with the key in the lock and pushing the door. Stu thought it'd be better surprising him before he broke in, and if that didn't work, where the man didn't run out of the building, then screaming in the hallway for the tenants upstairs to come help him. He unlocked the door and threw it open, gun pointing out. "What the hey," Dan said, his key still in the lock, laughed and said "You crazy kid. What's with the peashooter?" "It's a cap pistol. I thought you were a robber. Mom and Dad asked me to protect the house. They're even paying me, to baby-sit Natalie and Deb. You should have rung the bell. I could have killed you, you know." "With that?" and Stu said "Or scared you off. What are you doing home? Nobody said you'd be here," and Dan said something to explain it, that he got an army furlough or caught a ride in from school. "What did the folks do, change the lock since the last time? If so, I wish they'd told me," and Stu said "I don't know. They don't think I'm old enough yet to have my own key."

27

Harriet, around fifteen, running into the kitchen and saying "There was this awful man outside. He tried touching my chest and then talked dirty about my, excuse me, but this is the word he used, pussy, and also made disgusting expressions with his face. I had to run from him because I thought he was going to grab me and try to feel me all over and nobody was around," and their mother said "Sit down; one of you get her a glass of water," and went to the back staircase and yelled up it "Dan, come down," and Dan hustled downstairs in his socks and said "What's wrong, one of the kids being fresh again?" and she said to Harriet "Tell him what you told me and don't hold back on anything out of embarrassment," and after hearing a little of it he said "Which way was he heading when you ran from him?" and she said "He wasn't. He just kept standing there, grinning at me. When I got to our building and looked back to make sure he wasn't following

me, he was still on our side of the block but only now walking
to the park." Dan started for the door and their mother said "Put
some shoes on," and he said "Haven't time," and Jay and Stu ran
after him, their mother saying "Where are you kids going? It's
getting dark out; come back." They couldn't keep up with him
and saw him about a hundred feet away on the Central Park
West corner grab a man from behind just as the man was turning his head to him, and get him in a headlock and spin him
around before throwing him to the ground. The man said "Hey,
what are you doing? You nuts? Let go, you got the wrong guy,"
and Dan, holding the man down, said "You tried to feel up my
sister, you pervert, and used dirty words on her," and the man
said "What do you mean, me? I didn't do anything like that," and
Dan said "She said a guy around your age in a green checkered
jacket," and the man said "Oh, that girl. She came on to me,
honest. I didn't know what to do, for I sure wasn't looking for
that kind of trouble, a kid so young. So I tried pushing her away
and maybe hit her in the front too hard. I'm sorry if I hurt her,"
and Dan said "Horseshit, and you know it, you goddamn liar,"
and slapped the man's face and then looked up at Jay and Stu and
said "What should I do with the creep?" and Jay was about to
say something, when Dan let the man up and held him around
the neck and said "Next time I'll bust your windpipe and rub
your ugly face in dog turds and then turn you over to the cops.
Stay off this block, you hear? I see you on it again or ever come
near my sister, and you're really in for it," and let him go and
the man said "All right, you didn't have to get so excited,
although I can sympathize why you did. I hear you, big man.

Every sister should have a strong tough older brother like you; the city would be a better place for it. But next time will you please try doing it on someone who actually did what you accuse him of. Me, I was only making my way downtown to the IND subway, and where, if you let me, I'd like to continue to now," and walked away. "Let's go back; Mom will be worried," Dan said, and Jay said "Suppose it was all a mistake on Harriet's part, that she only thought he was doing what she said, just like he might have got the wrong idea about her?" and Dan said "She wouldn't have misinterpreted something like that. A girl knows when a guy intentionally grabs her breast. She also knows I'd be angrier than hell if she did make it up to get attention and I went after the guy and found out it was a lie." "She also never said anything about his green checkered jacket," and Dan said "I know, but you saw how he so quickly admitted doing it with that 'Oh, that girl!' Only later, when he saw I was letting him go, he recanted," and Stu said "What's that?" "Retracted, disavowed ... *lied again*, that should do it. Second I looked up the block I knew he was the one, just by the way he was walking. That slimy swagger and furtive glancing around. I hate guys like that, though it's a good thing thieves and punks like him can be so stupid." Another time about a year later. Harriet came downstairs to the breakfast room wearing pancake makeup and lots of lipstick and their father said "Where are you going to, a clown convention? I've never seen you with so much face stuff on," and their mother said "That's not nice, Mort. But you are wearing a bit too much makeup, dear," and Harriet said "All the girls my age wear it today like this. It's the style, like loafers, and it's only makeup and I can easily wash it off later." "Don't you want to take some of it off now?" and she said "But what for? And it took me a long time to put it on right," and Dan said—they were sitting around the dinner table having dessert; Harriet had excused herself earlier so she could dress to go out—"Do what Mom says. Take some if not most of it off." "Who the heck made you my third parent?" and he said "Don't argue with me. I said to do what Mom told you and Dad implied," and she said "Mom didn't order me to. She suggested and I just happen not to be taking her suggestion. You can't boss me because you're all of three and a half years older. You're not the king and I'm not your slave." He stood up and put his finger to her lips and smeared some of the lipstick across her cheek. "You bastard. I hate you," she said and burst out crying and ran upstairs to the bathroom there and slammed the door. Half an hour later, after the kids—not Dan; he'd gone out—had cleared the table and washed and dried and put away the dishes and swept the kitchen and break-fast room floors—they could still hear her sobbing upstairs. "She was supposed to meet her friends," their mother said. "They're going to be disappointed if she's not there. Someone should remind her." Before that, right after she ran upstairs, their moth-er had said to Dan "That wasn't necessary. We could have worked it out another way. And if she insisted on keeping all that makeup on, it wasn't the worst thing in the world." "She needed a lesson and I gave it. I don't like her talking back to either of you. She gets away with it, the rest of the kids will think they can too." Their father said "He has a point. Anyway, the damage has been done, so now, if nobody minds, I'm going to smoke my cigar." Stu said to his mother "I'll go," and went upstairs. It was quiet in the bathroom now. He knocked on the door and Harriet said "If it's Dan, save your breath; I'm not talking to you," and he said "It's me. Mom wants to know if you're still planning to meet your friends—they might be waiting," and she said "I'm not going. If they call, tell them I'm sick." "I didn't think, you know, it was right what Dan did to you, and also Jay and I think Mom thinks so too," and she said "Thank you for telling me that; it helps. He can be such a tyrant sometimes that I'm glad he moved out and I hope he never moves back or visits or even comes to dinner again. He does, I won't be here," and Stu said "He's not so bad, and he did once help you. When that man tried to feel you on the street and called you dirty names," and she said "He was only using that as an excuse to bop someone other than one of us. He's got a mean streak and can be such a bully. You've seen it too when he whipped you and Jay with his belt when he also said you were talking back to Mom or Dad." "Those times I did something wrong, while this time you didn't. Most of the time he can be a lot of help to me and everyone here and very nice," and she said "Believe me, I know him better than you. Think what you want, though. You're entitled to, and I'm not a dictator. Only one allowed per house. But if you have to excuse his beatings by saying he's also been good to you occasionally and that you were so bad you deserved to be whipped, then do so, and I'll have to settle for being the only one here to stand up to him." "I didn't say I deserved it. And he only hit us a little and hasn't done it for a long time, so I bet it's all stopped." "He's moved out, Stuart—you didn't think that might have stopped it a little?" "That's true, I forgot. But we most of those times had covers over us which he didn't always pull off, so it wasn't that bad and didn't hurt much," and she said "Good, I'm glad he didn't kill you. But I still hate him and am afraid of him both, though that's not going to stop me from talking back when he mistreats me or I think he's wrong about something I did. Do me a favor? Go downstairs with this phone number I'll give you and call and ask for Eileen and tell her I'm not sick but have too much homework to do for Monday to meet her." "Dan's left, you know—said he was going to see a friend," and she said "Then cancel what I just told you; I'm coming out."

28

In 1949 and '50 Dan was a reporter for a Westchester newspaper. He'd bought, with a loan from their parents, a used car to get to work, and lived home till he could afford his own place, but the family didn't see him much. He left at 5:30 in the morning, got back around seven at night, usually just to shower and change his clothes and maybe have a quick bite before going out on a date or to meet a friend or go to a movie, and never seemed to get home till past midnight. On his days off he slept till noon to make up for lost sleep, he said, and then left the apartment and most times didn't return till late. One night around ten their father went out for the early edition of the *Times*, something he rarely did. But this evening, instead of waiting till morning to buy the late edition on his way to work, he bought the early one to check the obituary page for someone's funeral the next day. He then thought, as long as he was outside he'd also break his routine of just a single daily shot of scotch (which he always had before he left his office for home, "and that one mainly for the heart" or "to clear the blood vessels," he liked to say) and stop at the bar on the corner of Columbus and 77th for a scotch and to briefly read the paper. "When who do I see there but our boy Daniel"—Stu had gone to his parents' room to say goodnight and overheard all this through the closed door. "What's he doing sitting on a bar stool by himself? I asked him, and he said to me 'Isn't this unusual for you too, because I've never seen you in here before? You come looking for me to drag me by my ear home?' I said 'Not at all; it's a complete surprise.' And he hasn't seen me here because it's the first time in probably ten years I've been to a bar at night to get a drink. 'But you seem to be a regular,' I said, 'what with that "you've never seen me here before."' He said to me 'It's just like you said. To be by myself, have a beer or two, watch some terrible TV, relax from the family and job—a home away from home whenever I want one, which I do periodically. And it's a nice quiet place, with the most comfortable padded stools of any I've been in.' I told him I wasn't familiar with that many bar stools to compare the one I was sitting on, and when I used to go bar-crawling at his age, we only stood. Then, though I knew he'd rather I get the hell out of the joint, I said I didn't like the idea of my son drinking alone. 'You're young, smart and good-looking,' I said, 'and with a beautiful crop of curly hair. You should be with a girl or your friends having fun. It's a bad sign, so early in life, drinking by yourself. It's also, because of the little dough you make, a good way of pissing it all away.' He said 'With all due respect, Dad,'

that it was his business what he did with his money and life,
so he wished I wouldn't butt in. To that, since it was the first
time he ever talked to me that way, I didn't know what to say,
so I just said 'okay.'" "He's right," Stu's mother said. "He's no
fool, nor is he the type to blow all his wages on drink. He needs
to unwind, and if no friends or girlfriends are around, he does it
alone at a bar. If he picks up a woman there, no matter what
kind, so long as he doesn't get something from it, what's the
harm? It's what you did before you met me, though always with
your band of cronies. So he's not the mixer and backslapper you
are. Who is?" "But he didn't just have a beer in front of him. He
had a shot glass, then another when I asked what he was drinking, plus another beer, and who knows how many before.
Drinking like an Irish sousehound who's been chased out of his
house by his wife." "Don't worry, he's only biding time till he
rents his own place." "That's another thing," he said. "Why would
he want to move out when there's more than enough room with
us? And the price is right, no? —Okay. So after I finished my
one drink in a hurry, I told him why doesn't he drink up and
walk home with me? He said 'Not right now.' He has some thinking to do concerning his job, so he'll see me later if I'm still up.
'What thinking you have to do?' I asked him. 'Anything serious?
Remember,' I said, 'if there's one thing you have to know about
work, it's never give up a job till you have a new one sewed up,
and never take the new one for less pay. You always have to
work up. And you always have to have money coming in,
especially when you're starting out. You never know when there
can be a sudden recession or glut in the job market for what

you're looking for, and you can be out of work for a year.'
He said 'That's precisely'—that's the word he used, *precisely*—
what he was thinking. And then that he'll see me at home, or
tomorrow when he gets back from work, unless I want him to
walk with me because I don't feel safe going alone or I just feel
a little unsteady on my feet. I said 'You think one drink would
do that to me? If you do, you don't know your old man. I'm not
boasting,' I said. 'One should never boast as to how much alcohol one can take. Though I will level with you: I used to be a big
drinker,' I told him. 'I got smart and stopped when I got married
and started thinking of all the kids I'll have to support for the
next thirty years and my health. But I never fell down once or
lost my way home like a stumblebum or even ever felt unsteady
on my feet from drink. Nor is this the kind of neighborhood I
moved my family to—a dangerous one, where we have to walk
in twos. It's just that I don't like'—I'm sorry, but I said this and
regretted it the second it came out—'I don't like to see you start
on your way to becoming a serious morose drunk.' He didn't get
angry or even look startled. And I don't know where that morose
word came from. In his typical way he smiled nicely and said
'You're way way off, Dad. But to be honest with you, though
there's no offense meant here,' and he whispered this, 'it's embarrassing your saying that within earshot of Ike, the bartender,
who's come to know me. But there's nothing to worry about.
I drink slowly. I hold my liquor well. I don't overtip or look for
whores here. I know I have to be up early the next morning,
and if I've been loaded in my life it's only been a few times in
college.' He was telling me to go easy on him, of course, but in

the calmest most respectful way. So, because the last thing I wanted was to hurt or push away such a good boy, I said goodnight and put out my cheek, which I guess I did out of instinct, since it's always how our kids say goodnight to me and how I want them to for as long as I live, and he didn't hesitate a moment, and kissed me. But I really hate seeing him become like that, a bar stoolie we used to call them," and she said "Take him at his word. He'd never do anything to jeopardize his job and health and bring shame on the family. He's fine and has to be left alone to solve his problems and run his life, unless he asks you for advice," and he said "What's that supposed to mean, I have to permanently keep my hands off and watch him fall into the gutter, if that's where he's heading? Okay. You're the boss, if that's what you want me to do with him," and she said "Nonsense. You're not listening. Let's turn in."

29

After Dan was released by the Chinese and wrote about it and then came home, Stu said to him "I know all about your capture and imprisonment and hardships and such from your articles. What I'm also interested in, since I'm thinking of becoming a newsman, is what it's like—the day-to-day stuff of being a war correspondent." "You know you can only become one after you've worked in the States a while for a newspaper or wire service," and Stu said "I know, and also that there needs to be a war. But tell me, were your living conditions better, when you were covering a company or platoon, let's say, than a private or officer?" "When we were reporting out of a city or area unaffected by the war, yes. On the battlefield, or near it, we lived like the average GI: ate their food, slept under the same conditions, washed as infrequently, dug holes to take a dump—the rest." "Ever in danger from the enemy?" and Dan said "Sure. Came under heavy bombardment twice, where we lost a reporter and photographer—and faced arms fire several times." "What did you do, if you were out in the open, put a helmet on and jump into a foxhole or trench with the soldiers and pray for your life?" and Dan said "Your helmet was always on when you were in a combat zone. And yes, I always took cover, once behind a mound of earth when a battalion of Red Army soldiers started charging up a hill." "You were at the top of it?" and Dan said "That's right." "God, what a thing to be confronted with. I guess it went okay. But what would you have done if they had tried to overrun the cover you were behind and even came at you with a bayonet— got that close, I'm saying, and couldn't tell you apart from a U.S. soldier, not that that might have made a difference." "You shoot them." "With what? I thought war correspondents, like chaplains and medics, weren't allowed to involve themselves in battle that way or carry weapons," and Dan said "They weren't, but most reporters who were in a combat zone did. This wasn't publicized, you know. But if there was a chance the unit you were with might be attacked or sniped at, you borrowed a gun from an officer and were quickly taught how to use it if you didn't already know." "Did you ever use it?" and Dan said "Never the pistol, which was what you'd get to protect yourself if you were attached to an army unit in a potentially dangerous area. For instance, when the unit I was covering went on a night mission to find and destroy enemy soldiers and another time to kidnap an important government official," and Stu said "They must have been scary—night, no light, just a pistol," and Dan said "They were, a little. But they made for good news stories, getting deep into the action like that and seeing it firsthand, though of course in the stories I never let on I was armed." "So you never had to use a gun?" and Dan said "I'll tell you something... though maybe I shouldn't. No, I will, but promise to keep it to yourself till after I'm dead," and Stu said "That means for the rest of my life then." "Fine, I'll go for that, both of us very old and kicking off peacefully at the exact same time. In fact, maybe all the kids could go like that—no sorrow. But seriously... the charge up the hill I mentioned before? They outnumbered the company of infantrymen I was with by maybe fifteen to one and were screaming and blaring horns and whistles. The sounds were supposed to scare us. The soldiers popped them with everything they could. I had my pistol with the six bullets in it but was saving it for what I hoped wouldn't be the right moment—maybe putting the last round into my head if things got that bad. They kept coming. A hundred dead, another hundred charging maniacs to take their place. Suddenly I was handed a rifle by a lieutenant, who said 'We need every trigger finger we can get to stop from being overrun. Know how to use it?' and I said I'd gone through basic training in '45 and the gun looked the same as the one then, and he gave me several magazines—magazines of cartridges— and said 'Kill as many as you can. You don't, you won't be around to write the story,' so I did what he said. Aimed and fired. Aimed and fired. It was ridiculous. They weren't shooting back. Just coming in droves, many of them dying with whistles and tin horns in their mouths. Their commanding officers probably thought we'd run out of ammo before the last thousand or so of their soldiers made it over the top. Then a bugle blew a few times from somewhere behind them and they turned around and ran back down and never came back." "How far up the hill did the closest of them get?" and he said "Twenty feet from us. I don't know how they weren't killed sooner." "Did you shoot at the ones retreating?" and he said "I didn't, but the soldiers, on orders from the lieutenant, did. Rifles, mortars, machine guns. A slaughter, but he thought that was the best way to keep them from coming back." "How many you think you got?" and Dan said "Do you mean kill, me, personally?" and Stu nodded. "Five or six, if the ones I shot at and went down weren't killed by someone else and my shots got their late or missed, though I doubt it. And interesting, because that's what the lieutenant asked me, and when I told him, he said 'In all that time and with the accurate rifle I gave you and so many easy targets, you couldn't have got more?' How do I feel about it now? Was that going to be your next question?" and Stu said "Maybe, but probably not. I wouldn't think you'd like my asking it," and Dan said "I never liked killing anything. Not even a bug, except a New York City cockroach or a mosquito keeping me from sleep or about to bite. But I had no regrets. I was saving my life, helping to save some soldiers' lives, so for about twenty minutes that's what I was, an involuntary, necessary and unlawful combatant, and then I wrote it up but without putting in the part I played. I also figured the lieutenant and soldiers would keep it quiet, but wouldn't have tolerated my refusing to fight. And for all I knew one of them might have got so crazy and incensed—slaughters do that, and also because the company lost a couple of men the day before—that he'd shoot me for not joining in." "What happened to the wounded and dead?"

and he said "For our side, they didn't throw anything at us but noise, so nobody got hurt. The lieutenant kept the Chinese from reaching their wounded for about twelve hours and then gave them thirty minutes to drag back as many as they could. That was the worst part of the next two days before they were allowed to get the rest of their wounded—the dead they just left there— hearing the groans and seeing these wounded and dying soldiers moving their fingers and their bodies jerking and also the smells from below. It was a tactic, the lieutenant told me, to show them how tough and merciless we were and what they could expect if they tried another charge. He also told me not to write how he dealt with their wounded and dead—a violation of the Geneva Convention, which could get him court-martialed. In fact, to write that the Chinese, after we chased them away, abandoned their wounded for two days and, much as he wanted to help, he didn't want to risk the lives of his soldiers by sending them down to get the wounded so we could treat them. In turn he wouldn't say that in a fit of anger I grabbed a rifle off the ground and began shooting at the advancing Chinese." "But you didn't grab it. He gave it to you, practically ordered you to shoot," and Dan said "I know, but you don't see his point? Anyway, Mr. War Correspondent, what would you have done in the same situation, used the rifle if asked, or pistol if you had one?" and Stu said "The rifle, just like you, though he'd have to quickly show me how to use it. Also because if the Chinese made it over the top they'd butcher me as fast as they would our soldiers no matter how many war correspondent credentials I'd wave. But I don't think I'd carry a pistol on one of those nighttime patrols.

I'd be afraid I'd hit a GI by mistake or a civilian instead of an enemy soldier," and Dan said "Sometimes their soldiers were dressed as civilians and would suddenly open fire on you," and Stu said "So even more reason not to have one—I wouldn't be sure who to shoot at unless I was up there at the top of the hill and the enemy was coming to kill me." "Good; better you don't carry a pistol. Those things can go off when you don't want them to, and there go your toes. And good questions too."

30

Harriet's oldest daughter got married in the banquet hall of a restaurant near the South Street Seaport. Stu's daughters were the flower girls. They were young then, four and seven, and fell asleep after dinner—Anita, the younger one, on his lap; Meera, with her head resting on her arms on the table. "I think we should get going," he said to Janice. "And darn, just when the dancing's starting," which he immediately knew was the wrong thing to say, since by then she could only walk with a walker. "Sorry, I wasn't thinking. —Gotta go, Mom," he said to his mother at the table, and she said "So early? Oh, that's too bad. But your two little darlings are staying," and he said "You serious?" "Yes. I'll look after them. Harriet or Dan will drive us home and they can spend the night with me. I've got more than enough room." "Mom, the kids have to stay with us. And they're already sleeping—it's way past their bedtime." "We're going too, Mom," Dan said. "Either Harriet or someone else will have to take you home, unless you want to leave now." "Just when the party's getting started? It's not past my bedtime, and how many affairs do I get to go to? Someone will drive me home," and Dan said "It's only that I hate this awful ear-splitting noise. It's given me a headache already. I also can't stand, though don't tell Harriet this, weddings that are so garish and big. What a waste of dough. It had to have cost them a fortune." "It's a beautiful affair," their mother said, "every part of it. The hall, food, decorations, Edith's gown, and these two gorgeous flower girls in matching dresses. Tell me, where'd we go wrong in raising you? You're my treasure anyway," stroking his cheek. "Both my boys are." "You know, I wouldn't mind staying another half hour and getting in some dancing," Melody said. "Then maybe Mom will let us drive her home. And she wants to dance—your mother was a professional dancer—so you'll dance with her," and their mother said "I'd love that." "I haven't danced in twenty years," Dan said, "and have had two left feet for sixty years, so I'm not about to make a fool of myself out there now. Besides, the band's probably constitutionally against fox trots, which was the only dance I could do." "I'll request one," Melody said, "or two, the second one for you to dance with me after your mother," and he said "Listen, sweetie, I have to help Janice and Stu with the kids. Let me carry one of them to your car," he said to Stu, and Stu said "Don't worry, we'll manage. Meera will walk and I'll carry Anita." "But look at Meera. Dead to the world, and you can't be parked too near here. Just give me one, preferably the lightest." "Really, I don't want to make it a burden for you," and Dan said "How can it be a burden? Anita's a feather. And this'll help me get out of here, you idiot." They said goodnight to their mother and sisters and a few other people and left the restaurant. Dan and Stu carrying the kids, Melody and Janice walking slowly behind them over cobblestones to get to the smoother part of the sidewalk. No cars were allowed in the area—a pedestrian mall or whatever it's called. Stu thinking How nice this is, my brother carrying my kid, two of us walking side by side, exchanging smiles, talking about the party and how good all the grandkids looked. And Mom seemed fine, more lucid and chipper than usual; she actually seemed to have a good time. "The whole thing wasn't as bad as I said," Dan said. A lovely night, perfect weather, and how lucky they were there was no rain when a storm was predicted. Dan speaking very low so not to wake the kids, though Stu said "Talk as loud as you want; a gunshot wouldn't disturb them now. You must be tired from the walk," to Janice when they got to the first street cars could go on. "Stay here with Melody. We'll get the kids in the car and drive back. —Okay with you?" and Dan said "Sure, anything," but looked tired, so Stu said "Maybe I'll take Anita from you and leave Meera with them," and Dan said "Come on; you can make it, I can make it. I'll even trade with you if Meera's getting to be too heavy a load." "No, no; it's good." Then it was just Dan and Stu, carrying the kids, silent except when Dan said "Left or right at the corner? And if you don't mind, for I am getting a bit pooped, how far's your car from here, just so I know what to expect?" "Next block in the lot under the Drive. I'm sorry; Anita's heavier than she looks. Big bones and thick hair like her mother," and Dan said "Not that I'm trying to make excuses for myself, but it's late for me and too much food and drink, so I haven't the stamina I had when I got to the wedding. I'll be fine." They put the kids in the rear seat.

Dan tried to strap Anita into the children's car seat and then said "Better if you take care of it; I don't know how it works. They didn't have them when my kids were this little, or there wasn't a law that you had to use them, so we didn't. Wrong of us, I realize, because I even did a public television documentary on auto safety and went to Sweden to interview Volvo and Saab people and the Minister of Safety and Health on the effectiveness of various safety features their cars had to have and especially this seat. Now I remember. Melody was all in favor of them and asked me to bring one back. I scoffed at the idea, saying it was too heavy to carry to the plane and we'd have to drill several hooks into the rear seat for it and that'd be expensive and also lower the resale value of the car. Don't say it. It was long ago." Then driving back, each kissing the other's wife goodbye, Stu getting Janice into the front seat, saying "Hey, this was fun," and kissing his cheek, one of the first times, maybe the first, he did that, which they continued to do just about every time they met and also when they said goodbye after. Thanking him again for helping with the kids, getting in the car, waving goodbye and driving uptown to their apartment. "That was so nice of him to carry Anita," he said in the car, "but I think she got to be too much of a strain for him the last two blocks." "Really?" Janice said. "Because for a man his age he's in terrific shape. Anyway, and not so he could get out of the party, it was obviously something he very much wanted to do." "Why's that?" and she said "What do you think?" and he said "Of course; what a stupid question."

31

Streak got his name because of the gray streak at the top of his head. Other than for this mark, he's all white. Dan knew this, had seen Streak in their New York apartment. Stu had joked to him, as he'd done to others, that Streak was also called that because of his mean streak. He attacks people, can't be trusted. Is affectionate one moment, purring and rubbing himself against your leg, and vicious the next. They lock him in a bathroom when a young child's in the house. He once chased a plumber from the door when he bit his hand—the man was petting him—and then went for his leg. Has scratched and bitten Stu and his daughters several times. Once, late at night, Stu opened the kitchen door and called for Streak to come in, he wouldn't, so he picked him up to bring him in and Streak clawed Stu's arm through his shirt-sleeve and leaped out of his hands and ran off. "Screw you, you freaking bastard," Stu yelled—Dan laughed when Stu told him this on the phone—"and as punishment you're staying out till morning... who the hell wants you in here anyway?" and slammed the door, but Janice later told Stu to let Streak in when she heard him tapping on their bedroom window. When she's being wheeled up the ramp from the carport into the kitchen— Dan really got a kick out of this when he told him—Streak, almost every time if he's around, leaps onto her lap, usually rests one front paw over the other, and stays there till he's taken or pushed off by Stu or, once the wheelchair's in the kitchen, he jumps off and goes to his food or water bowl. He's also rung the kitchen doorbell when he's wanted to come in. On the average of once a month. Gets on the ledge under the bell and uses his paw or head or the side of his body to press it. "People have said it has to be an accident," Stu told Dan, "but I swear I once saw him butt his head against the bell till it rang," and Dan said "Clever cat you got there. But because of everything else you've told me about him and his having five to six claws on each paw, not one I'd want to mess with. Based on his size, bite and ability to chase people away, you should be calling him your watchcat," which was what Stu had referred to Streak as to Dan a few months before, also "attack cat," but said then "That's good; I just might. And put a couple of signs up around the house: 'Beware of Cat.' Maybe even hire him out to neighbors to guard against burglaries, which we get a lot of around here. You know how we got him, don't you?" and Dan said "If you told me, I forgot." "We owe it all to Harriet. She and Mom were visiting us in Maine. They went with Anita to a take-out shack, one where you can get lobster and crab rolls and where they also keep small animals in cages by the picnic tables for people to adopt. Rabbits, kittens, owls that can't fly, ducks. Harriet called us from it and said 'We've found the most adorable kitten for Anita. The owner of the stand says he knows the kitten's family and all the adults in it are unusually small, so not too costly to feed, and love children and learn to use the litter box early and are never a problem. Anita's fallen in love with it and named it Streak and won't put it down,' Harriet said, 'so you have to let her have it. If it's a matter of expense in taking care of it, I'll buy the cat carrier and litter box and whatever else you'll need, and pay for all its shots.' 'All pets are problems,' I told her. 'You can't leave them alone for more than a day, so there go our two-day trips. And very few motels take them, so what do we do driving back? Besides the ticks and fleas the cat will bring into the house the next few years and soiling our rugs and tearing up the couch and its hair-balls and vomit and foul litter-box smells.' She insisted we see the kitten before we decide against it, no doubt thinking we'd fall in love with it. Anita, when we got there, begged and swore she'd never ask for anything else in her life—you know how it goes— plus buckets of tears. Janice said to me on the side it was my call to make since for a while I'd be the one taking on a lot of the responsibilities of the cat. Also, Mom said 'She wants it so much, give it to the little darling. I always gave you kids whatever you wanted.' True? No. At least not me. And Harriet? 'Anita will benefit from it in so many ways,' she said. 'It'll make her a more nurturing person, which'll help her later on when she becomes a mother, and be a companion while Meera's away.' Meera was at sleepaway camp then, and it's true the two are very close, but everything under the sun thrown at us to back up their argument till we finally—or I did—caved in." Dan's response over the phone? Forgets except that he remembers him laughing a lot during the telling. If Dan were alive, he'd certainly tell him what happened to Streak today. This morning he let him out around 5:30. That's the time he usually gets up to turn Janice over in bed, ask if she needs anything else, do it if she does, pee, drink a glass of water in the kitchen with his vitamins and glucosamine pills and get the *Times* and *Sun* from the driveway where they'd been thrown from different cars around four. Streak, as usual, was waiting at the door to go out when Stu got to the kitchen. After Stu tried to read the *Times'* headlines without his glasses, he went back to bed till seven—again, like the pills with water and letting Streak out, what he did every morning. Dan knew this routine. Stu had told him of the many routines he'd developed over the years and wished he could break free of. "I've got my ruts and routines too," Dan said, "none of them important." "Mine aren't important either," and Dan said "But most of them are funnier and more interesting than mine." Stu's: reading the newspapers for half an hour in the morning before getting Janice up, and always starting with the *Times* obituary page. Same light breakfast every day and morning hot drinks in the same order. Preparing most of his and Janice's breakfasts and washing the next day's salad the night before. Even filling the teakettle and getting the drip coffee ready the night before, where all he had to do next morning is pour the boiling water. Getting the dining room table set up for writing before he reads the newspapers in the morning: rough draft of his manuscript to the left of the typewriter, clean and second sheets in different piles to the right, finished part of the manuscript on a chair pulled out to the left of the one he'll sit on. Anyway, about twenty minutes after he got out of bed and brushed his teeth, washed, shaved, brushed his hair—always fifty strokes, which he counts as he does them—and put his boxer shorts on and did a hundred pushups and dressed, he went into the kitchen to boil water and finish the preparations of Janice's breakfast and the evening salad and to let Streak in to give him his food and a fresh bowl of water. He wasn't there. Normally, a few seconds after Stu came into the kitchen, Streak was banging the front door with his head or paw to be let in. Stu looked around from the opened kitchen door, didn't see Streak, and washed his plate and put food on it and set it and a fresh bowl of water on the floor. Then he cut up the salad and put the salad bowl, covered by the dishtowel he'd dried the salad in overnight, on the bottom shelf of the refrigerator because it's supposed to be not as cold there as the shelves above it and he didn't want the salad to freeze. The water boiled, he made himself tea and opened the door again for Streak, though he hadn't heard him behind it. He'd say to Dan "I wasn't worried for him, you know. Once a month or so he didn't come back from wherever he went after I let him out, till around eleven or twelve. He might have caught the scent of some animal those times or was lying in wait for a bird or chipmunk or mouse. I've seen him do that for hours, hiding behind a bush or in the grass. He'll be back, though, I thought." Around 8:30 he woke Janice and asked if she wanted to get up now or sleep another fifteen minutes, which she often did and he took advantage of by having a second coffee and reading more of one of the newspapers, but she said no, so he folded back her covers, exercised her legs, got her up and her food and drinks and portable phone on a tray-table in front of her, got her tape player within reach of her on the floor and the next tape of the book she was listening to in the breast pocket of her nightshirt, made the bed and went into the dining room to write. By this time Anita had left for school in her car. The doorbell rang around ten. Streak? he thought, or a delivery. He went to the door. A neighbor. "I'm afraid I've very bad news for you," she said. "Yours is the big white cat, very furry?" and he said "What's wrong, what he do? Something happen to him?" "It's a male? He ran in front of my car just after I turned left onto Acadia, in front of your house. There was no way I could avoid hitting him. I put him on the side of the road. Believe me, he came out of nowhere. I applied the brakes—" "Oh no," he said, "what am I going to do?" He ran across their little footbridge to Acadia, saw Streak lying in the weeds by the road. There were no marks. Turned him over. No marks. Felt his head and nose; no sign of breathing. Shook him; nothing; eyes stayed closed. He wasn't bleeding and hadn't bled. The woman was standing behind Stu—he was kneeling beside Streak—and said "I'm so sorry. Is there anything I can do? If not, do you mind if I go? And please, if there are any expenses—" and he said "No, it's okay, these things happen." He put Streak into a cardboard box and brought him in. Meera was away at college and Anita wouldn't be home till after two. He went to the back to tell Janice. "I'm really sorry; he was such a nice cat to you. Jumping into your lap; following you around when you went outside; sitting in the chair next to you when you worked at your computer. You were the one he liked most. What a thing to happen. I thought he was indestructible. Never sick or hurt. Threw up a lot, that's all. What do we do now, bury him or wait till Anita gets home?" and she said "Wait, of course. Technically, he's her cat." "Maybe I should go to her school, take her out of class and tell her like I did to both kids with your mother, and if she wants to come home, let her." "I don't see the point. This will be a terrible shock and she'll feel miserable for a while and never forget him, but it's different than it was with my mother. We'll wait." He went outside and looked inside the box. Felt him and he felt stiff. Some ants were crawling across his stomach. He brushed them away, closed the box, dug a hole big enough for it in the grassy area inside the circular driveway, a few feet away from where he'd buried the metal box containing the ashes of Janice's mother three years ago, and put the box in the hole. Anita came home at two-thirty. He said "Mommy and I have some very bad news for you," and they told her and she said "Oh no; oh my poor Streak," and he wanted to hold her but she put her head on Janice's shoulder and started crying. He put his hand on her back and kept it there. A few minutes later she wiped her eyes and said to them "Thanks for waiting for me, but you should have buried him right away. By now he must smell." "No, it takes longer than that," he said. "Okay, we'll bury him. It's all ready. Should we have a little ceremony before?" and Anita said "I think we should just close the box and cover it up and put a stick or something there so we always know where he is. You do it, Daddy. I'm too sad over it," and she went to her room and cried there for more than an hour.

He wheeled Janice outside, sealed the top of the box with masking tape, shoveled dirt over it, flattened the mound on top, put a few stones on the spot where the box was. "No words, I guess," he said. "That'd be silly, wouldn't it?" and she said "I don't think so. Perhaps just what you said about him before. He was a wonderful cat and we all loved him," and they started crying. "It's something," he said, "how emotional one can get over the death of a pet. I remember with her parakeet, Ned. He was just a bird and we had him less than a year, but we all broke up when he died suddenly. And her hamster, Trey or Troy. Same thing. So it's not surprising, all this emotion with Streak. He's a cat and we got him as a kitten, and he was around for years and so sociable and always a presence. But with the others—there was even Meera's goldfish, whom I think I dropped a tear or two for, maybe because she was so sad—it was surprising." Around four he said to Janice "Like to go out for a walk?" and she said "That'd be great. I get to feel so cooped up in here on nice days." He wheeled her around their property to see what flowers were coming up and which were fading and how the trees and shrub he'd planted for her this spring were doing. They were in the circular driveway—he'd pulled toward her a rose on a bush for her to smell—when they heard scratching. "What's that?" he said. The flattened mound of earth where Streak was buried started to move. "My gosh," she said, "he's alive." The ground opened up a little and a paw stuck out, pushed some dirt away, then a second paw and then Streak climbing out. He mewed, shook the dirt off him. "Anita," Stu yelled, "come outside," and Streak looked at them and ran into the house through the opened door. They went in after him. He was drinking from his water bowl and then gobbled up the rice and cat food mix Stu had set out this morning. "Streak, my dear sweetie," Janice said, "we're so sorry," and he looked up at her and ran to the back of the house into their bedroom closet and is still there. Whenever Stu or Anita looked in on him, he stuck his head up behind a pile of sandals and shoes and hissed. Dan would have liked this story, Stu thinks. He would have said, first off, "Jesus, that's fantastic." And then something like "Never heard anything like it. With people, yes—isolated instances of victims of the Germans during World War II, crawling out from under hundreds of machine-gunned bodies and slipping away—but a cat? It's straight out of Poe— you know, the one with the black cat sealed up with the murdered wife. And that these things are always happening to you and your family. Meera falling off her friend's balcony and a pedestrian just happened to be on the street to cushion her fall. Anita, alone in your van, disengaging the hand brake and it rolling down a hill. Other incidents equally extraordinary and hair-raising, but all of them turning out favorably, or let's say, no one hurt. This is the most bizarre of any you've told me. But let me ask you. It's the old newsman in me speaking. Discounting the possibility of a resurrection, why were you so sure he was dead?" and Stu would say "He was hit by a car. And not just a car but an SUV. Hit from the front, square and hard, the driver said. And she told me he was dead and that she had lost two dogs in the last few years that were hit by cars—not hers, she made sure I knew, and true, these cars were going faster—but the point is she was familiar with dead animals. And he looked dead when I saw him lying in the grass. And she'd carried him there, so she had the chance to feel his body for life. He had all the signs of a dead cat, both of us thought. He didn't seem to be breathing. His body was cold and he gave no impression of being anything but dead. And maybe they're not the same, so I shouldn't use this to justify why I thought he was dead, but I've seen and felt dead people. Mom, Dad, Deborah, and once on the street a man who had a fatal heart attack in front of me and I tried to revive him—you remember the story—so I think I have a good idea what's alive or dead, even though I proved wrong here," and Dan might say "This woman said she witnessed the deaths of her dogs, not cats. That could be different. Same goes with you comparing people to your cat. I've seen dead people, plenty of them when I covered the Korean War, and a couple of state executions before I became an overseas correspondent, and just general local stories—killings and a feature piece on emergency rooms. And Mom too, though not Deborah or Dad, except in their caskets, I think, and that doesn't count in what I'm trying to say. A person, when he or she's dead, you know it. It's the face and body, and nothing's alive in it except maybe the gas passing through." "But he was absolutely stiff," Stu would say, "and already had ants crawling over him and flies on his face, and he didn't try to shake them off," and Dan might say "He could have been in body shock to conserve his life force, for want of a better term, till he recovered enough to move and get away. That happens in animals, I read. And it's not called body shock. Everything reduced: heart rate, breathing, excretion, the whole body apparatus down to nearly zero, and as a self-defensive measure also, to instinctively play dead," and Stu would say "Actually, now that you speak of it, I remember driving back from Maine the first summer I was with Janice, and a dog ran out—there was nothing I could do to avoid hitting it—and slammed into our car and flew over it and landed on the road. We stopped and thought for sure it was dead. Truth is, I didn't know if I was going to stop—that's how sure I was it was dead and I also didn't want to risk getting into trouble and for our trip back to be delayed the next few hours—but there was a car right behind us. That car stopped and so did a few others. Everyone, after looking at the dog, thought it was dead. It just lay there, stiff, no movement whatsoever. A young woman even rested the dog's head on her lap and stroked it and said she felt no sign of life. Then, when some of us were talking as to how to go about finding the dog's owner to tell him it was dead, because we couldn't just leave it on the side of the road—though again, I'm afraid I could—it stood up and hobbled a little and then ran into the woods. It was a county road, the one between Belfast and Augusta. You might remember it from your visit to us the next summer; it's the one you take from Route 9 or 1 to get to 95 and the Portland airport. Anyway—no houses around, and the dog had no tag and by now had disappeared, so we were told to get back in our car and continue our trip, the dog will be fine." "Both are great stories," Dan might say, "especially how they turned out. Streak alive and hissing; and Anita, how thrilled she must have been when she heard he was okay. For you and Janice it was probably, for a few moments, like a miracle, seeing him claw out of his grave. As for the dog you hit and that you might have driven away from without stopping if there hadn't been a car behind you—well, that's your business, though maybe your thinking's changed since then. I would have stopped and done what I could to find the owner, maybe even have driven to the nearest store and called the state police to report it and then met them back there—that is, if the dog had stayed dead."

32

After Dan was released from prison and got back to New York, he urged Stu to quit his waiter's job at Schrafft's and concentrate on his college studies. This came after he asked Stu how he was doing at school and Stu said not so hot but things should improve. "You attend classes a few hours a day, work nights waiting on tables five days a week, how do you expect to get good grades? You're taking tough science courses and need to be alert and have more time to study," and Stu said "How am I supposed to get money then?" "Dad should give you an allowance, because look how much he's saving on tuition by your going to City," and Stu said "I'm too old for allowance. And Dad's tight with cash, so if he did give, how much you think he'd part with?" "Listen, you want to get into dental school and later make a good living, do what I say. I'll work on Dad for you," and that night before Stu left for work, they went to their father, Dan doing all the talking. "You want your little juney boy here to graduate in good standing if not top honors his last three years and get into dental school, don't you?" and their father said "I hope one of my sons does. I actually hoped for all four, a huge practice in the Chrysler Building where you'd eventually buy me out after we worked together a while, each of us treating patients in different rooms and maybe even with different specialties and with one receptionist for the five of us, but who could be so lucky? And one of you had to croak before he had a chance to go to college, though he was the weakest prospect to become a dentist. No interest in academics. Since Stu's the only son left interested in my field, sure, I want him to do well in school, so what are you driving at? I feel a big touch coming on," and Dan said "You're right. You've got to give him an ample allowance for the next two years at least so he doesn't have to work and can do better in his courses, especially the sciences." "Why? I worked starting from the time I was in third grade. And when I was at NYU for dentistry I worked full-time at night for the post office while taking the regular courseload in the day, and I still managed to graduate near the top of my class," and Dan said "Not to detract from your accomplishments, but that was then. It's much more competitive to get into dental school now, and did you have to take as many pre-dental science courses in college as he does?" and their father said "We were allowed to go straight from high school into dental school, same for doctors. I took the sciences in high school, all of them, and more when I was in dental school my first year. Anyone can do it, work and school, if they study hard and don't piss away their free time," and Stu said "What free time?" and Dan said "Let me. —He's right; the kid has no free time. And if he switches his schedule and works days and goes to night school, it'll take him twice as long to graduate and by then he might lose interest in dentistry. Look, you going to give him a weekly allowance, and one he can take a date out on once a week, or do I have to do it myself?" and their father said "Don't try to shame me; it doesn't work. You guys must think I'm made of money, but I'll do what you say. You're the head cheese in this house while you're still living here, right?" and Dan said "I never said or suggested that. Just, if he has to work nights, get home at one or two sometimes, he'll never—" and their father said "Okay, already, I heard you the first time and then the second and third. Now how much you think I should shell out a week, five bucks?" and Dan said "Come on, Dad. That'll barely cover his lunch at school." "Let him bring a bag lunch like I do every day to my office. —All right, ten, max," and Dan said "Twenty's what he needs, that's not asking too much of you, and a five-dollar raise the next academic year," and their father said "You joking? Fifteen, tops, and suspended when he gets a job over the summer, and we'll see if he rates a raise of even a dime the next year by how well he does at school." Stu quit his job, spent more time studying, started getting better grades on his papers and tests. Dan was transferred to Washington a month later and soon after that their father stopped leaving the allowance by the kitchen phone every Friday morning before he left for work. Stu had to ask him for it that evening or the next morning, and the first few times his father said "Oops, forgot," or "Sorry, forgot again," and then "Oh boy, but you know me with money.

When it comes to shelling it out, it's the last thing I think of."
Then: "The truth now why I've been so tough in giving it up?
Aren't you just a little ashamed to still be getting an allowance?
To your mother, it's understandable; she's got weekly expenses
for the house. But you should be earning your own dough and
doing well at school both, and who says it has to be a five-to-six-
hour-a-day job? In other words, be more independent, which you
used to be a lot and which in its own way is more important in
your life than anything you're likely to learn in college," and gave
him the money. "It's fine with me," Stu said. "I was only taking
the allowance because Dan wanted me to so I could study more.
I'd much rather earn my own money than to have to beg you for
it every week," and his father said "Who's asking you to beg? All
I'm saying is if Dan and Jay were able to hold down a job while
in college, and they were no brighter than you, I don't understand why you can't too. But you speak to Dan, don't let on
you're going back to working, or I'll never hear the end of it.
He's too damn persuasive, and he can sometimes, with his high
moral talk and insinuations, do you guys call them?, go too far
in trying to make me feel like two cents. But he's a good kid, you
all are, but if he has to find out, let him do it naturally when he
visits and you happen to head off for work and he asks where
you're going, and so on. You got to promise, though, your grades
will stay as good as you've been getting lately so I have an argument when he starts in on me. Even if they don't turn out to be
the highest, I know some dentists on the NYU admissions
committee, or know some people who do, and I'll get you in there
or some other low-charging dental school." Dan called soon after
their father got Stu an afternoon job in the Garment Center as a

shipping clerk, and said "So, everything still going well at school?" and he said "Fine; doing a lot better in the courses that count." "Dad being okay with the allowance?" and he said "Sometimes it's a little hard getting it out of him, but he always comes through." "How long does he stall before he forks over?" and he said "Not long; day, two," and Dan said "That's not right. He shouldn't make you grovel for the lousy fifteen bucks. I'll speak to him," and he said "Really, it's not necessary. He explained it's just a question of his remembering to give it to me on Friday, which is usually his busiest day and he comes home tired, or that he doesn't have enough cash on him for the weekend and I'll have to wait till Monday when the banks open," and Dan said "What? He's full of it. Half his practice is in cash. No big bills, either. Mostly he gets walk-ins—quick extractions and cleanings—so ten, fifteen dollars each. Listen, if what he's giving isn't enough, I'll send an additional ten once a week. It's no great sacrifice—I'm making a good salary now and my expenses aren't steep—and I want you to have some fun in life too. I got you into this by telling you to quit your job, so let me help out." "Thanks, but I don't need it. I'm living on the cheap and it's good training for the uncertain future. It also keeps me in, pounding the books, or a word I got out of a Dostoevsky novel, lucubrating," and Dan said "What's it mean?" and he told him and where the word came from, "or maybe I got that wrong, but I think the lamplight's right. Ah, what am I stringing you along for? I went back to work, but different; fewer hours and not as hard on my feet. It wasn't just Dad being tight with the money, but my feeling dependent on him for it and you for arguing him into giving me it when we both knew he didn't want to. If I don't get into dental school, no great shakes. All the sciences come too damn hard for me, so it's obvious I wasn't cut out to be a dentist." "Geez, I don't want to put any more pressure on you than you've already had, but you're the last male hope in the family to become one and he'll be so disappointed if you don't apply to dental school." "Don't worry about it," Stu said; "I don't. He'll be sad when I tell him—that doesn't have to be for another year yet—and then get over it as he did with Jay and you," and he said "It'll be much worse, though nothing we can do. I should have stayed out of it. But I thought your becoming a dentist—relieving people of pain, plus all the respect and money you get and you can choose your own hours—was something you'd like." "It was, not because of the money, or not since high school, but to please Dad. Like you, how long can you do that if what'll please him is the toughest and last thing you want to do?" "Next time I nose into your life like that, tell me to buzz off," and Stu said "Oh yeah, I can really see myself doing that." "Why, am I so fearsome and forbidding a character?" "No, who said that? It's just you always give good advice—or invariably—so I listen and usually take it. This, quitting work to study more to get into dental school, was probably good advice too. Twenty years from now, if I'm broke or have a crummy or deadly dull job I have to stick with, I might regret not having taken it," and Dan said "Now you're making me feel even worse. Okay, got to go; wanted to talk to the folks too, but my dinner break's over. Really, next time, on something like this, do us both a favor, will ya, and remember to put me in my place."

33

Their mother's will stipulated that Dan be the sole executor of her estate. She wrote in it "I hope this doesn't cause friction among my children. Thankfully, if it does, I won't be around to witness it. I feel that Dan, being the oldest and, I think, the most capable of my four surviving children (something I never would have said while I was alive, which I still am, of course, but writing this as if I'm dead) should be the one to run things. Also, because of his experience producing television news shows and overseeing large staffs and running the news division of a large public radio station, if that's what his last job was—I was never clear about that and whenever he explained what he was doing, I could never understand, most likely because of my advanced age and diminishing comprehension and my fatigue throughout most of the day (and a bit of a drinking problem, I admit, because I know that's what you all would have said if I hadn't)—I feel he has the necessary managerial and financial skills and patience and even temper to handle the executorial problems that will no doubt arise. If anything should happen to Dan before I die, God forbid, or even after my death but before the estate's settled, then Stuart, my other surviving son—oh my, to have so many of your children go before you—should become executor. (I apologize for these un-will-like interjections. My lawyer, Emile Drenner, will no doubt ask me to strike them out. But suddenly hit with my losses over the years and also that I have to draw up this document and that when it's opened I'll be gone from the rest of you forever, the personal notes just naturally came out.) I'm also sorry if Harriet, my next eldest surviving child, is hurt for my not choosing her as succeeding executor (isn't this lawyer language I'm trying to effect without Mr. Drenner's help dreadful?). I feel that my boys are more easygoing than my girls, so less likely to antagonize the people the executor has to deal with and thus better able to handle my estate, which, as you all know by now because I've talked about it with you a number of times, will be evenly divided among you minus the costs the executor will have in carrying out this thankless job. I think that does it. We won't meet again, since I'm convinced there's no hereafter or stopover or any place like that. It's just burn or rot—you'll have decided which for me by now, for I know I can't. I think I fear fire more. But a burial and everything accompanying it are much more expensive than a simple cremation (in addition to being more morbid and time-consuming), and I want you to come away with as much of my holdings as you can short of donating my body to science. That—the idea of being picked to pieces—

irrational as this must sound, I fear the most. In closing, let me get one more thing out. Despite what some of you may think, I had no favorites of my children (and I'm sure I'll continue not to till I die) and loved the seven of you equally and deeply. It's so hard to leave now, even in this silly but I suppose practical paper, but I have to end sometimes so I'll do it with a traditional good-bye. Goodbye, goodbye, goodbye, goodbye." What she left was a five-story brownstone in good condition, with six rented apart-ments, a professional office in front, and her duplex, with lots of valuable furniture and antiques. Very little cash, though, and no stocks or bonds. Most of her savings and the monthly rents went to the upkeep of the building and paying round-the-clock caregivers the last eight years. Dan decided—"It's within my pre-rogative as executor to make these unilateral decisions, though if any of you have any objections and they make sense to me, I'll change the decision"—to sell all the furniture and antiques other than for some pieces they might want for themselves and, to a lesser degree, for their children. "We don't want to keep too much of the more valuable stuff. As a future corporation, which I'll be setting up soon with your help and outside legal advice, we'll eventually have to pay a huge inheritance tax. What I'd like to do now is take out a mortgage on the building—the rates are at an all-time low and the place is free and clear—and use the money to renovate Mom's apartment. Really, a first-class job. Once it's done we can rent it for about nine thousand a month, realtors tell me... a floor-through duplex on the West Side right off Central Park West, with a laundry room and playroom in the basement? Then, after a few years, we sell the building when we get the price we want, which we can do—hold out—since we'll be earning a terrific income from it. So, those are my plans. Anybody want to address them?" and they said things like—they were all having lunch at a restaurant, which Dan said the corporation-to-be was paying for—why should they object or even quibble when he'd be doing all the work managing the building and supervising the renovation? "Good. Total harmony. What I'd hoped for and sort of expected. Remember—anyone think I'm being too pushy or extravagant, since I also have plans for the building's facade and entrance area, vestibule and hallways, don't hold back. As for Mom's possessions—Harriet and Natalie get her jewelry, such as there was, and whatever clothes they want, which I feel is right. As for the furniture, we should choose what we want by the end of next week. Keep it to, say, three big pieces each and one for each grandchild, but no more than six per family. Not the piano, though. That we'll get a few thousand for. A Baldwin, next best thing to a Steinway, with the original ivory keys. Quicker we clear out the apartment and get the renovation done, sooner we can start making an income from it. That wouldn't be bad, right? Just living off Social Security and my pension, our stocks having taken a tumble—I know we can use it. As for the antiques, there are so many, so we'll say five or six, but not of the more valuable ones—keep that down to two—and nothing for the kids unless you give them from the ones you take." Stu and Janice didn't want any furniture and he only asked for three tiny ivory Japanese figurines—they go by a Japanese word he always forgets but thinks it means "toggle"—that were in the foyer curio cabinet and were his favorite pieces as a kid. "They're carved so true to form, right down to the miniature fingernails and eyelids, that they were like real characters to me. I used to stare at them through the glass and in my head make up stories about them. The woman with hamper and baskets, the fishmonger chopping a fish in half with a cleaver, and the third one, I'm not sure what he does, but the reed pen and what looks like paper on a block in front of him, so maybe an artist or poet or accountant or scribe." And two bronze candlesticks and a small bronze piece that goes with them of a naked boy sitting on a tree stump reading a book, because they were Jay's favorites and the only things he once said he wanted from the apartment. "You're asking for almost nothing," Dan said, "but I can understand. Melody and I don't want anything either but a lamp—any one of them—that I need for my study, and a couple of serving platters because both of ours fell off the shelf and broke. But listen. The leaded glass ceiling fixture in the breakfast room is yours, right?" and Stu said "It once was. I bought it from a friend ages ago; he was a collector of Louis Tiffany shades. This one isn't, but when he saw it in an antique barn upstate, he thought it could be. Later, he said he had more than enough Tiffany-type shades in his closet, so he offered to sell it. I was at his apartment, admiring the real ones. I bought it for forty dollars, which was a steal even then. I lugged it home on the subway, almost dropped it, it was so big and heavy, regretting that I'd blown so much money on it, and then, by myself, took a whole day to hang it, one of the toughest jobs I've ever done." "You should have asked for my help," and he said "I didn't want to bother anyone and I don't know if you were around." "So when I came in on a visit," and he said "Anyway, when I went to California in '64, I gave up my apartment and Mom said the shade would look good in the breakfast room. She had an electrician install it, and I was glad to have a place to leave it. And of course that she liked it so much, and Dad, never one for aesthetics, seemed to too. I think it reminded him when he was a kid, when lots of homes had the cheap fake ones, lamps and shades." "So it's old and probably worth something, and you should have it. It'll be the last thing to go in that room. Once the lamps are gone, your shade and fixture will be providing the room's only artificial light." "I don't want to take so much money away from the estate. I bet in an antique store that shade goes for close to a thousand now. The glass and lead are real and individually soldered, and it's an unusually wide shade, even for a fake, and in great shape," and Dan said "It's obvious you only loaned it to Mom and didn't ask for it back because she liked it so much, so the shade belongs to you." "That is what I thought I was doing then, and also why I didn't ask for it back. That and taking it down and getting another fixture up in its place. Okay, I'll take it, thanks. I'd love to replace our ugly dining room ceiling fixture with it, which came with the house." A few months later Stu was in New York and Dan wanted to show him the progress being made in renovating the apartment. "Let's start with the kitchen first. It's supposed to be the room that sells the place. As you see, we're not done yet. Though the new windows and cabinets and walls are all in, and how do you like the corked floor?" and Stu said "Is that what it is? Looks fine, very smart, nice colors and pattern." "You don't care for it. Well, it's not what I'd like to live with either. But the contractor told me it's what rich young couples with small children want today, and that's who the realtor thinks will rent it. It's a heck of a lot better than the linoleum tiles Mom had down for the last forty years," and Stu said "Maybe even longer. I remember how she used to complain about our scuff marks. 'Pick up your feet,' she said, 'don't slide or drag.' Cork probably won't do that," and Dan said "I don't see how." Dan led him into the dining room—"They're going to pull up the pine strips and put down oak planking. It's going to look beautiful, and no chance of splinters as you have now," and Stu said "I'm not even sure it's pine. It was the cheapest kind of flooring under the original carpet, which Mom had me tear out around thirty years ago and stain the floor to give it the look of hard wood. I can still feel all those deep splinters in my feet, when I made the mistake of walking barefoot on it or in socks. Dad, too, when he shuffled around in thin-soled slippers or I exercised him around the table that was here or back and forth through the house. I used to pull or dig them out of him with tweezers or a needle, a hell of a job though he never complained of the pain," and Dan said "So by getting rid of it I'm doing something right," and he said "What do you mean? The place is being transformed, and so far it looks great. Of course, and this is no criticism of Mom, nor to lower in value the work you've done, but anything would be better than the way she let it go the last fifteen years. She didn't have the energy or time to look after it," and Dan said "Or the money. And once she moved downstairs to the breakfast room, she never saw how bad the second floor was getting. And the basement. Jesus Christ, it took days for several men to clean out the mess. Most of the stuff was her kids', going back sixty years, but it would have taken too long for all of you to choose what you wanted to keep, so I just dumped it. Not a buck to be made out of any of it." Next the foyer. "New paint job and floor and that door to Dad's old office Sheetrocked and plastered over rather than concealed by the breakfront as it was since Dad went to prison more than fifty years ago. Not much else to change here, except the staircase will have a thick carpeted runner so that the ideal couple who rent the place won't have to be too concerned if their kid happens to fall downstairs." "Jay and I used to do it—on carpeting then too, but to get the attention of guests who just came through the front door. We'd start at the top and roll over and over down the stairs till we got to the bottom and would play dead. Scared the hell out of some people." "Something like that never entered Newton's head or mine. The folks must have relaxed quite a bit with you two, since they never would have allowed it with us. Good thing you didn't break your necks." They went up the staircase to the living room: huge antique mirror above the fireplace taken down and restored and reattached to the wall, new windows and window gates, carpet removed and oak floor sanded, fireplace de-electrified and flue and chimney cleaned. "Imagine having fireplaces in the living and dining rooms and never using them because you were afraid the place would burn down or one of the kids would fall or crawl into it. That was their excuse, but part of it with Mom, I'm sure, was the soot. Actually, after hearing of you and Jay throwing yourselves downstairs, I can understand their anxieties. Now, all the fires the tenant wants." The apartment centrally

air-conditioned, "which meant, while we were at it," Dan said,
"rewiring the whole building, with circuit breakers instead of fuse
boxes. All the tenants can now use as big an air-conditioner as
they want in every room. I didn't want our lower rental tenants
shorting the building, where our big renter here would suffer. At
ten thousand a month or so, you don't want to think you're living in a tenement. In the long run it'll jack up the value of the
building when we sell it." Front bedrooms: both had been completely redone, even new radiators and doors. "What do you
think of the marble floor?" Dan said in what was first called the
baby's room and then the boys' room and then the girls' room
and then just Deborah's. "It was waiting patiently for us under
two layers of linoleum and one of carpet for sixty years. The
room was the original entrance hallway when the building had a
stoop, before the folks carved up the place. Marble doesn't quite
work for a bedroom floor, but I didn't have the heart to rip it up,
and it wouldn't have been worth anything if I did. Maybe they'll
end up using the room as a studio or office." "The crystal chandelier with all the beads and balls on it," Stu said in the master
bedroom; "where'd it go?" and Dan said "The contractor said it
was two hundred pounds too heavy for the ceiling and he was
surprised it hadn't fallen long ago. We got twenty-five hundred
for it. The antique dealer said it hung in an opera house on
East 14th Street, before the original Met." "It was here when
they bought the building, the folks said. Not in this room but
another... I think in the living room of Brooker's old apartment,
3R," and Dan said "That'd make sense. It would have been the
living room of the building when it was a one-family house.

Ours was the parlor. Anyway, I didn't want it crashing down on someone. They'd see it hanging there, they'd think it belongs. It also didn't fit with the remodeling of the apartment and, unlike the marble floor, it couldn't be covered up." Dan showed him two of the four bathrooms. New tubs, showers, sinks, and so on. "The medicine chests aren't the best, but I had to cut back somewhere. A recent city law says all renovated bathrooms have to have lower-water-usage toilets, so I had to replace all of those too, and one was relatively new. I ran into these things all the time. The regulations and codes are endless and often arcane. That's why the renovation, and also the size of it, is taking so long. That hurts when you think how much rent we're losing every month," and Stu said "I'm sure it's taken a lot out of you too." "Actually, it's been interesting. I learned a lot about contracting and buying and such. If we have to do one of the other apartments in the next year—and if one becomes available, I'm doing it, because it really pays off—it'll be, by comparison, a snap." Workers were painting and plastering the two back bedrooms and the long hallway connecting them. "Original floors are good here too," Dan said. "Sanding and staining and a polyurethane coating will be all they need after the walls are done, and a piece of wood here and there glued in, but where it doesn't look as if they've been inserted." They went down the back staircase to the breakfast room and out to the L-shaped backyard. It had a new wooden fence and an outside steel door to replace the corroded iron one, and the outside window bars had been replaced by inside metal ones that folded into the new window frames and disappeared. "Clever, eh?" Dan said, back in the breakfast room, demonstrating. "Expensive, too, but I didn't want our tenants feeling as if they were living inside a prison cell, and you need gates on the ground floor. Which kid was it who walked in on a robbery here—where the thieves came through the pried-apart bars while the folks were sleeping upstairs—you?" and Stu said "Second I came in the front door I knew that a window on the first floor was open and someone had broken in. It was late and cold out, so the folks never would have left one open, and there was almost like a gust blowing toward me because I still had the front door open. I grabbed one of the fireplace tools from the fake fireplace—it's something I think you would have done—and banged it against the dining room table and yelled 'I'm going to bust your fucking heads in, you bastards,' and ran to the back. They were already out the backyard door—I could hear them scrambling over the fence. Sounded like two of them, and they were so agile and fast that they had to have been kids. Who knows what they would have done to Mom and Dad if they'd gotten upstairs—killed them, or beaten them up for hidden jewels and cash, they'd think. Dad was in the back bedroom then, and only later, when he couldn't make it upstairs, moved down here, just like Mom did twenty years after he died. All they got was her pocketbook, which she always hung over the doorknob leading to the base-ment." Then he noticed the hole in the middle of the ceiling with wires sticking out. "Oh look, the shade's gone," and Dan said "Last month. We got five or six hundred for it. Let me see—I've an itemized list of what we got for each object, most of which, you know, doesn't go into our pockets but to the building. —It's not here," after looking through a file folder he'd been holding.

STEPHEN DIXON

"Has to be in my briefcase," and Stu said "It's all right. Whatever you got for it is fine with me." "No, I want you and Harriet and Natalie to know. I'm curious myself now. I probably got robbed on some of them. Though I did do research on the pieces a former colleague of mine who knows something about old furniture and antiques thought would bring in the most, like the leaded shade. I also got more than one estimate on almost everything. Some of it—actually, a lot—I had to give to the Goodwill on 79th Street and that Housing Works store down the block—the profits benefit people with AIDS. Manny helped me bring it to Goodwill, but Housing Works, which is more selective, came over to choose and later picked theirs up. If neither of them was interested, and if none of the nieces and nephews wanted it, I'd put on the street whatever was left, and everything there but a couple of pots without handles was snatched up in an hour. Mattresses and such the city picks up in a special sanitation truck once every other week, but you have to call to make an appointment and there's a limit to how much they'll take, so this went on for months." "You could have... no, you never would have, left the extra big trash in front of other buildings the day the truck came," and Dan said "Right; they'd get fined. Some of the junk, after the workers left for the day and I'd totally forgotten about it, I had to drag out myself," and Stu said "I'm sorry." "It was the kind of exercise I didn't need, but I didn't want sanitation to think I was calling them up for nothing. Next time they might not have come." He went into the kitchen, came back with several sheets of itemized lists. "'Leaded-glass lamp'—I don't know why I called it lamp here," and Stu said

250

"You were probably in a hurry." "Could be. 'Five twenty-five.'
Now I remember. She said five, I said six, we settled on five
twenty-five. In parentheses I wrote what I thought its value was:
'six to eight hundred.' I'm a lousy haggler. But I couldn't begin
to compete with this shrewd fast-talking but pleasant dealer spe-
cializing in things from that era—what did she say, 'fin de
siecle'?" and Stu said "That's close enough to the time." "Am I
pronouncing it right?" and he said "Sounds good to me. That
'siecle,' or however it's pronounced, is a toughie." "She said it
would have been worth a few hundred more but needed that
amount of repair work to make it salable to her clientele. Some
new leading, many of the glass sections were cracked and needed replacement, and that kind of glass was difficult to match, and
she'd have to get an artisan to do all the work." "What is she
talking about?" Stu said. "It was in good condition last time I saw
it. Maybe a few cracked pieces—I didn't pay that close attention—but the leading seemed okay, none of the pieces falling
out," and Dan said "That's what she told me and I wasn't going
to argue with her, since the shade was part of a package of about
ten things she bought. I think the shade was the most expensive
of them. The biggest items—not from her, and not the piano
either. That one was a major disappointment. Harriet—others—
said it was worth eight to ten thousand. That new it would fetch
twenty or thirty. I called around for weeks—music schools, dealers. Also had signs hung up in Julliard and Manhattan School of
Music and so on. Only two dealers and a pianist came over to
look at it and all said it would take five to ten thousand to bring
it back to perfect playing condition—they didn't want anything

less. Some of the wood was cracked, and the strings, soundboard, almost everything inside was damaged or shot, and the keys would have to be replaced. So it went for"—he looked at one of the sheets—"twelve hundred fifty. The 'fifty' I practically begged the buyer to throw in. Don't ask me why, it was so petty of me, but I felt gypped for us all." "Did you find the bill of sale for it? As far back as I can remember, and maybe even since the late Thirties when the folks bought the piano at an auction, it was in the drawer of the living room side table—the one to the right of the striped love seat opposite the two green chairs," and Dan said "As provenance it might have been interesting for this woman to have, but too late for that now. I don't think I ever opened that drawer in my life, not even when it was sold. I suppose, since it never seemed used, I never thought anything was in it." "Well, with me, even though Mom didn't want us in that room, I sometimes played with my little cars or toy soldiers in that particular area—the fireplace fence as a huge wall for the soldiers to climb over and such. And occasionally looked in the drawer—there was never anything in it but furniture casters and curtain hooks—and hid under the love seat. It was only about four inches from the bottom of the seat to the floor. I can't believe I was once so small," and Dan said "You were always very skinny, and if you sucked in your breath?—although I bet you couldn't turn over. Anyway, twelve-goddamn-fifty for the piano. But it cost her eight hundred to get it out of here and truck it to the piano-repair factory near Kingston, New York. And then, after it was rehabilitated, she called it, to tip-top form, probably another five hundred to get it into her New Paltz home. She said she'd always

wanted this very same model Baldwin and that she was going to
have a glass-enclosed soundproof room built for it off her den and
overlooking her swimming pool. Okay, she was loaded, but she
knew what the piano was worth as is, or convinced me she did,
and I wasn't getting any other bites. By that time I was feeling
hopeless I'd ever sell it and even thought maybe it'd be a strong
selling point to rent the apartment with a grand piano in the living room, but the realtor nixed the idea. First of all, the piano's
barely usable, she said. Second, corporate lawyers and stockbro-
kers, etcetera, don't play music; they listen to it on thousands of
dollars of audio equipment. As it is, I'm glad it found a good
home." "Oh, we let it go, the poor piano," Stu said. "We should
have had it tuned every year and promptly fixed whatever got
broken. And my memories of it—I mean, even in that enormous
room with its twelve-foot ceiling the thing stood out, especially
with the cover up—Mom going upstairs alone to play *'Für Elise'*
or that Russian song 'Dark Eyes'—*'Ochi Chernie.'* And Jay,
Harriet and Natalie all took lessons and played on it for years,
the only times Mom let us in the room and for her parties," and
Dan said "And you too, though you couldn't read a note, if I'm
right. Your extemporaneous eight-movement concertos for one
performer and no orchestra. The furniture that got the most
money were the two breakfronts in the living room and the
dining room table with its heavy cumbersome leaves that took
two people to put in. Its eight chairs I had to sell as a group
separately. They went, says here, for nine hundred; they all needed serious reupholstering. The table: three thousand, bashed-in
end from your poker, I presume, notwithstanding. The dealer

pointed it out but didn't say he was taking anything off because of it. And almost sixteen hundred each for the breakfronts. Who knew they were so valuable? I didn't even have them down on my list as possible top-dollar items—just a question mark in parentheses—and my former colleague wasn't impressed by them and my research in antique books turned up nothing. The dealers who priced them gave the same figure, so I got lucky, but it shows how I might have screwed up sometimes. The table, it was so long and old—something you'd expect to see at Monticello or the White House—and in relatively good shape, we both knew would fetch a high price. I'll make copies of these lists and send them to all of you." They went to the basement. New floor, walls, windows, overhead water and plumbing pipes now out of sight. "Dropped ceiling," Dan said, "but easy access to them for leaks. The real estate broker thought we needed a playroom. It's nothing like the dump of a rumpus room when we were kids. I don't know why the folks didn't make more out of the space. Seven kids? You'd think they'd want them out of the way and where they wouldn't be playing and falling over the expensive furniture and antiques, and the room was always warm because of the oil burner in the next room. Now we have baseboard heat. What's left? The laundry. All the appliances—even the slop sink, though the realtor gave it a more elegant name—instead of being down here will be tucked away behind louver doors in the kitchen. There, I've given you the grand tour. What do you think?" and Stu said "It's terrific. Really a great job and more to come. Thanks, not only for showing me it but for taking care of all this." When they got upstairs, Dan said "Remember when I said we might get eight to ten thousand a month for this place and you sort of slapped your face, thinking 'Is he deranged?' Now the broker thinks—and she said she's usually no more than a couple of hundred dollars off—because of the size of the apartment and all the improvements and the quality of them, and also to the building, we'll get eleven-five to twelve," and Stu said "Never." "You, Harriet and Natalie—you each say the same. But you see what this neighborhood's become. West Side in the Seventies is as desirable a location as anything on the East Side, and this block's one of the best. I kid you not: twelve's the going rate. For this apartment alone we'll each, after expenses, earn about twenty thousand a year. For the other apartments and the office, add another ten. We'd make more if we could buy out the rent-controlled tenants and do a quick renovation on their apartments to bring them up to fair-market value, but both told me they're only leaving feet first. So, thirty thousand; almost doesn't make the building worth selling. But we're all getting on or already there, and I don't want the building ultimately finishing me off, so in four years, I'd say, we sell. What do you think?" and he said "Fine with me. I'll be happy to get rid of it, if just to reduce the work on you." Later they went out for lunch. At home Stu told Janice about his tour of the apartment and what Dan said they'd be making from it, and she said "That's all very nice. In three years Anita will also be in an expensive college, so it couldn't come at a better time." Then he told her about the shade and she said "You know how much I admire and like Dan, but that wasn't right. He's worked hard at getting the apartment and building in shape and dealing with all the other things related to it, but that shade was promised to you." "He must have forgot," and she said "Who are you kidding?" and he said "You're right. One time today, when we were reminiscing about the place, and he was talking about me as a young kid, he said 'You see? I remember more about you than you think,' so I don't see how he could have forgotten the shade promise in four to five months." "But you didn't say anything," and he said "I made as if, with my silence, that the shade was part of the estate Mom left to us all. I didn't want to start anything. You talk about all the work he did for the building. We don't pay him, though, or do anything to make the load lighter for him," and she said "He didn't want help. He said so, or that's what you told me." "Not from Harriet, who offered and is the only one who lives in the city and could help him," and she said "She's also an interior designer, so she could have been a lot of help." "Yes, but he must have felt he could do it better without any interference from us. Or just by telling us what he was doing or planning to or what he and the architect and contractor had come up with, and seeing if we had any objections. Maybe that is the best way. His judgment's good, he's able to narrow things down quickly and organize them well, he's careful how he spends the money, and he's put in a lot of time learning what goes into renovating an apartment and building," and she said "I'm sorry, but I still don't understand. I know you're trying to protect him, and that's fine—he's your brother and you don't want to think anything bad of him. But he had to know the shade was rightfully yours, so all I'm saying is why did he act as if he didn't know?" "Maybe he had it taken down when the ceiling was painted, was planning to give it to me next time

I was in town and could pick it up, but it got mixed in with all the other things on display in the living and dining rooms for the furniture and antique dealers. Because we're talking about nine big rooms and two long hallways, not to mention things like the mini chandelier and Art Deco etched-glass shower doors in two of the bathrooms, so a lot of stuff, and only after it was sold and carted off did he realize he'd promised it to me." "Then he could have admitted his mistake and offered to give you the money he got for the shade, which I'd think, because he is so honest and direct, wouldn't be hard for him to do," and Stu said "Okay, then this possibility. He thought—he had a rethinking, I'm suggesting, since he first spoke to me about it—that the shade belonged to Mom after hanging in her apartment so long. But he didn't want to raise the issue with me because he didn't want to get into any kind of dispute, not that I would, or hurt my feelings. And maybe, technically, he was right that the shade had become legally or rightfully hers and thus the estate's. It was there since 1964. That's thirty-three years. It also could have been that he recalled that even she, through something she said to him, considered the shade hers, because, to be honest with you, I don't ever remember her saying she wanted to give it back to me after she died. And she spoke about things like that a lot. You know, what she intended to leave to each of us, though none of that was in her will, according to Harriet and Dan. I never saw the details; didn't want to. Of course, the last few years, her memory wasn't good. But even before that, all she would say were things like 'Isn't the shade beautiful'—we'd be sitting in the room—and 'Look at the warm color it brings to the walls,' and so on, but nothing that it was mine or thanking me for giving or loaning it to her or first suggesting she hang it in the breakfast room. Or this. Maybe, with all the work he does for the apartment and building—clearing the place out, supervising the renovations, taking care of all the things that need to be taken care of in a five-story brownstone and its tenants, and two of them are lulus, and the city and the lawyer and accountant and realtors and taxes and permits and regulations and so forth—he's just been overworked and that's why this lapse of whose is what occurred. But please don't bring it up to him. I don't want to embarrass him or make him think he did something wrong and that I was looking forward to getting the shade back and hanging it in our dining room," and she said "Why would I? I never would. Though I still don't think it's fair."

34

Also, he wonders what Dan would say about his fears for Janice and his kids. For Janice—she hasn't been well, several recent setbacks, and by "not being well" he means worse than before and that things might get worse for her, much worse than she is now—Dan would say on the phone "Have you tried everything that might help? Maybe her doctor doesn't know as much about her disease as you've said and you might want to search around for someone else." "No, he's among the best in his field and is current with every new development and treatment and medication for it in all its stages and is doing important research himself. Besides, she likes him. Some of the treatments he's put her on worked for a while, her condition improved a little or at least didn't get worse. But she eventually had serious side effects with all of them, the last one resembling a heart attack and where she had a lot of trouble breathing, and she had to be taken off them."

"Have you gone online to see what's there? Melody does it for almost everything regarding our health. If she's thinking of taking a new vitamin, even, she goes online and researches it and then moves on to chatrooms to find out what people who have taken it have to say. There could be things Janice's doctor doesn't think much of. Alternative medicines, bee-bite therapy, medicinal herbs. Or, because he doesn't want to get your hopes up, treatments having some success in other countries but which aren't licensed here yet and may never be or not for many years. For instance, drug companies, having spent billions developing the drugs now used in America and making a fortune from them, not wanting the competition, so putting the screws on government licensing agencies... money talks, as Dad liked to say." "Her doctor's not like that," Stu would say. "He tells us of every new drug that's possible for her, now or in the future; gives us all the time we need when we see him and answers every question we raise—never a rush act. As for going online, I wouldn't know how if I wanted to." "Learn," Dan would say, "so you can search out all these things for her. If that's really a problem for you, although you're a quick learner, then ask one of your kids. Or a computer-wizard student of yours; pay him. Or Janice. She uses the computer." "She's slow but she gets things done on it. And she has used it for that. Couple of years ago when she learned to use the voice activation system. Said there was little on it about her disease and especially the stage she's in that she didn't already know, though plenty of crackpot theories and remedies." "There could be good places she hasn't located," Dan would say. "I'm not much more than a browser myself, but

you have to keep looking, Melody says, and asking the online
nicknames you trust in chatrooms for directions where to go."
"Janice said she covered everything and whenever she goes back
online for it there's still never anything she didn't know." "Look,"
Dan would say, "isn't it possible your fears are somewhat exaggerated, which'd be normal because you're worried and projecting
the worst?" "They're based on what I see she's going through. I
told you about her trouble breathing and the coronary-like chest
pains. Okay, that came in the middle of taking infusions. The IV
was removed, she hasn't been on it for months, but a few times
the same symptoms, though less, came back. She's also weaker.
Her leg spasms are stronger. Her feet are twisted inward and
cause a lot of pain. Her vision's poorer, speech is worse, she gets
tired more quickly, and things drop out of her hands and she
knocks things over more than ever. Even her handwriting—
though we can live with this; but still—which had been improv-
ing like almost everything else since she started the infusions
four years ago, has become illegible again, all squiggles and
scrawl. So at times, because of all this and that there doesn't seem
to be anything new that's going to help her or arrest her disease,
she wonders openly why she still hangs around." Is there nobody
else he can tell these things to? He doesn't think so. His sisters.
They're sympathetic and listen but they get too sentimental
about it. Friends? Not really. There used to be two, up till
around three years ago. He could tell them anything and they the
same with him. One lived in Baltimore and they'd go out for
lunch every month or so. The other in New York he spoke to on
the phone once a week and would try to see a few times a year

when he was in the city. But the first one moved to Indiana with his wife three years ago and seems less and less interested in keeping in touch by letter or phone. The other has early Alzheimer's, it may even be beyond that by now, so of course has his own problems and for the last two years has seemed too out of it most times for Stu to talk about Janice's illness. They usually just sit in his friend's kitchen having coffee and Stu, sometimes with the guy's wife and son, does his best to try to get him to reminisce. People at work? Many are pleasant enough and clever and smart but also pedantic, careerist and annoyingly self-absorbed. Academics, he's found, even the one who teach fiction and poetry writing, can be such cold fish, so he feels uncomfortable telling them anything very personal. And his fears for his kids? Some are irrational and exaggerated, he knows that. Anita drives a car. He bought it to have a spare one when their van is on the blink and also so she could drive it to high school her senior year and after school and weekends to work or whatever she needed it for. The car's small. When he bought it he knew he should be buying a bigger car but was thinking of the cost. If this one gets into a head-on collision at a speed over fifty miles an hour, she's finished, he's thought, or seriously hurt. She hasn't been driving long. There are a lot of daredevils and just lousy drivers out there. "Why," he would say to Dan, "do so many young guys have to drive like maniacs, weaving at top speeds in and out of lanes and tailgating and frightening you and endangering the lives of other drivers, especially inexperienced ones like Anita?" He fears for her every time she takes the car. Fears when she calls from the mall, for instance, and says she'll be driving home in half an hour so please hold dinner for her. But the biggest fears for her are when she drives in the snow or heavy rain or when there's ice—this most of all—on the road. Fears, when she parks at night in front of her friend's rowhouse downtown or is going to meet friends at a concert somewhere, that some guy will grab her from behind—two or three guys—and mug or rape or kill her. He fears for Meera at college. It's in a small city with a high crime rate. She has her own apartment and it's on the first floor in back, easiest one to break in to. Her building does have a good security system: vestibule intercom with TV monitor, razor wire on the fence her apartment faces, floodlights and infrared motion and glassbreak sensors all around the building, and it's in a pretty good university neighborhood, but he's heard no neighborhood in New Haven is that safe after eleven or twelve at night. "What is it with so many American cities?" he would ask Dan. "Why can't they be as safe as cities in Europe and Canada and Japan and their inhabitants more like the people in those cities too? Why do so many American men have to be so angry and aggressive and predatory? Oh, these are stupid unanswerable questions for the most part, I know. Drugs, guns, poverty, money, the wrong influences, no fathers, the country's violent history, the cultural mix of its cities, the whole works, am I right? Psychologists and sociologists or just urban experts of a particular sort might have some of the answers, but nothing to stop the break-ins and street muggings and such." Her apartment has an alarm system, but suppose someone was able to deactivate it and get in before she did or while she was sleeping? "Despite the elaborate security system her apartment and building have," he would tell Dan, "and that it's a busy commercial street she lives on—lots of restaurants and the university's art building and museums—some criminal types know how to break in to anyplace or would take the chance for a quick robbery or rape, or am I letting my fears get the better of me again?" "From everything you've told me of Meera's living arrangements," Dan would say, "it seems her building and apartment have adequate protection to stop them. But you ought to find out for sure how safe she is, and if you're not satisfied, get her to move to a safer place. After all, you're paying the rent." True, he should, but she likes her apartment and its proximity to the art building, and would never leave. He fears she'll be mugged on the street when she walks home late from her art studio or on the front steps or in the vestibule when she's entering her building. He thinks what would he do if one of his daughters was murdered or died in a car accident? He'd crack up. He wouldn't leave the house. He'd eventually pull through enough to go out, but much of his life would come to an end. He'd quit work. How could he teach students again who'd be her age and then the next year and so on what her age would have been? How could he even be on the same campus with them? He'd take care of Janice. That'd be about most of what he'd do with his life. They'd live frugally to make up for the money he wasn't making. He'd be overprotective of his other daughter. He'd be a mess. He'd never stop being a mess. He'd get sick and wouldn't care if he died but then would think he has to get well and stay alive for Janice and his daughter. They'd suffer as much as he but he really wouldn't know how to deal with it.

Nothing would be enjoyable for him again. He couldn't write. He wouldn't want to have sex. He'd drink a lot. Get drunk every night. Or drink enough every night to fall asleep. He wouldn't want to read anything but newspapers. And never the *Sun* again because of all its murder and car-crash stories. Wouldn't want to travel anymore. The only people he'd see would be family and he'd keep that to a limit. He wouldn't want to listen to music much and when he did, only sad pieces. And what if something like what he imagines would happen to one of his daughters also happened to the other? There's no one else he could talk to about things like this. About his daughters, yes, to Janice, but not as much as he could to Dan because it'd upset her. Dan was always understanding, analyzed his anxieties well, asked the right questions—just good questions—leveled with him and gave good advice. For the things Stu didn't think he could speak to Janice about, there was always Dan to call up, and he always seemed to be home. "Am I going a bit over the top with this?" he asked Dan a couple of times, and he said "They seem normal to me. I had them. Not for Melody but the kids. They'd leave the house in a car, either theirs or as a passenger in a friend's, and for sure when Manny had a motorcycle for a while, I often got worried. I can remember plenty of times staying up late when the kids were out and worrying about them till they got home. Melody I knew could take care of herself as well as any woman. Some punk came up to her from behind, she'd sense it seconds before and would, without even turning around to look, blow a police whistle she always has around her neck when she's out alone at night, and run away. She's still faster than most men. Or she'd spin around and kick him in the groin and then mash his face in with her shoe. She did that once. About ten years ago. I never told you? Ran once, too, without doing anything and another time blew the whistle and scared the guy off. But the time after that— she'd had it, you see; this was her third mugging in two years, all in the city where she was going for her master's at night. So she did what I told her to in such a situation: kicked the creep in the nuts—he'd jumped out of his car and tried dragging her in. Then, when he was on the ground, and this wasn't something I told her to do; all I said was poke in his eyes or go for the balls— she kicked him in the ear. She wasn't aiming at it—just his head. But it must have hurt, and the more the better I say and I hope he lost his hearing in that ear, and then ran away. She called the police from the next block and said he might still be there, she'd kicked him so hard both times, but he wasn't, and the tag number she was quick-thinking enough to get was for a stolen car. My fears for my kids, though, I don't think were ever as great as yours. But all you've gone through and you've lost so much, it's easy to see why they'd be more active, I'll put it, than mine." "Why do you say that? We both lost the same. We each lost a baby before it was born. Maybe Janice's long progressive disease is the one thing I have going that way that you don't. But Jay, Deborah, Mom, Dad, Newton, whom I hardly knew. I mean, I knew him, but nothing like you did," and Dan said "But you and Jay had probably the closest relationship of any two kids in the family. And you had to be much closer to Deborah than I. I was thirteen when she was born, and in college and then the army by the time she was four or five. You also helped take care of Dad for years while I was raising a family. And Mom, let's be honest, had a special affection for you. Possibly because you stayed around so long, living at home all through college, then coming back to help her with Dad, while from the time I was seventeen I only wanted to be out of the house and on my own. As for Newton, we had one of those classically hellish relationships only two brothers very close in age could have, the opposite of you and Jay. For the first dozen years of our lives we were always fighting. He once split my head open with a Boy Scout canteen. And I once went after him with a hatchet but couldn't catch him. Those weren't accidents or isolated incidents either— I think I've told you how we destroyed my violin and his drums—just maybe the worst. When we fought, there was often blood, and a number of times Uncle Ben had to come over to sew us up." "But losing him—that must have been some blow. You two slept in the same room for years, and later double-dated and so on." "Sure. We made adjustments and got it together the last few years of his life. And I suppose, despite our different interests and personalities—he was so much darker than I at first, then lighter and a lot more sociable when I became very serious and not a dancer and party-type guy like him—would have become closer the older we got once we were both married and had kids. But that's the way it goes; something else to regret. As for you, I wish you didn't have these disturbing thoughts about your family and other things. But I can understand why you do and I'm glad you feel you can talk about them with me."

35

It's complicated. Dan's covering the Korean War for a wire service. On a week-long break he meets a freighter captain in Hong Kong and they become good friends. The captain and Dan and another newsman covering the war buy a 42-foot schooner and plan to sail it to one of the French Polynesian or Fiji islands when they can arrange a month's vacation at the same time. Stu isn't sure it was a schooner. The word just popped into his head. A few years ago when he was talking on the phone to Dan about the time he got captured he asked what kind of boat it was and Dan told him but he forgot. The length of the boat and its name, though, stuck. So, a sailboat of some kind, a very large one—Stu had seen newspaper photos of it with Dan and the other two men on deck—with several tall sails and an engine and it slept eight, Dan said, "not uncomfortably." The three men, with a crew of four Chinese, one of them the girlfriend of the freighter captain,

Len Krakow, take the boat on a trial run from Macao to Hong Kong, or maybe it was Hong Kong to Macao. Soon after they bought the boat, Stu forgot to say, Len taught Dan and the other man, Phil Apfelwhite, how to sail. Also, Len lived with his girlfriend at the time in Hong Kong and to stay close to her he only worked on ships that traveled between Southeast Asian ports, which is how Dan was able to see him so much. A Chinese gunboat stops their boat in international waters, though claims it's in Chinese territorial waters, and armed sailors board it and the three men are accused of being spies and taken to the mainland—the boat's never returned to them—and kept in a string of prisons there for around eighteen months, each one, Dan said, more dismal and primitive than the next. The four crew members are put on another gunboat, beaten for working for known spies, imprisoned for a few weeks and then released on the mainland, the girlfriend eventually slipping back into Hong Kong where she gets a job as a bartender while she waits for Len. The men are released six months after the armistice ending the war is signed. Phil Apfelwhite had German and English citizenship, Dan said, so there was continued pressure on the Chinese from those two countries for his release. And Chou En-Lai, the Chinese prime minister and foreign minister then, thought it was a good time to improve relations with Europe and, to a lesser degree, America—"It was all about trade," Dan said. "To create a huge war machine and produce your own H-bomb that won't blow up in your face, you can only go so far on slave labor; you also need real dough." Dan returns home, works a short time for the wire service in New York, and gets a much better job with CBS News in DC. Six years later their brother Jay is in Paris, at the end of a round-the-world trip that lasted a year. Dan's still in touch with Len Krakow, who at the time is the captain of a freighter leaving England for Baltimore in two weeks. An interesting note: before Jay started out, Dan told him to look up Len's ex-girl-friend in Hong Kong, where she now owned a bar bought with money Len gave when he split up with her. Len was married to a Cuban, and when he wasn't working on ships, lived in Havana with her and her two kids. Jay wrote Stu from Hong Kong, saying he'd moved in with Len's ex-girlfriend and for a while thought he might stay with her indefinitely and teach English to foreigners for a living, but decided he wanted to continue his trip more. "She's ten years older than me and ravishingly beautiful, if for once in your life you'll let me use such a trite familiar phrase, and the sweetest most generous and naturally bright women I've ever met. She also cracks up at my paltry jokes, thinks I'm a great lover and that I've gorgeous legs, and is teaching me street Chinese. But don't breathe a word of this to Dan. He might think it too weird if not even a bit immoral of me, living partly off a woman." Years later, Stu did tell Dan. His reaction: "Jay, I can understand. He wanted to taste a stomachful of exotica and also get laid. I'm surprised at her, though. All I thought she'd do for him is show him around Hong Kong, give him a few good meals and introduce him to some nice syphilis-free Chinese girls his age." Dan arranges for Jay to sail back on Len's ship. He'll be signed on as an apprentice seaman, he tells Stu, "do menial chores, but nothing too strenuous or time-consuming, if I know Len. Just enough to learn rudimentary seamanship and relieve

the boredom of a long crossing with twenty other seamen, none
of whom speaks much English." From Paris, Jay asks Stu on the
phone what does he think he should do, "stay here another month
and then return home on the liner I've a ticket for or get most
of my fare back and go as a paid seaman on Len's ship in a
week?" Stu says "No question in my mind: take the freighter. It'll
be a new experience, one that can be useful to you as a writer as
it's been for so many others—Melville, Lowry, you name it.
You'll also have all that money from the ticket and your pay. And
Dan says that just from this one sailing and maybe Len stretching the truth as to what kind of work you did and how much time
you put in, you'll be able to get better-paying positions on other
ships if you find from this one it's something you want to do.
I know it's what I'd do in a second if I didn't have the good job
I have now." "But I'm with a woman I met hitchhiking in Iran.
She drove me here and has an apartment and doesn't want me to
go so soon, so I'm sort of torn. Though you're probably right.
I'm almost broke and the experience looks interesting, so I
should take it," and their father cuts in on the upstairs phone
extension and says "Don't listen to that jerk. He doesn't know
what he's talking about and only wants you back sooner so he
can pal around with you. As for Dan, he's only arranging this
hookup because he feels he has to, you and this Krakow guy coming across the ocean around the same time. Do yourself and us a
favor and stay there, finish out your trip, get this traveling bug
out of your system and come back when you intended to. But on
a regular passenger ship with good food and music and not
some tin can, and then start getting serious with your life again.

You know me—I'm tight as a boxer's fist with money, although I like to think it's because I know how hard it is to get, and I'd ordinarily jump at the freighter deal as a good break for you. But your ocean fare's paid for, when you get here I'll loan you what you need till you get back on your feet, and I'll even wire you some now if you want me to. Besides that, who knows how safe this freighter is, for look what that guy did for Dan: got him interested in boats and landed him in a Chinese prison and almost got him killed there. Even if it is safe, it's bound to be an uncomfortable old tub you'll be seasick and miserable on. So enjoy yourself while you can and we'll see you when we see you, and Stu—keep your trap shut about saying anything else to encourage him," and Stu says "Okay, I will, but he already knows what I think," and their father says "Idiot. You think you're so smart sometimes, but you sound like a fool," and Jay says "Dad, lay off him; you're being unfair." "Oh, now I've got both of you against me when I'm trying to do some good." Jay returns on the freighter. In a letter to Stu from England: "My decision was half made to me by our least favorite royalty, Ole King Moolah. I want to have some when I get back so I don't have to sponge off you and Dad. And just as you said, the freighter's too intriguing an experience to pass up and also a potential work opportunity, for who can say if I won't take to the mariner's life for a while? To get paid and travel free to faraway enchanting places like Shreveport and Baltimore and drink lousy coffee for twenty days? Melville, move over, here comes Jay." Stu's been a newsman in Washington for two years, a job he got through Dan, and plans to take off a few days so he can meet Jay's ship and spend time

with him. Dan's now married to Melody and is the chief writer
of a network radio news show in New York. Stu's having a drink
in their apartment—he comes in every third or fourth week to
see family and friends—and Dan says "There's something I want
to talk to you about." "Uh-oh, your voice," Stu says; "it's bad;
what? The baby?" and Dan says "No, but if Melody were losing
it, devastating as that would be so late, it wouldn't be as bad if
what I'm about to tell you turns out as it seems it might." The
Ari, Len's freighter, which left Cork five days ago, hasn't been
heard from in three days and the ship's company headquarters in
Greece and now the Coast Guard and the UK equivalent haven't
been able to make contact with it either. "It's possible the ship's
all right and its radio and transmitter and emergency distress signal and everything else like that, including the entire electrical
system, aren't working. Though most nautical experts I spoke to
say all that happening at once and for the ship not to be in
tremendous danger if not to have sunk already is unlikely," and
Stu says "Oh God, that can't be—it couldn't have happened," and
digs his nails into his wrist and shuts his eyes. Melody, seated on
the couch next to Dan and holding his hand, says "I know, I
know, we've felt the same the last two days," and he finishes his
drink and Dan says "Want another?—I would," and pours more
Scotch into Stu's glass and says "So, I'll go on? There was an
unusually fierce storm in the North Atlantic area the *Ari* would
have been in two to three days ago. Storm's still going on, same
intensity, making search efforts all but impossible, and if the
ship was spotted or its radio or distress signals picked up,
rescue attempts totally impossible till the storm lets up some.

If I'm being too blunt here, say so. What these people I spoke to
think happened—and remember, this is mostly speculation, albeit
based on a lot of things: past incidents, etcetera, so they could be
wrong. A couple of them—one a very knowledgeable Coast
Guard spokesman—say it's fifty-fifty the ship's still afloat and
can be found and saved, or at least the crew can. But the others:
that the *Ari* split apart or took a huge iceberg it didn't see or
hear coming, or driftwood—whole trees—causing a hole in the
hull and what that brings. Or because of hurricane-force winds
the ship listed as far as it could without turning over and took
in too much water, and then keeled over because of the water and
went down. If the crew made it into lifeboats—no reason they
shouldn't have; it's rare, I was told, for a ship to go down right
away, even those split in two—they wouldn't have lasted an hour
in those choppy, frigid waters. If some had to jump overboard to
reach the lifeboats, they would have died of shock seconds after
hitting the water. Considering what else was available to them,
that had to be the best way to die," and Melody says "Dan, watch
what you say; you're going too far." "Okay. But Mom says, Mom
says—right? Mom always says 'Let's face it,' and we should. A
small freighter or tanker a year like the *Ari* is lost there. Never
a passenger ship, it seems. The ship companies are more careful
with them—lots of passengers, big fares, lawsuits that'll break
them. Or maybe they meant one ship a year is lost in the entire
Atlantic, though the North part's the roughest in the ocean
around this time, December, January. I wasn't aware of this
myself till two days ago. Coast Guard, ours and UK's, are
calling off what little search there's been because the chance of

locating the *Ari* is so small that it isn't worth losing a search plane or vessel. They'll resume when weather conditions improve, though I think they think it'll be too late by then. If only I hadn't gotten him on that goddamn ship. Hadn't known it was leaving England for America. Or was docked there, anything. Hadn't even known Len or kept in contact with him all these years. Had listened to Dad, but then I never did, but this time did and didn't interfere in Jay's trip home. Or if I did tell Jay—well, of course I did; what am I saying here? But then realized my mistake and said I changed my mind about the ship—the owner's a cheap bastard, has a reputation for cutting corners, making money off of insurance—all of which I only found out now but didn't take the time to look into for Jay... I was so busy with other things, but what bullshit. And he would have listened. If he didn't—got caught up in the adventure and bargain ride—then I would have told Len not to let him on. Or just never thought of taking up sailing years ago when I was covering the war. What a dumb idea that was. It never entered my mind to do anything like it till then. Then Len would only have been a passing friend, someone I met at the International Press Club in Hong Kong— and what the hell was he doing sitting alone there at the bar anyway? Probably just there for the subsidized booze and free buffets. No no, he's my friend. And if it came to this, he'd do everything he could to keep Jay alive, see that he was okay—make sure he was the first into the fireboat and warm—so I shouldn't think these cheesy things about him. And I have to assume the *Ari* was a safe ship. Otherwise, Len never would have taken it out of port, and for sure not with Jay aboard. But if I hadn't bumped into him at the bar or just did so casually—one or two drinks, that's all, never spoke about sailing or saw him again—then Jay would be boarding his Dutch liner in a week and heading home that way. What a disaster it's turned into, the worst thing imaginable, and all my doing," and he grabs his hair and pulls it and says "I want to tear my fucking hair out, my fucking brains. I could kill myself for what I did," and Melody takes his hands away from his head and holds them and stares at him till he looks her in the eyes, and says "There, that's better; stop it now, my sweetheart. Jay will be found. The ship will, Jay and Len, everyone on board and the ship intact," and Dan says "If it isn't, I'll never forgive myself. I might look one day like I have, but I never will." "Drink up, drink up," and gives him his glass and they all finish their drinks—Melody's is just soda water and a slice of lime—have another, says nothing for minutes till she says to Stu "We've had dinner, but I can get you something. There's chicken, rice, salad, some soup," and he says "No thanks, not hungry," and to Dan "You shouldn't be taking this all on yourself. I'm as much at fault as anyone in this." "It's no one's fault," Melody says, "and everything's going to be all right. You're all—your whole family except your father—entirely too lugubrious and pessimistic." "It's true. It's those damn family tragedies and misfortunes we've had. Dad in prison and losing his license. Deborah with her cancer. Dan and the Chinese. Newton, of course, and now Jay. I don't know why they haven't hit Dad worse. Look," he says to Dan, "what I meant before is I also told Jay to take the freighter when it was obvious he was having second thoughts about it or didn't know what to do when Dad told him not to. No, Dad told him that after I told him to take it, and the truth is I didn't let up when Dad told me to clam it. I thought it was a better arrangement for Jay. More interesting than any passenger ship, and there was the pay and what he'd save on the fare. And Dad was right in this too: I wanted him to come back sooner than the liner would have brought him, and Baltimore's so close to DC I could be at the place the *Ari* docked at in an hour. But I agree with Melody. I don't believe anything happened to the ship other than for things like all the lights and communication going, where they temporarily can't beam out or be heard or reached by radio. If a ship a year can disappear in the Atlantic, then one a year can lose its power in a bad storm. And then ride it out and get some to all its power back and continue to Baltimore or back to Ireland or England if it's been damaged in some way. Or not get any of its power back but be found in a day or two anchored or drifting," and Dan says "I'm sorry, and I hope to hell I'm wrong, but I don't think that's it. You know me; I like to see things as they are. Maybe it comes from being a newsman so long or it's what sent me into the work. Ah, that's bullshit. But what do I think? You want to know?" and Melody says "Let's drop it; it won't help anyone," and Stu says "Go ahead; it's not going to change my mind." "From everything I've learned about it the last two days," Dan says, "and also common sense and what I knew about sailing before, I think the ship's finished, all the damage has been done. Structural defect and it split apart. Or got knocked over by winds and waves, or something hit it or it exploded because of an engine problem. One of those or a combination of a couple, and everyone on board went down with it or into lifeboats which quickly capsized and sunk. To believe anything else would be fooling myself and not preparing myself for what I'm ninety-nine percent sure I'll be told in a few days," and Stu says "You can't be that sure. You don't have all the facts; nobody does. It's too soon, and there are too many possibilities. It's an enormous area and they've been at sea several days and the ship could be any place in it, off course by a hundred miles so they could get out of the storm and so not where the searching people have been signaling or looking for it." "About not sticking to their original route—that could be so," Dan says. "And other things we haven't thought of. Okay. We'll wait and see what happens. Maybe I'm too much of a pessimist. But we won't tell the folks anything till we're sure either way or they start asking questions." "I can help you out with that if the news is bad," and Dan says "Better you go back to Washington. That way they won't get suspicious. If the news is the worst, I feel it's my responsibility to deliver it and I'll do it alone. You'd just break down and then I'd lose control and it'd be a mess." Years later on Jay's birthday, when Dan and Stu talk on the phone, and they always do that day, one of them calling and a few minutes into the call, one or the other saying something like "You of course know what today is," and the other saying "Main reason I called" or "He's been on my mind all day." "I'd give anything to get him back," Dan's said a few times on Jay's birthday. "It's so stupid to say and also self-aggrandizing, but my health, life, everything I own." "Always, day of his birthday," Dan's said a couple of times, "I get so upset, and sometimes starting the night before, that I can barely function and I usually have to stay home from work, as I did today.

My own birthdays come and go without my noticing them most
times till very late, but also because my family's instructed not
to remind me with presents and 'happy birthdays.' Mom, who
always used to send a card, I suppose doesn't remember anymore.
Imagine, her firstborn, and she's forgotten his birthday. But I
shouldn't kid about any of it." "Don't you think by now I should
be able to let Jay's birthday go by once without letting it disturb
me so much, as it did today?" Dan's said. "Melody thinks I should
see a therapist about it, but what's one going to tell me that I
don't already know?" "I should have thought something could go
wrong on that trip," Dan said on one of Jay's birthdays. "Late
November, early December, North Atlantic, start of the storm
season or the very peak of it? And a small old freighter owned
by a sleazy foreign operator and flying under an even different
foreign flag? What the hell was I thinking? That he was in the
best of hands with Len, first off. I had to have thought that.
Len took chances and could be a real adventurer—gunrunning,
smuggling, sailing with no lights on into a mined port to rescue
refugees, but all in the late Forties to make money on the side.
He was the youngest man ever to make master ranking in the
merchant marine, or in the last fifty years, he said. He knew
everything there was about the sea and ships and celestial
navigation and so on, and I know, because of the kind of man he
was, that if he thought... oh, I'm sure I've told you all this, but
if there was any possible danger to the ship he never would have
let a friend's brother get on it. But he had to know the company
that owned his ship was a piece of shit. But the *Ari* still could
have been in perfect shape—he'd see to it—although there's
always the possibility of unforeseeable danger when you take any

vessel out into the ocean, even in the best weather and calmest sea. All the research I did, after the ship disappeared, and I still haven't a clear idea what actually happened to it and why," and Stu said "Nothing ever found from it, right?, except two life preservers washed up on the Irish coast," and Dan said "One preserver, one saver, both with the ship's name. And the English coast, which could mean they fell off the ship before it reached or even headed out for Ireland." "Another mystery," and Dan said "No mystery; these things are lost off ships all the time. It could be they weren't battened down well. And then there's always— you wouldn't think it—vandalism aboard. Sailor gets drunk or mad, throws them over, even lifeboats." "But as I've said before, we were both involved in Jay being on that freighter. Me in more ways than you because I know if I'd told him to take the ocean liner then, he would have. He was that indecisive and wanted my advice, which was unusual for him with me, not you, in asking what I'd do in his place," and Dan said "Still trying to take the blame off me, but it won't work. I don't mean for this to be com-petitive guilt, but if it wasn't for what I did, Jay would be alive today. He at least would have been alive after the *Ari* disap-peared, because who knows, with our family luck, what would have happened to him after that." Once—Dan was in his sixties and Stu in his fifties by then—Dan called late at night for them— past eleven—and said "What happened? True, it's not midnight yet, and sorry for calling so late on a weekday—but for the first time in more than thirty years we didn't talk on Jay's birthday. What's it mean, that we're finally getting used to his disappear-ance or are just tired of this phone ritual?" and Stu said "I'm sure not, on the first, for either of us. As for the ritual, I didn't call, after not hearing from you, because I thought it was enough that you probably thought about it at least once today and I didn't want to remind you of it again because I know how much it affects you." "I didn't think of it all day till about twenty minutes ago, and then it hit me worse than it normally does, maybe because I realized I'd forgotten it. It was only while I was lying in bed with a book that it came to me. I have a small framed photo of Jay on my dresser—been there in the same spot forever, it seems—and looking up from the book, I saw it and then thought of him and what today was and so on. It's the last photo we have of him, taken by his girlfriend Paddy, whom he'd hooked up with a month before their relationship fizzled again. I think she gave it to us, in fact. He's standing in front of a tiny Fiat they were driving from Turkey to Paris, where I think they were to drop it off with the car's owner, a Frenchman." "I know the photo—I have a copy somewhere myself. Jay in a dark turtleneck jersey and V-neck sweater, snow all around him, though it was early fall, so he must have been pretty high up, and in sneakers and sunglasses and holding a cigarette. Always the cigarette. The smoke killed me for years when we slept in the same room. Everybody in the family but me smoked and eating dinner with you all was pure hell for me. But it wasn't Paddy who took the photo. He told me over the phone that last time of another woman—Lael, a Belgian. They'd met in Iran and I assume became lovers and drove together all the way to Paris, where she had an apartment and wanted him to live with her. What I also recall, the Fiat was hers and the photo was among the things she sent us of his after she wrote him in New York and I had to write back telling her what had happened," and Dan said "Then how does Paddy figure into it, for I know they were together on his trip for a while?" "That was in the Philippines, soon after he left Hong Kong. She had family there—aunts, grandparents—and had flown in. You arranged for him a stringer job there with AP for a month," and Dan said "What a memory you've got. Mine's fading, which sometimes is no great loss. By the way, how was Mom today? Her girl said you were going to visit her. I should have come down to see you, since you don't get in much, but I thought you wanted to be with her alone—I see her plenty. I bet, bad as her memory's become, she still always thinks of Jay on his birthday and then remembers, but quickly pushes out of her mind, that I was the fool who got him on that ship—another reason to stay away on his birthday," and Stu said "No she doesn't. And she was fine, ate well when I took her to lunch. Had a drink, though I know you've said not to offer her one, and was unusually talkative—before the drink, even. But she didn't mention Jay and I didn't bring up what day it was for the same reason I didn't call you. Why remind her? It would only spoil her good mood. One thing I'm curious about, though, is what happened to the insurance that was supposed to be paid by the *Ari*'s insurers because Jay was officially listed as one of the crew? Did Dad get it and then just sock it away someplace?" and Dan said "All of it; that's what the ship company wrote me when Mom had me check into it. At the time—this was a year after the *Ari* was lost—I told her 'Let him keep it if it makes him feel better,' and I still think I was right in not asking him what he did with the dough. It was just money—she didn't want any of it;

called it 'ghoul *gelt*'—and I didn't think anyone else in the family did, though I never asked. Not that it could have gone to anyone but the parents. Maybe he had some fun with it to drown his sorrow, we'll say—I didn't want to know," and Stu said "It was a good deal of money, from what I remember them first offering—ten thousand or so. Then Dad coming back at them that the settlement was too low, so they might have doubled it just to keep him quiet. But you're right. Like you, I wouldn't have touched a cent of it."

36

Two things, both dealing with his daughters. The first, three summers ago: Anita stuck at Logan Airport on her way to Maine after a month at an academic camp on the Hamilton College campus. Plane from Syracuse to Boston went without a hitch. But the Boston-to-Bangor flight kept getting delayed and then was canceled. Something to do with electric storms in the South and Midwest. Planes heading there were diverted to major Northeast airports, causing more arrivals there than air traffic controllers could handle and jamming the skies and runways. If that's unclear as a reason why every scheduled arrival and departure from Bangor was canceled for the night, it's mainly because it was never made clear to Stu and, he thinks, to the other people waiting for the Boston plane to arrive. When he first went up to the airline counter to ask what was causing the delay, the woman there said "Weather," and he said "But it's beautiful out.

Every star in the sky can be seen and there isn't a hint of a storm," and she said "Not here but in most of the country west of New York and south of Richmond, and we're affected." He'd gone to the airport with Meera. Janice wasn't feeling well—stomach upset—and thought she'd feel even more nauseous if she drove with them to the airport an hour away. When the Arrivals screen listed Anita's flight as canceled he went back to the counter and said "So what happens now that everything out of Boston's canceled? Do you put my daughter in a van to Bangor with the other passengers on that flight or do you put them up for the night in a Boston hotel?" and the woman said "Neither, I'm afraid. It's the passenger's responsibility what to do if a flight's canceled because of natural events like bad weather. Our sole responsibility is to get them on the next available flight to their destination. Because of her age and that she's traveling alone, she should be on the first plane to Bangor tomorrow morning," and he said "What the hell are you talking about? Excuse me, I didn't mean to curse, but maybe you don't know exactly how old she is. She's thirteen, just a kid. You have to do something for her now. I've talked to my wife. She's spoken to our daughter several times on the phone and she's stranded and scared and doesn't know what to do. And we know no one in Boston or anywhere around there to come get her or send her in a cab to their home. And it's almost midnight and I have to take my other daughter home and I also have to look after my wife there. She's alone and not well and has been glued to her wheelchair the last five hours because of all your flight delays. The plane's ten minutes delayed, then an hour, then two hours? If you had told me sooner it would be canceled—" and she said "We didn't know sooner. I only found out twenty minutes before it was posted on the board. If you had come up to me, I would have told you. I'm sorry," and she started to close down the counter, "but there's nothing more I can do for you." "Wait, what are you doing? Closing up or taking a break at a time when I need you to help me?" and she said "I've done everything I can, so I don't see what that help could be. According to the attendants at Logan I spoke to, all the other passengers on your daughter's flight who don't live in that area are doing what passengers always do in situations like this, finding hotel rooms or a place to bed down in the terminal, so that's what I suggest you arrange for her. That said, her plane was our last scheduled arrival tonight and we're not expecting any more diversions from other airports. So yes, I'm closing up and going home. I've been on the job six hours straight without a break and have been the only attendant here the past three hours. And excuse me, sir, but I also have to tell you I don't like your tone of voice to me, nor some of your language. I sympathize with your predicament, but you've no call to snip at me. It isn't my fault your daughter's flight was canceled, or the airline's. That decision was part of a much larger one made by the FAA and air controllers, and after considerable deliberation, I'm sure, to help relieve a national flight emergency and prevent an airplane disaster, maybe several of them. If you want to complain further you should call our customer service line," and she wrote down the phone number for him. "They're no doubt very busy now, but you'll eventually get through to someone if you hold on, though don't be surprised if they tell you the same things I did. If you want to complain about me, here's my name," and she wrote it next to the phone number, flicked several switches behind the counter and walked out of the terminal carrying a thermos and knapsack. He called Janice. She said Anita was getting more worried by the minute because the airport was emptying out. "Next time you speak to her—she's by a public payphone, right?" and she said "I've the numbers of two of them side by side"—"Tell her I'm trying to work something out for her and not to panic, it's going to be all right and that you or I will be calling her about it," and he wrote down those two numbers. He called the airline's customer service. It took half an hour to get off Hold and to speak to some-one, who said there was nothing they could do for his daughter. "If you'd paid the extra fee for our escort service for minors, a representative would have met her Syracuse plane, stayed with her till the Bangor flight was canceled and then got her a hotel room at our expense and probably something to eat too, and tomorrow morning—it's still Saturday where I am—escorted her from the hotel to the plane. And our first flight to Bangor, also, since the twenty-five dollar fee is more a courtesy on our part, considering all the man hours this service eats up." "I was told she was too old for it," he lied. "That's what your airline person said on the phone when I bought the ticket and wanted to buy the service. That twelve was the maximum age for it, and not twelve through thirteen but her twelfth birthday," and the man said "I don't know who could have told you that. It's different with each airline, but the fourteenth birthday's our limit and we've been known to stretch it to the fifteenth when asked by a parent or guardian." He said "Look, this is getting me nowhere and I need to get help for her fast. You can't help me, let me speak to your supervisor," and the supervisor he was connected to told him the same things: his responsibility, not theirs, so nothing they can do for him. "Speaking as a parent," the woman said, "I'd call Logan Security and ask them to look after her. Tell them you think their airport wouldn't want a thirteen-year-old girl getting molested or worse in one of their lounges, as can happen. I don't have their number, but Boston phone information will." He called Logan Security and was told they couldn't keep his daughter in their office overnight as he suggested. "No room and too many weirdos tend to come in here uninvited. We're also low on staff after midnight because the airport gets deserted. Tonight should be busier for us with all the flight cancellations, putting an even greater strain on my diminished force. And sometimes we have to lock up the office if we're out inspecting something in the airport. But if she parks herself in a seat by her airline's ticket counter, we'll make sure to check in on her plenty of times on our patrols." He called Janice and she said "I don't go for it. Who knows what people, pretending to be waiting for flights, are just predators or thieves. And sometimes those security men have longer criminal records than the crooks they're supposed to be protecting you against. Late as it is, call Dan. I called friends I thought might know someone in the Boston area who could help, and don't know why I didn't think of him. He knows so many people through his work. Maybe one, as a favor to him, will go to the airport and stay with Anita till morning, or he might have some other ideas. He's great at that."

Stu called him, apologized for the time, as it was obvious he'd woken him up—"Don't worry about it; what's up? Because I know it has to be important"—and told him about Anita and everything he'd tried to do so far. "Hotel idea was all wrong," Dan said. "You don't want her in a strange place, maybe miles from the airport, alone, nobody you trust to look after her. I know a few people in Boston and all of them will be happy to help out, but first let me try my luck with the airline. Who'd you speak to there and what's the phone number?" and he said "They're not going to do anything; they made that clear over and over," and Dan said "Just tell me," and he said "I never got a name. They were just people in Customer Relations, from the first guy I spoke to, to a woman higher up. His supervisor." "You should always get names. Then they know you mean business and if they're at fault you're liable to report them. Let me see what I can do," and twenty minutes later—he was going to give Dan half an hour before he called him—he was paged on the public-address system to go to Security, and a woman there said "Your brother called. He said to tell you your daughter's been put in a limo by the airline and it should be getting here around five and for you to phone him for more information." Dan said "There are two women in the limo with her, one a military officer at the Air Force National Guard base by the Bangor Airport, so she's in safe hands and they're even going to ask you for a photo ID." "How'd you pull it off?" and Dan said "I guess I got to the right person who thought what I was asking for sounded reasonable and quickly put together this limo with several other people stranded there," and he said "I'll always be grateful to you, not that I haven't been anything but that for all the other things you've done for me the last sixty years," and Dan said "Like the time I threw a pillow at you and you tripped and split your skull? But what are you going on about. Anytime, for anything, call me." Stu and Meera drove back to the rented farmhouse. She went right to sleep and he took care of Janice, got her into bed, slept an hour and then drove to the airport, getting there just as the limo was unloading its passengers. A few weeks later he got a voucher for a roundtrip airplane ticket to anywhere in the continental US, no restrictions, along with an apology from the company's vice president for the way the airline's personnel at the Boston and Bangor airports mishandled the situation with his daughter. He called Dan and said "Tell me, so I know from now on how to get things done with bureaucrats and petty tyrants when I'm totally in the right and they're flagrantly wrong. What did you say that made the airline not only drive Anita first-class to Bangor and probably include in the ride free two women to look after her and now send me this voucher and apology?" and Dan said "I didn't want to tell you—thought you might object to my appropriating your name in a lie—but I said I was you and that I was outraged at their unwillingness to take care of my daughter in so perilous a dilemma," and Stu said "I told them the same thing, so it had to have been something else," and Dan said "Then I suppose it was my gravelly voice and choice of words and that I was extremely pushy and emphatic, if not, when they continued to stiff-arm me, bordering on the maniacal in a way that only a parent can be who's trying to protect his child from imminent danger," and Stu said "So was I, even the voice, which all the boys in the family inherited from Dad, though my word choice probably wasn't as good as yours and I tend to hem and haw," and Dan said "Then I don't know. Anyway, whatever it was worked." The other thing involved a woman he knew from thirty-five years ago. She was married and living with her husband but not sleeping with him, she said. "Oh, sleeping in the same bed with him most nights, but you know, not screwing." She had driven in from Michigan with her three-year-old daughter to see old college friends and spend a week away from her husband. Stu was in from California, where he was living with a woman he knew just a few weeks and her two-year-old son. Dan had called him to say that Deborah, who had a rare form of cancer the past twenty years, was in the hospital again "and it looks like she's dying, so if you want to see her again, come now." Stu saw her every day for a few hours—she died the next year—and met Trudy at a party and was immediately attracted to her. Nice smile, good sense of humor, well educated, literary, caring to her daughter, who was running around and then suddenly so tired that Trudy had to leave the party early to get her to bed, intelligent face and things to say. They arranged to meet at a restaurant the next night—the friend she was staying with would look after her daughter—and ended up in bed in an apartment a couple he knew had loaned him for a few days. This was August; the couple was on vacation. Soon after they made love, Trudy said "I believe I did something quite stupid. No, I'm positive. I didn't think anything like this would happen, so I left my diaphragm behind in Ann Arbor. I don't even think I know where it is, it's been so long since I made love. I knew this was my fertile period and I was planning to ask you to withdraw before you ejaculated. But I got so lost in the act that I forgot to—as I said, it's been a while and my head and body were spinning—and I'm certain I conceived. This will sound foolish to you—I think I know something about your nature already—but I felt the same sensation of a sudden short eruption and the most infinitesimal start of something down there that I had with Louise." "Oh, please," he said, "that's ridiculous. I'm not saying you didn't conceive, but that you felt the conception," and she said "We'll see. If I'm right, I'm not sure what I'd do. I've been longing to have a second child and one as close in age to Louise as possible, since I want them to be tight loyal friends should anything happen to me. My husband has his own sweeties for his sexual exigencies— his grad students. He never lays a hand on me even when we're sleeping naked and I assure him it won't take long and I'll do all the work and it's not as if I have to have an orgasm and it'd only be so I can have a second and final child and Louise a soulmate." They made love several more times that week, always with a condom. She said he didn't have to put one on. She was beginning to like the idea of his fathering her child, if it turned out he hadn't inseminated her the first night. He said that much as he'd like to be a father, in or out of wedlock, having one with her wouldn't seem the right way to go about it if she was living in Michigan with her husband and he in California with his girlfriend, with little chance they'd see each other the next couple of years. She returned home, promising to inform him if she had conceived, and a few weeks later she wrote him "Congratulations, you're going to be a biological father. Yup, that means I'm keeping it.

I discussed it with Frank. I caught him on the way out to one of his trysts, so the conversation was fleeting, and he said he doesn't mind the baby's from another man so long as he doesn't have to spend more time with it than he wants to, and that he's very happy for me because he knows how much I wanted a second child. I apologize if this complicates your relationship with your woman friend. Tell her, if she's at all interested, I won't make any demands on you, financial, paternal or otherwise." Her next letter to him said she had the baby, a girl, Catherine. Stu and his girlfriend split up over other reasons. He saw the baby a number of times the next year when both he and Frank got jobs in LA, and after he left his and moved to San Francisco, Trudy drove up with her daughters a few weekends to see him. Then he moved back to New York and Frank got a research grant in Thailand for two years and his family went with him. She said she'd write Stu soon as she got a permanent address, but never did. He wrote her care of her old LA address, but the letters came back saying the person he wrote left no forwarding address. He called the friend who'd given the party Stu had met Trudy at, and the guy said he hadn't a clue who he was speaking of. "Who'd she come with?" and Stu said he didn't know, though he knew her name then and the address—"something Downing Street, in the Village. I was sure, though I don't remember talking about it with her, that you were all at Stanford together—that that's how she knew you," and the friend said "I did have lots of my classmates at the party, but this Trudy doesn't strike a bell. Tall, slim, blond, pretty, long legs and a tiny nose? That could describe half the coeds at Stanford. And she came with her young daughter? I always tell my guests to leave the kids home. Why are you so interested in finding her?" "I guess I never told you, which I really haven't done to anybody— I didn't think she wanted me blabbing about it—but I had a child with her," and the friend said "You, a father? That's something. And you're that sure it's yours?" and he said "She said I was the only guy she was sleeping with then, and she had the baby almost exactly nine months from the first time we had sex. Also, the girl, last time I saw her, looked just like my brother's two daughters did when they were around that age, and my brother and I, despite the huge age and height difference—I'm much younger and taller, though he takes better care of himself—could almost be taken as twins." "She might not have been leveling with you. She could have had other men then and didn't want you to know. As for the girl looking like your nieces, lots of young kids look alike." "But even her husband, whom she said she hadn't had sex with for a year and they might still not be having it, more than intimated the kid was mine. I was calling Trudy and he answered and in the background the kid was making noise and he said 'You should be here so you can deal with your daughter when she gets in these meshuggener moods,'" and the friend said "Don't be deceived. He could have been toying with you too, and after the call they both had a good laugh on you." A few days later, while on the phone with Dan, he said "The other day I told some guy I don't even like that much this news, so I don't see how I can withhold it from you any longer," and he went into the story how he'd met Trudy more than three years ago and what happened from it. "How come you didn't tell me sooner?"

and he said "Mainly, and this guy's the only other person I've told and it came out accidentally with him, is that I thought you might think my behavior unprincipled—frigging a woman who was still living with her husband, even if they weren't sleeping together and he was messing around with any number of women," and Dan said "If he didn't object, why should I? Although usually I think it's best for the marriage to be over and the couple living apart before another guy starts in with the woman. But the question I want to ask is how can you be so certain the little girl is yours?" and he said "The woman said so, and so did her husband to me." "Not enough. She's trained to be a college English teacher, not a geneticist. And he might be the brilliant scientist you say he is with a medical degree and post-doctorate, but he didn't put you through any scientific tests to prove the girl's yours. It could be—I'm assuming you were all taking some drugs at the time—that he had sex with her while she was dead drunk or out-of-her-mind high or asleep and didn't want to tell her because she could then say 'You're tooling me while I'm unconscious, why not while I'm awake and can enjoy it?' Okay, not a great example as to how he might have impreg-nated her and she didn't know. But you can only be absolutely sure you fathered the girl if she, you and her mother take these elaborate blood tests within forty-eight hours of one another. I know that for a fact. I contributed to an hour-long news spe-cial on it. The tests are so accurate that they can stand up in court in almost every state. So, much as it seems you want to believe you're the girl's natural father, and I can understand that yearning, because what are you now, thirty-three? But I'd stop thinking of it till mother and daughter reappear and you have the money for the tests. It's a lot, by the way. More than a thousand for the three of you. That is, if she consents to them taking it and her husband has no objections that his child do it. Then again, why would you want to go through all that, plus the expense? The girl has a father who's given her his name and provides for her and seems to treat her well, by what you've said the mother's said. Your horning in will only confuse the girl. Okay, another instance of my finding out what I really think by talking about it. You were wrong. You never should have shacked up with this woman while she was still married, no matter how sour or unfulfilling the marriage was for her. Look, you'll meet someone and get a good job and marry and start having kids of your own. That's the right way and the least upsetting for everyone concerned." Fifteen years after he last heard from Trudy, he got a letter from her, sent from California to his mother's address and forwarded to him. She apologized for not staying in contact all these years, said Frank had died six years ago and that she only recently told Catherine that Stu was her biological father. The girl wants to get to know him and one day reasonably soon meet him. At the very minimum, have him know some things about her. "She feels it's important. If you wish, you can ignore this request entirely. You'd be justified, considering our absence from your life for so long, which I confess was all my doing, not hers, of course, or Frank's. She'd love to write you but at this moment is too shy to, so wonders if you could begin the correspondence with a letter or postcard or even a greeting card with a brief message—'Hi from the Big Apple' or wherever you are—to show you'd be receptive to hearing from her. For her sake, I hope you will be." He didn't know what to do. Janice didn't see a problem in his writing Catherine, but wasn't sure what he should say. "That you're married, have a two-and-a-half-year-old daughter, are expecting another daughter in three months, and you're teaching for a living now and perhaps something about your writing—I don't see the harm in any of that. Maybe you should call Dan. He can probably advise you." Dan said "It can't hurt to write the girl, though stick to the essential facts about your life. Don't admit or even mention the possibility of your being related. You do, it could get legally sticky for you later on. If she brings it up, don't respond to it, and if she insists in future letters, say it was never proved and you'd rather not talk about it. As for the mother, from everything you've said about her I doubt, at this late date, she'd pressure you for child support or for part of your children's inheritance for the girl. But you never know what even the best-intentioned people will do if they're strapped for cash or goaded by strong influences—friends who say she deserves some of your money, after she brought up the girl on her own the last six years and now that you're earning a good income from your job and books. Or just parents who feel something hasn't been given their children that will greatly benefit them or is their due. Money more than anything does that to people." Catherine and he exchanged letters about twice a year for fifteen years. He also called her about once a year and sent her a hundred dollars every year for her birthday, till Dan said "Excuse me, but if you are going to give a gift like that for so long, why not raise it to two or three hundred? A hundred is worth a third of what it was when you first started giving it," so Stu raised it to two hundred. He saw her once when he was on a West Coast book tour, took her out to dinner. They spoke a lot about Trudy, who'd moved to Catherine's town after she had a stroke that paralyzed one side of her body. He'd made plans to visit Trudy, but she called it off. "She's the least vain person I know," Catherine said at dinner, "but her face is so twisted and speech so bad and her mind erratic and forgetful, that she doesn't want to be seen by you this way. She's glad we continue to write each other and now have met, and wishes, in case anything more happens to her—and she asked me to tell you this, otherwise I never would have mentioned it—that we saw each other more and that you finally acknowledged me as your daughter." "Tell her I'm giving it some real thought," he said. Trudy had another stroke. A few months after that her house burned down when a potholder she was using caught fire and because of her paralysis she couldn't put it out in time and dropped it on some bags of paper she was saving to be recycled, and she had to crawl out of the house. She had no home owner's insurance, Catherine wrote. "She couldn't afford it, so she's now practically destitute, living off Social Security and food stamps. She won't take anything from me except physical help: shopping, getting her on the toilet or in a shower and even feeding her sometimes when she can't do those things herself. She says that with a rigid macrobiotic diet and the right yoga exercises she'll eventually get through this and be back to the abysmal physical state she was in before the second stroke. As for my sister, if you're wondering, she never offers money or help." Trudy later rented a trailer with her new boyfriend, whom she met in rehab and who was in worse shape than she—"They say they're taking care of each other," Catherine wrote, "but other than for companionship, I don't see how." He had to move into a nursing home a few months later, "a place she wouldn't be caught dead in, she said." The trailer also burned down. Something to do with a kerosene stove falling over when she fell on it in her wheelchair, Catherine wrote. "I never got the story straight because she only vaguely remembers it happening. That one she had to be rescued by firemen. I know she didn't start the fire on purpose, since she lost one of her two treasured show dogs in it. The male, no less, which cost her four times as much as the female, and which she felt was her last chance to become financially independent again: breeding them. She had no place to go now, since no landlord would trust her in an apartment or trailer after the two fires, so she finally relented and moved in with me." "That poor woman," Dan said on the phone. "Every suspicious thing I said about her, I take back. And that wonderful daughter of hers. She was obviously brought up right, but there was something more. We should all be as fortunate to have such a selfless, caring child." A few months ago Stu got an envelope from Catherine—it was summer and he was in Maine with Janice—with a photo of Trudy inside and on the back of it directions to a Santa Cruz beach where there'd be a memorial for her. The memorial took place the day before he got the envelope, which had been forwarded by his post office in Maryland. In a separate note Catherine said "Where are you? I've been calling you for days and always get the same recorded voice: a girl's.

I have to reach you. Please call me." He called her home and work numbers—she was a massage therapist and had her own business—and only got her answering machine for two days. In each message he said how sorry he was to hear about Trudy and gave his phone number. She didn't call back. At dinner a few days later, he said to Janice "When both girls get here I'd like to sit them down and tell them about Catherine. Nothing that startling at first. More like there's this thirty-six-year-old woman in California, and she, and her mother when she was alive, thinks I'm her father, but there was never clear proof I am. Her mother, in fact, was living with her husband at the time she claimed I'd knocked her up, but said she wasn't sleeping with him." "Why would you want to tell them any of that?" and he said "I'm not sure. Trudy's death certainly has something to do with it. But mostly because they'll find out one day. Either from Catherine somehow, though maybe not, or someone else on the outside. One of Dan's kids. I'm sure all of them know—you know, dinner conversation, when Dan or Melody just talk casually about it but spill the beans. They also might have told some of their other cousins, and one of them will forget it's supposed to be a secret from our kids for the time being, if they were told that, or think 'Surely they know by now,' or one day it'll slip out of me. That probably won't happen, if it hasn't so far. But longer I wait, more angry and upset they'll be, when they do find out, that I didn't tell them sooner. Catherine found it puzzling and was even a little bitter once that I hadn't told them. Of course, she was talking about her actually being my daughter. I always told her they were too young to know anything about it. Now I don't have that excuse, but it'll still hit them pretty hard, no matter how I put it to them, or maybe not." "There's bound to be some reaction from them," and he said "But what kind is what I'm really worried about. If they sluff it off, act blasé, as kids do, would I believe them? Catherine also said she'd like to meet them—said it lots of times, and always asked for photographs of them and I sent a few over the years—but would I want that? Would they? To meet her, I'm saying. What would be the point, especially if I'm still so unsure she comes from me? There's never going to be any sure proof with blood tests, now that both her parents are dead. I told you that Frank, Trudy's husband, died in a motorcycle accident, didn't I?" and she said "I thought you said it was a car." "Maybe it was. Something with wheels that went over a cliff. I once wrote about him that he rode a motorcycle, so that might have been why I thought it. I found that more interesting. A research scientist with a medical degree who specializes in the most intricate parts of the brain and who also races souped-up motorcycles. He died when Catherine was ten. Trudy and he were still together, I think. The last time—the only time— Catherine and I met as adults, in California, was the last time she asked if I'd told the kids about her yet, and that was six or seven years ago. Ninety-five; my only book tour. So seven. She also said at that meeting that that would be the last time she'd speak to me about it. So what am I saying? I'm getting a lot of things mixed up. What was I getting to with all this?" "You know what? You're obviously disturbed by Trudy's death, and maybe even a little guilty about it, and also conflicted about mentioning anything about Catherine to the kids. Think it would be a good

idea to discuss it with Dan?" and he said "Why?" and she said
"Because you've spoken about it to him before. He knows the
situation and you admit you're confused and he may have some
good advice. He has the distance from it we don't, no emotional
involvement in it that can influence his judgment, and he'd be
thinking on your behalf and would be straight with you. I'd also
be interested in what he has to say." He called Dan and said
"Janice more than I wanted me to call you about this. But okay,
here goes. You and I talked about it a few times and you told me
never to admit being the father of this girl, Catherine—well, a
woman now—but the daughter of this woman I once knew who
died recently, Trudy," and Dan said "I'm sorry to hear that. She'd
been sick a long time, though, right?" and Stu said "It was probably another stroke. I got it all in the mail, but very brief. So
things, I feel, have changed. Because Trudy died I feel I should
tell my kids about her. And that her mother and the legal
father—her mother's husband and the one who raised Catherine
and who died in an auto accident—" and Dan said "Jesus, the
things that women went through and which never seemed to
stop. Strokes, burning houses, something about all her pets going
up in one, and forced to live on the dole because she was now too
disabled to work. I didn't know about her husband dying so tragically," and Stu said "If I did tell you, it was long ago, so no reason you should have remembered it. Anyway, I was thinking of
telling my kids that both Catherine's parents thought I was the
one who fathered her and that they never, far as I know, thought
otherwise. If Trudy was lying to me—that I was the only
guy sleeping with her when Catherine was conceived and that

Frank hadn't screwed her for a year—then she would have changed her story later on—after her first stroke when the doctors thought she'd die, Catherine wrote me—wouldn't she?" and Dan said "Wouldn't she what? Change her story?" "Yes. Come clean. Told Catherine who the real father was. But right to the end, or till a few years ago when Catherine told me this, Trudy said that if she dies soon, which she thought she would and certainly after her second stroke, which was worse than her first, at least Catherine will be better off than her older sister in one respect: that she'd still have someone she could call her parent. That isn't really leaving her anything, she said Trudy said, since up till then I hadn't acted much like her biological father. Two-hundred-dollars-a-year birthday gifts and a letter or two and semiannual phone calls, if that, and one meeting on the run in California. Though she felt—again, this is all what Catherine said Trudy told her, and I think Trudy said this in the hospital right after she got part of her speech back after her first stroke, so a death-bed confession, and I'm not trying to be face-tious, just underscoring my point—that something more could develop between us after she dies and maybe even with my daughters." Dan said "I still don't think you should say anything to them. Number one, your paternity was never confirmed, and now it never will be. Why open up something that doesn't demand being opened up? Look, she was penniless and had nothing to leave her kids. So for one of them she left the only thing she could: a second father who might be able to help her out with money after she dies. Left her it, I don't like saying, by possibly lying regarding your role in having the child. I mean,

I didn't participate in it, except for a couple of tokes at a few parties, but this was a loony time then, the Sixties. Drugs, free love, the rest. And she was sort of a free spirit, it seems. Took psychedelics with her husband for years, you've said, and once— though it could have been more often—with you. And I'm sure plenty of pot, and because he was a doctor-research scientist, he had access to other drugs like that. So anything could have happened during that period when the baby was conceived. It didn't just have to be on your night. It could have been someone a week or two before, a lover or her husband, which is how she was able to say she was so sure she conceived with you. I don't care if her husband went along with her and called you the father. He was a bit of an oddball, right—the motorcycles and such?" and Stu said "Why, what else?" and Dan said "You told me of those slides of brain cells. How he got so excited by them and shut the lights and handed you a joint and put the slides in a pro- jector and had you look at them on a huge screen. And too many psychedelics make people nuts. I did research on it for a program that was never aired. But number two, I don't see how telling your girls, could help anyone, including you and Catherine. As for them, they're sixteen and nineteen, so I think it'd still be too upsetting to have something like the possibility of a half sister suddenly thrust into their lives. They might want to meet her, or they might get mad and not want to have anything to do with her, which'd end up hurting Catherine if you told her. Or sup- pose one of your girls wants to meet her and the other doesn't? In other words, who knows what could happen, but all of it to me this minute seems unnecessary and maybe even wrong.

Because now that I think of it, why would they want to meet her and possibly have a relationship with her when their own lives are just opening up to other things that are much more important to them. College, graduations, serious men friends, budding careers. And she's so much older than them, and they've never been closer, you've said, so they don't need another sister. When they're a few years older they might respond to a... well, they'd just be more mature and settled in their lives, so more open to it, I think, that's all. So, much as I'd love to welcome another niece into the family, especially a daughter of yours, I'd say that for the time being you hold off. Let's talk about it in a year, what do you say, when things have calmed down. Then you won't be so affected by the mother's death and jump into something you normally might not want to," and Stu said "That's probably the solution. Yeah, I'll do what you say and we'll talk about it in a year. I'm even going to jot down on the last page of my daily reminder book.... I have it open in front of me now... to, quote unquote, 'Transfer the following notation to next year's daily reminder book to, 0–3 August 16th, talk to Dan on the phone about Catherine and the kids.'"

37

Stu was working in LA as a technical writer for a systems analysis company. He compiled, through research and interviews he did with employees, information on the expertise the company had in a variety of areas. He wrote it up in three-to-five-page reports— and sometimes, with graphics and photos, in one-page capability bulletins, they were called—in clear journalistic language for the proposals division of the marketing department, which used them in applying for contracts. Some of these contracts and subcontracts were with the Army and Air Force and NASA for more than a hundred million dollars. He told people he didn't really know what he was writing about—"You have to understand this is a very sophisticated high-tech company with more PhDs working for it than at most research universities, but my boss keeps telling me I'm doing a great job. I'm not even sure what systems analysis means, though I've been told and looked it up a dozen times." Six months after he started working there, a writer friend in New York called to tell him of a job opening at a San Francisco public television station: writing an hour satire on the Democratic and Republican conventions coming up that summer, and if the show goes well, then writing another hour satire on the presidential and congressional elections. "You'd be a natural for it, and your present job must be boring you stiff. First of all, you've a degree in government—" and Stu said "International Relations, which I think is political science, history and economics... and just a BA," and the friend said "So tell them you concentrated on political science; they're not going to ask you for your college transcript. Also, you've had a few funny short stories in some good magazines, one of them major, with plenty of quick scenes and snappy dialog. One even on a US vice president, I remember, who's hounded off the ticket for a second term because he's so bright, articulate and honest that he makes the president look like a corrupt putz in comparison," and Stu said "Something like that. Maybe, as a possible part of the political satire, I could show them that story," and the friend said "Why not? But you've time, so let things come. Most important, though, is that you worked for a radio news service in Washington for a few years covering the Senate and House, which'd be right up their alley," and Stu said "It was only two years, and the White House, also, when our regular reporter for it was on vacation or just drunk and not around. Also the '60 Democratic convention in LA when Kennedy won it. And then the campaign, following him but mostly Johnson around for a while, in DC and the states bordering it, and New Jersey and Delaware," and the friend said "Even better. You've more qualifications than they ever hoped for, besides being single and unattached and able to make the move. Apply. I bet the job pays well and it could open up all kinds of things for you in commercial television and possibly writing for Hollywood too." "The only problem I can see is that my brother's head of special events and public affairs at NET, so he might be in charge of handing out some of the money for the show if the station's going to ask for it—I think that's how they operate in public television," and the friend said "Your brother's a bigwig at NET? Same one who got you the job at that Washington news service?" and he said "He told me of the job. The three fellows who started it were former colleagues of his at INS. He also told me of an associate producing job for CBS Radio in New York when he was working for its news bureau in Washington. At the time I was an editor on what were called dick magazines—detective—but I got the job and stayed at it—this daily half-hour interview show of people with interesting or quirky professions or pursuits or in some way in the news with a twist—till it got pulled. And if you really want to go back, he got my brother Jay a job as copyboy for the NBC weekend news show *Monitor*. When Jay graduated college and got a reporter's job—Dan had made the contact for him on a Galveston paper—I inherited it and worked there for two years till I graduated, so you can say I got the job from Dan once removed." "So tell him about this job. Say you heard of it from me and you're applying. He obviously liked helping you and your brother get jobs and advancing your news careers," and Stu said "This one would be a conflict of interest for him.

Better I apply without mentioning Dan. We've a common enough last name, so they might not suspect. If they do and ask if we're related, I'll say yes but that I didn't want to say anything because I didn't want there to be even a suggestion of nepotism involved, and also that Dan doesn't know I've applied." "Good for you. It's not what I'd do—I'd use the brother connection to the hilt. But you want to get the job on your own and I'm sure they'll respect and even appreciate that. I never knew of your CBS work. That just adds to your qualifications. So all that plus your integrity—I'd say you'd be hard to beat." Stu wrote the producer of the show and included his résumé and two published short stories, including the one about the vice president, and a one-act play he wrote when he worked in Washington, which takes place in the Senate cloakroom and the alcove at the entrance to it where senators come out to talk to reporters and other people who have sent a page in for them. The producer called him and said he liked his writing—"Busted my gut, some of it. You have the various dialects and parlance and nomenclature of politics and politicians down pat, or they sure seemed believable to me. I have to confer with the station manager and then I'll get back to you." He called the next week to say Stu was hired. "You'll have to relocate to San Francisco for the five months it'll take to get done, since we're now aiming for two shows of an hour and a half each. Still willing?" Stu quit his job, drove to San Francisco and rented an apartment a few weeks before he was supposed to start work. He was there three days when the producer called and said "This is awful, unforgivable, I could kick myself from here to Vancouver... but all right, no icing. Very bad news I hate like hell telling you after all you've given up and gone through to get here," and Stu said "You can't hire me, had second thoughts when you found out I'm a philatelist, or the show's been canceled," and the producer said "The last one, and both shows, when I thought they were in the bag. And you know who put the kibosh on them? Your brother Dan. Why didn't you say you two were related?" and he said "I didn't think I had to." "Oh yeah? So I had to hear it from him when he called this morning and said much as he'd love for his brother to work on a script for our station, after talking it over with people at NET in New York he's changed his mind about doing anything satirical on politics. It's because of the war and all the protests and the unparalleled seriousness of the presidential race. That our timing was all off. If we want to go it alone, that's up to us, but he knows as well as anyone we haven't the funds to produce even one of the satires for just a local audience and a couple of other public TV stations that might buy into it," and Stu said "I'm sure he withdrew his support because it didn't appear kosher his dispensing government money—that's where NET gets theirs from, right?—on a project his brother was working on." "I didn't say that; only that I didn't especially like hearing it from him first." "Bah, what an idiot I am. I should have told you when I applied for the job. How'd he find out?" and the producer said "You've been in radio; you should know. I had to submit a budget, which included the names and salaries of all the top people working on the show. That's how he decides how much to give us," and he said "What if you told him I don't have to work on the script. That I've taken myself off the show because I suddenly realized the possible conflict of interest. In other words, that I'm stupid and I never told you he was my brother because I didn't want you to be influenced in any way—" and the producer said "Don't bother; it's final. Your brother has a terrific rep in this business. I've never dealt with anyone in his position who was more deliberative, direct and fair, and that once he makes a decision against something—he's not as fixed when he's for it—it's irreversible," and Stu said "That'd be my take on him too, the stuff about being deliberative and above-board. As for never going back on a decision when he's against something, that I didn't know." "By the way, you did tell him you were moving to San Francisco, didn't you?, because I'm curious what he thought you were coming here for," and Stu said "For different reasons than the job. I said I wanted a change of venue from LA. Or maybe I said 'milieu,' but a city more like New York. Anyway, what's the difference now? I'm screwed." Next time Dan and Stu were on the phone, neither spoke of the canceled show and Stu losing the job because of it. "What have you been doing with yourself?" and Stu said "Looking for work." "I thought you moved there because you hated LA and wanted to live in a real city to write," and Stu said "I did, but it's a much more expensive city than I bargained for, and I've also had major car trouble." "Need a loan?" and Stu said "I'm good for now, and I'll find something before I go broke, but thanks." "Then let me give you some money. I know I keep offering and you keep refusing, so it could almost seem I'm being insincere about this, but I mean it. I want you to work on your writing a while without struggling to come up with the rent. My own personal creative writing fellowship, you being the first and last to receive it and where it's not renewable," and Stu said "It'd be nice to have a real one, without having to go to writing classes, but honestly, I'm fine." "What sort of work you looking for?—maybe I can help," and Stu said "In news. I can't think of anything else that'd pay as well and I've experience in and which'd have some kind of future for me, because the writing's sure not going to do it." "You've been out of news since '61. It's not going to be easy. They'll ask questions: 'What have you been doing the last seven years?' They'll see it's had nothing to do with news, except the technical writing job a little, and that one you quit after several months," and Stu said "Then on an alternative newspaper. Or a newsletter or magazine; there are a few out here. It'll be an adventure, or maybe I'll change fields." "Good way to look at it. But keep me in mind for a fellowship, or fraternalship, it should be called. It's open-ended, apply anytime, and you're guaranteed to get it unless our roof caves in between now and then or Melody thinks we're not putting away enough for the kids' colleges." Stu called the producer and said "You sure my brother knew of my being on the show? When I talked to him, though I never brought it up, he acted like anything but," and the producer said "More than likely to spare the feelings of you both. Like I told you, your name and salary were on the budget sheet I sent him," and Stu said "Just out of curiosity, how much was that going to be? Shows how truly stupid I am or how much I wanted the job—I never asked but assumed it couldn't be less than what I was making in LA, which wasn't half bad," and the producer told him and Stu said "Whew; I could have put a chunk of it away every week and lived off it—not here or

New York, but in some city—for a year and also got my car completely fixed." A woman he knew told him he was eligible for unemployment insurance. "You left a job for a better-paying one, which was then eliminated before you started it—that's what qualifies you," and he said "It's funny. My father would call me an idiot for not taking it, while my brother would approve. He'd say I took a chance, lost, so I shouldn't go on unemployment because of a shortsighted impetuous decision I made," and she said "So what, what your brother thinks. No disparagement meant to him, but you'd be losing out on twenty weeks of payments, and the government's talking of a three-month extension of it because so many people have been out of work for so long." "Well, it's important to me what my brother thinks, and he'd be right on this. I made my move and now I have to pay for it. And not taking unemployment insurance will give me the added incentive to find a job fast." He was interviewed for some newswriting jobs, didn't get them, looked around for other writing work, wasn't any, so he got a job as a waiter, one that took two weeks to find. A month later he was laid off because business was so bad. He drove a school van for a while, at the same time did a little artist modeling and was a salesman at minimum wage in a department store nights and weekends. After a few months of this he decided nothing was keeping him here—not job, woman, prospect or any special attachment to the area, and he was working longer and harder at three part-time jobs than he'd worked in LA at one and for around half the money. So he sold his car and went Greyhound to New York and lived with his parents and worked at a number of temporary jobs till he got a teacher's license and a job teaching social studies in a junior high school in Brooklyn and could afford his own apartment. Seven years later—he taught for five years, became physically and emotionally drained by it and was now a bartender in a brew-and-burger restaurant—he was having dinner with Dan and his family in their home in Westchester. The presidential conventions were a few months away and Stu made up some funny stories about the candidates and just American politics and politicians in general and kept everyone at the table laughing. Melody said "You know what? You could tell me to peddle my own fish, Stu, but I think you're making your living in the wrong profession. Maybe even fiction-writing's not what you should be doing either, and I only say that because you've worked so tirelessly at it with little payoff and publication. You should be writing political satire. You've a knack for it, even a gift. Not so much for newspapers and magazines. They might be tough to break in to with short pieces and I know from Dan they don't pay well, but for television. You could write several skits and playlets similar to the routines you've been doing verbally for us. With your skill for dialog, and since these pieces would be almost all dialog, it shouldn't take you long. Then, I guess, you send them to whoever deals with such things at the networks and individual stations and ask, what with the conventions and elections this year, if they've ever thought of doing a prime-time political-satire special. Am I wrong, Dan?" and he said "No, I like the idea. Freelancing isn't easy—I've been at it with mixed results for two years—but go on, I'm listening. Stu *is* funny and does write well," and she said "Because the time might be ideal for such material. I'm not aware of anything like it on TV. Certainly not on public television, and only a silly smattering of it on what I've seen on late-night talk shows. I bet it's what people would like: to laugh for a half or full hour at the ridiculous shenanigans and hypercritical fakery of the candidates and their handlers and party chieftains and most of the promises they always make but never deliver on and also the millions of dollars spent on these obscene races," and she gave Dan a look as if saying "Am I still making sense?" and he said "No, it's good, first to last. It might not pay as well as tending bar at a ritzy hotel, if Stu found a place like that to work in. Or be as dependable an income, and then, of course, there's his own health insurance to pay. But it'd beat the late hours of barkeeping, and there'd be less sidestream smoke to inhale." "Be serious," she said, and Dan said "All right. You made some very good suggestions and directed it to the guy, of just about anyone I know, who could carry them out. Well, maybe I'm going too far, but he could quickly learn it and his background is good. But, I repeat, getting work like that is hard." "It's interesting, though, that you say all this," Stu said to her, "since that's practically where my great writing career was heading eight years ago." "Oh yes?" she said. "Where? How? I had no idea," and he said "When I was living in California. A job writing just that—a political satire special. Two, in fact; one on the major primaries and political conventions in '68 and the other on the elections. For KQED, the San Francisco public TV station. One of the best in the country then and maybe still." "Still," Dan said. "More serious syndicated news and public affairs shows come out of it than from anywhere but Boston and

New York." "I was hired for the position and quit my LA job at that systems analysis company I was working for to move to San Francisco. Clay Street, steep climb up the hill from Haight. In a house with what was called the Peace Garden in front and back. My landlord, an old guy, was against the war and planted peace and anti-war signs in place of flowers and shrubs, all with literary horticultural references. Shakespeare, Milton, Tolstoy, though don't ask me to quote. Pro-war pigs burned down the house a year or so after I left, so good thing I got out when I did. My landlord wasn't hurt, thank God. But the show was cut a few days after I moved to San Francisco, and that's my story," and she said "What a shame. It could have been a wonderful break for you and it no doubt paid well," and he said "Very well. But that's how it sometimes goes and one usually doesn't get another chance like that. I tried but with no luck. So I waited on tables instead, drove an after-school van, was a department store salesman in the men's shop—you name it. Even posed nude as an artist model—it paid a dollar more an hour than if you wore a strap—and wrote a few stories that might not have been written if I was working on the satire show. By that time, writing two things at once, no matter how different the subject matter and form, no longer worked for me, which is why when I had the technical writing job in LA I mostly painted to get my creative kicks," and she said "I can understand that. Though I've read where some writers have succeeded in separating the various forms by writing on different typewriters in different rooms: for essays, poetry and novels. I don't know if they also did their short stories in the novel room, but I assume so. But three forms, three rooms, and they can do all three in one day," and he said "Not me. I have to zero in on one thing at a time for however long it takes, till it's done and then on to the next. Besides, in San Francisco I only had one room and a tiny toilet. For a kitchen I had the bathroom sink and a mini refrigerator and hot plate." Then he realized it was the first time Dan had heard him talk about the political satire show, and he looked at him and Dan said "You never told me any of that about yourself. The LA work I knew and that you moved to San Francisco. But I'd always thought it was because you saved a pile of dough from the job and wanted to give yourself time to write and also to be part of the scene there. Too bad, though, losing the job. It would have been a good change of career for you and more in line with what you could do and had done than the technical stuff. But things turned out okay without it," and Stu said "What do you mean?" "You're still writing, haven't given up. You got some fiction done you wouldn't have if you'd held that job. You've worked at a number of different jobs since, all more interesting as material than technical or television writing. And though what you're employed at now isn't what you like and there's no future in it, you'll make it in fiction yet, I'm sure." "Even so," Melody said, "what a lost opportunity then. And you might have settled in San Francisco if you'd started the job. Might still be living there— married, kids, everything, because the salary would have only got better over the years if you had stayed in TV," and Dan said "Nah. Stu's a New York person and he also would have missed us too much, right?—only kidding. But he would have come back after the show was over or in a couple of years. Also because there are so many more television news-writing jobs in the East than out there, and a greater share of the specials like that. And just having worked for KQED would have impressed plenty of other public TV stations and even the public television network here. But you wouldn't have wanted to stay in television too long. You wanted to write your own things, and you said yourself you can't do both at the same time. Am I right or not?" and Stu said "I don't know. To be honest, maybe I could have, but I haven't thought of it much." "Okay. So I was wrong." The political satire show and Dan's part in axing it never came up in conversation between them after that. Surely, Stu thought a few times and spoke about it with Janice, Dan didn't believe that business about Stu quitting the LA job to write fiction and be part of the San Francisco hippie scene. Just didn't seem possible—not with Dan's mind—he forgot what really happened. Nor did it seem like Dan not to want to talk it over with him, and that maybe he regretted what he'd done; anyway, to clear it up. So Stu didn't know what to think about it and he'd rather leave it at that.

38

He hangs up and Janice says "It's unbelievable," and he says "Don't tell me, I don't want to hear. It's impossible, not unbelievable; not possible, that's what it is. He can't be dead. It couldn't have happened. It hasn't, hasn't, I'm telling you—turn that thing off, turn it off," and she flicks the television off with the remote and says "The sound wasn't on and I forgot about the picture. I was listening to you on the phone. And please try to take it easy, my darling. This is too much for you, too upsetting," and he says "I don't want to hear about it; it isn't too much. I've got things to do; Manny said so," and she says "That was Manny? I wasn't sure," and he says "Of course, Manny; you answered the phone, didn't you?" and she says "No, you did. You came into the room when I yelled out I couldn't reach my portable. I sort of guessed it was him or one of his sisters," and he says "Yes, Manny, Dan's son. Dan's dead, he said. That's what he told me.

I couldn't believe it when he did. That he didn't want to but had to, that's what he said. 'Dan's dead, Uncle Stu; Dad's dead. I have some very bad news for you,' he first said. 'Dad's dead.' So what am I going to do now? What *can* I do? And that he's sorry, he said, can you imagine? 'I'm so sorry for you, Uncle Stu.' The kid loses his father and he's sorry for me. He's past forty, not a kid, but it is his father. And he told me how. A tree, possibly. Or he fell and had a heart attack or stroke and that thing with the blood clot or he had one when he was running and then fell. It's too early to tell, he said. A root on this godforsaken path Dan was running on may have tripped him, breaking some ribs in the fall and one went into his lung and he bled to death. That could also be the case, because no one was with him or around. A man walking a dog walked by maybe an hour later, they estimate, and now I have to call my sisters, he said he can't. Or even foul play. Based on the bruises to his head, someone may have hit him with a tree branch. They don't know yet, doctors or police. It just happened this afternoon around three. Or he was found around three and it happened around two, I forget what Manny said. That makes what, seven to eight hours or so. I'm going crazy over it, crazy," and she says "You should sit down. Come here," and holds out her arms and he says "I don't want to move from this phone yet, someone might call. It's because he doesn't like Harriet and Natalie that I have to call them. He doesn't want to speak to them, even, over this, or he just has other people to call," and she says "Or he's too emotionally shaken to call them and also feels it'd be better for it to come from you. Calling you was probably all he could do, but he felt he had to because of how close you and Dan were," and he says "That too. Or that a tree branch might have snapped when he was running under it, because of the ferocious wind. You remember the wind. We were what? This is so crazy. We were there, how far away from where it happened? Because it happened in Yonkers in a remote part of the park he was running through. He liked to run in those kinds of places, out-of-the-way. To stop and see and smell things and maybe there'd be animals he couldn't see in runs in regular places. And we were driving back from where around that time today?" and she says "Yorktown Heights." "To attend an art opening of your friend's at an arts center, or the town center or community hall, but someplace there. I forget whose," and she says "Leonore." "We drank some wine, ate crudités. While Dan was doing his weekly Sunday run but without the doctor friend he usually ran with on Sundays, can you imagine? Always ran with, Manny said. A doctor who could've helped him, but he had to be at a family function, Manny said. A funeral, he thinks, can you imagine? So Dan ran alone and got killed by a heavy tree branch or a whole tree that fell, or could have, since one seemed freshly down near where they found him. And we were possibly passing on the Saw Mill River Parkway at the time, or close. At the most an hour after he was hit or found, because we got back around eight. It was a fast trip and an hour after we got back you wanted to have your dinner in here because you wanted to watch a special program at nine. I thought of dropping in on him. I didn't tell you this, but I swear I thought it when we were approaching Dobbs Ferry. But I knew you wanted to get home. Sooner the better, because it can be excruciating for you, sitting in your chair so long. And you also wanted to watch that documentary, so I continued to the bridge without saying anything because we still had a three-and-a-half-hour drive. I thought he might be there. I didn't know he ran every Sunday. That was news to me; I only found out now. I thought he might be home and we'd stop to say hello to Melody and Dan and maybe one of their kids if one was there and possibly the new grandchild, whom we've never seen. Maybe wouldn't even have to get out of the van. Or you wouldn't have had to—I would have gone to the bathroom there, which I always do at a stop—and because I haven't seen him in a while. And now I have to call my sisters and tell them, and which one do I call first? Harriet, because she's older, but what do I do?" and she says "About Harriet?" "How am I going to do it? I'll go crazy over the phone. I'll break down the second she says hello and you'll have to get on and tell her," and she says "Wait, then; don't call right away." "And if her answering machine answers, what then? Do I tell her that way? Of course not. So do I say who it is and that I'll call back later, and then call Natalie? Or do I hang up without saying anything and call back later?" and she says "The latter. Moment you hear the answering machine, hang up. But wait with both of them, as I said. Give it more time. You don't have to call right away. Make yourself a drink. Try to get control of yourself before you call, complete control or as much as you can get." "But it'd be unfair for them not to know now if they're around," and she says "Why?" and he says "Because, I don't know, but it just seems that way. I have this information and they don't. And I want to get it over with, even if I do fall apart on the phone, so I don't have anything to do after I tell them but help you get to bed sometime later and then get to bed myself. So I have to call them. But I won't be able to control myself, before or during the call. So I have to think about this, think about it hard, think what to do. I have to get out of here and away from this phone," and he leaves the room—Janice calling out "Stuart, please"—and the house and walks on the driveway to the mailbox. It's dark out, lots of tall trees around, just a little light from the streetlight on the main road about two hundred feet away, and says while he walks "It can't be. It couldn't have happened. Please don't say it has. Not Dan; not my brother. I was going to see him today. He didn't know that but I did. It would've been short but it would've been something. But he was out running. Now what am I going to do without him? Who am I going to speak to? If one of my kids gets very sick, in a car accident, dies, who am I going to call? I've nobody to help me like that, nobody. If Janice gets worse, almost dies as she almost has, what am I going to do? I'd call him, right? Call him first thing and he'd talk to me and help me through and give me good advice. That's what he's always done. Isn't it enough I've lost two brothers, do I have to lose three? Because Manny wouldn't fib on this. What he told me must have happened. That my brother Dan... that Dan, my last brother, is dead. It can't be, that's what I say. I don't want to hear it, don't want to think it," and sticks his hand into his mouth and bites down hard on the knuckles. He knows he was talking too loud, maybe shouting. Shouting; don't lie! So calm down, do what she says, get control, get yourself a drink, and takes his hand out of his mouth and shouts "Dan can't be dead, he can't," and bites down on his knuckles again. "Shh." Speak low, he thinks; everyone doesn't have to know you're crazy, and says "I'm so sad; I'm so nuts. I can't take it. Literally, I can't. Why'd it have to happen? Tell me. Everything was going along fine with him. He was retired, healthy. He was having a good time just being home. Reading a lot, doing things. Running, that fucking curse running. And swimming, playing tennis with his wife, seeing his kids and grandkids, even fishing, and doing volunteer work. Soup kitchens. Just recently, started rereading all of Dickens. 'I'm slow,' he said, 'more so than I used to be, so I've a long way to go, but what of it if I love it?' He was content. That's what he told me, content, when he didn't think he would be, not having a project to work on. A son in Hawaii; he was flying out to see him next week. It really shouldn't have happened. Why do these things always have to? Enough. I'm not making sense. I hate it out here. But you'll also hate it in the house. But people will hear me out here because I know I'm going to talk too loud or shout," and runs back to the house and goes inside. "Now what?" he says. "What am I supposed to be doing?" He looks around the kitchen; it doesn't look right. Something seems to be off or askew, or it's the light. It's definitely darker, or it's just my glasses or eyes, and he takes the dishtowel off the refrigerator door handle and cleans his glasses. "Oh, yes." He opens the refrigerator freezer. Anita! He turns on the driveway floodlights and carport light outside the kitchen door. She's still out and will be coming home soon, tomorrow's school. "What'll I tell her?" he says. "It can't be what I have to tell her. The freezer." He grabs a few ice cubes from the ice container in it and drops them into

a coffee mug from the dish rack and fills the mug with vodka.
He goes into Janice's study and calls Harriet from the wall
phone there. She answers and he says "It's Stu, I have to be
quick," and she laughs and says "Do you remember that Groucho
Marx greeting—you, of anybody, would, my font-of-information
brother—when he bursts into a room and says to the hostess at
a grand party something hilariously absurd about being in a
hurry?" and he says "Please, I've got to," and she says "'Hello, I
have to go.' What's the rush, Mr. Quick? I'm much aware from
previous calls with you that you don't like talking on the phone,"
and he starts sobbing and she says "What's that? Are you joking
with me?" and he continues sobbing and she says "Stu, what's
wrong?" and he tries to speak but can only sob and she says "Is
it Janice? Does it have to do with her illness? Stu, you can't call
like this and not tell me; what? One of the kids?" and he says
"Dan... Dan..." and she says "I should call Dan to find out? Just
say yes or no," and he shouts "No," and then says in a normal
voice "He's dead. Manny called. I hate telling you, but he asked
me. Hit by a tree or branch, or something. In a park. Yonkers.
An out-of-the-way path, running. Later he was found. It's terrible, Harriet; I can't take it. I think it can't be, it just can't, but
Manny said—" and she says "Oh my goodness... oh no... I can't
believe this. It's awful, horrible. Oh my goodness, Stu, what a
shock," and he says "I know. Neither can I. But it's true. He
called fifteen minutes ago, ten, I don't know when. What's the
difference what time? It happened today around three. Said his
father was running and might have tripped. They don't know. He
was alone. He's still at the hospital, I think, Dan is; Manny called

from Dan's home. A tree or tripping on a root or rock, or he had a heart attack or stroke. But he had bruises," and she says "No doubt from the fall," and he says "From the fall, that's what he said, or he might even have been mugged. I've got to go. I got to call Natalie and tell her," and she says "I'll call her; you're in no shape or mind to," and he says "No, Manny said I should call you both," and she says "Who cares what Manny said. I mean, I know he means well and my heart goes out to him—to his whole family; it's terrible—but I'll call. It'd be better for you and Natalie," and he says "No, please let me; then you can. It's true I feel a bit crazy, but I'll do this one more thing and then take something. I've a glass of vodka right here, but so far—" and she says "Good, drink it and then rest," and he says "That's what I'm saying. I have it but I haven't drunk it. But I'll drink it now and maybe another after I do these calls and then I'll take care of myself. I'm sorry, Harriet; so sorry for us all," and hangs up and dials Natalie. She says on her answering machine she's either away from the phone or on it and to leave a brief message "and please speak slowly and clearly. If you think I know your number by heart or have it written down or can find it if I do, you'd be greatly mistaken, so repeat it twice," and after the beep he says "Natalie, it's Stu; I have some terrible news. The worst thing imaginable's happened. But I won't be able to tell you. I can't this way, on the machine. It's not my family; it's Dan. I shouldn't have even told you that. Call Harriet; she knows. Though she'll probably call you very soon too," and Natalie says "What about Dan? I didn't want to talk to anyone tonight, so I was monitoring my calls. Did he have a heart attack? A car accident?" and he starts crying and can't speak and she says "Stop that for a second; what is it? Should I call Harriet right now to ask her?" and he says "Manny called me. I'm sorry. I hate breaking it to you but he asked me to. One call might have been all he could do. All right; it's very bad. Dan died this afternoon; an accident or something else. Please let me finish," because she's screaming "What! What!" "This is tough to get out and if I fall apart again I won't be able to say anything," and she says "Okay, I'll be quiet; go on." "A tree or someone. It was in a park, on a remote path he was running on, near where he lives. Or he tripped and hit his head or had a heart attack or stroke, but something killed him," and she says "I don't believe this. Not our Dan. Why does everything have to happen to our family? One stupid death after the other. What the hell will be next?" and he says "What I feel too. Not Dan, not Dan, it couldn't have happened, can't be. I've been running around like a madman saying it, screaming. Outside. I had to come in. He was too healthy, too smart. He could get out of anything, I thought; get through, I mean. Prison; shot at by the Chinese; that boat across the Atlantic that almost sunk. I know this is selfish, but what am I going to do now?" and she says "I understand. You two became very close after Jay died. Much closer than Harriet and I ever were with him." "So close. I was just thinking before. Or I actually thought it now. If something were to happen to me, who'd look after my family? The kids would eventually be okay, and Janice could probably work things out for herself and she has several good friends, so maybe I'm exaggerating. But Dan would step in to make sure everything was taken care of," and she says

"Nothing will happen to you. You're healthy, too, and nine years younger than Dan. It's reasonable, though, what you're saying," and he says "Excuse me, but what was I? That business about my loss, I guess. I can't get it out of my head, that and his being dead. But it's everybody's, I know that. But I have to go. I've told you, did what I was asked. I'm glad I got you so that's over with. I'm sorry, that must seem awful of me to say. I'll speak to you," and hangs up and goes into the bedroom to tell Janice he told his sisters. She's in her wheelchair, same place near the TV she was before, watching the public television program. It's about Lewis and Clark. "I needed a distraction; I'll shut it off," and he says "No, leave it; what's the difference?" "How are you doing? A dumb question, inappropriate, and I know how you're doing— I could hear you—but you know what I mean," and he says "My drink; wait," and runs back to the study and looks for the mug. "Damnit" he shouts, "where the fuck are you?" Sees it on top of the toilet's water tank below the wall phone, and grabs it and drinks several gulps and goes back to the bedroom with it. She looks up from the screen when he comes in and says "Honestly, I'll turn it off. I just don't know what to do or what I can do for you. It's so awful—Dan—and I'm stuck in this horrible chair. I can't go out and run around and tear things unless you push me," and he says "I wasn't tearing anything. What do you mean, 'tear'? I was screaming. That, everybody heard. I'm sorry. It's just... but I'll try to stop. I don't know how to absorb this, though. I should drink up," and he finishes the drink. He puts the mug down on the dresser and turns to her. She says "Watch out, the mug!" and he turns back around and the mug's fallen over, he doesn't know why; he set it down right, and the ice cubes slide off the dresser. He yells "Goddamnit, won't anything go right?" and slams the dresser top with his fist and the mug jumps up and falls off the dresser and he shoots his foot out to cushion the fall and it bounces off his shin and breaks on the floor. "Now look what I've done. Our favorite Maine mug. One thing after another after another," slamming the dresser top with his fist, "and it's goddamn endless; it's pathetic," and gets on his knees to pick up the mug's handle and three broken pieces and ice. "Don't cut yourself. And we'll get more of the same mugs this summer," and he says "I don't want any more. I don't want any more of anything," and picks up the pieces and ice and dumps them into the wastebasket under his work table, and she says "The ice will melt. And if there's a hole or just the seam's not sealed tight at the bottom of the basket, it'll get on the floor." "Let it, it's only goddamn water." "Of course," she says, "I don't know why I said it. It won't hurt the carpet. And the carpet has a special stain resistant on it, or did," and he says "But it's water, it's water, it can't stain," and she says "I know. But the phone receiver. Excuse me, but it was knocked off too," and he says "Fuck the phone; fuck all calls. Fuck the world. Fuck the trees, all trees, the wind, everything, everything." "Stu, I know how you feel. Remember, I went through almost the exact thing with my mother last year. The shock of hearing it. Even the phone call, except it was morning. But listen... Oh, I don't know what to say. Maybe you should have another drink. Relax yourself more, get tired, then go to bed. We'll go to bed earlier. I'll shut off the TV and come to bed with you, if you get me ready," and he says "I don't want you to shut off anything, I've already told you that. If I haven't, then I'm telling you now. I don't want to do anything, you hear?" "Then please put the receiver back. I'm not able to reach it," and he says "That I can do," and puts it back and the phone rings and he says "You answer it, I can't." She takes the portable off her lap and is about to press the Talk button, when he says "No, I will, it might be Manny," and says into the receiver "Yes?" and she shuts the TV off and Manny says "Uncle Stu, it's me again; I was concerned about you. I didn't know what to say to you before," and he says "Nobody knows what to say to me. I'm sure they don't to you either, but they keep saying things, and I should really be the one concerned about you. I'm so sorry for you and your family—your sisters, your Mom, Isaac," and Manny says "I'm doing all right. We all are, considering. I spoke to Issac. He's worse off than the rest of us because he's by himself out there since the divorce, but he says he'll be all right too, that we shouldn't worry. But you were in such bad shape when I told you about Dad that I thought—" and he says "I'm still in that shape. I feel I'm losing my mind, Manny; I don't know what to do. I loved your father. I never told him that, I don't think— you don't tell your brother that—but that's how I felt and I feel totally lost without him. I don't know what to do. I said that, but it's true. It's going to be a rough night, that's what I have to face up to, unless I drink myself to sleep. But then I'll wake up. But Manny, I have to go. I can't stay on the phone or by it or even in this room. I'm sorry, I have to say goodbye," and he hangs up. "You know, despite everything you're going through," Janice says, "you have to remember he did just lose his father."

"Why, what did I say? Did I hurt him? I didn't want to. If I did say anything to make him feel worse, I'm sorry, but what can I do now, make it even worse by calling him back and reminding him what I said and apologizing?" and she says "No. I was just saying for the next time. Look, what if I call Dr. Morelli to prescribe a tranquilizer or sleeping pill for you?" and he says "How we going to get the pills?" "I'll call Chris to go for them," and he says "And where would we get them? Look at the time. It's Sunday and late—the pharmacies are closed or never opened," and she says "There must be one open now. A 24-hour Giant, and I heard of an all-night pharmacy in the city; Morelli would know. Or one of our friends would have pills and bring them over," and he says "I don't want any pills. I only want to get through the night. And tomorrow night to get through that night. And on and on the nights, but this one first. I only want to think about it, about him, everything. I'm not making sense. What I meant... well, I don't know what I meant, but I meant something," and the phone rings and he says "Goddamn freaking phone. I can't stand the ringing. Answer it if you want. I'm through talking to anyone anymore, even if it's Manny or one of my sisters," and he leaves the room and she says on the portable "Hello? Oh, hi." As he's leaving the house a car pulls up in the circular part of their driveway. It's Anita, driven home by a friend. He doesn't know if he should go back in, leave again through the living room door where it's dark and go over the footbridge to the main road, or dart through the carport and past the car, as if he hasn't seen it. "Hi, Daddy," Anita says as the car drives off, and then "What's wrong? Your face," because he's staring at her, tears coming out, and she says "Mommy?" and he says "Uncle Dan. He died this afternoon. Hit by a tree. He was running. Manny called. They're not sure what killed him. Tripped, maybe, and maybe hit his head and got a blood clot or stroke. Or a heart attack or even mugged and murdered," and she says "God, not Uncle Dan. And murdered? By who?" and he says "Not murdered. They don't think it's that." "And it couldn't have been a tree that hit him," and he says "Yes, it could have, that's what they said—Manny, probably the doctors and police, or something else. But most likely the tree. It was down, in this park, right beside him, I think, on this remote path, and his head had been bruised, maybe crushed—that, Manny didn't say. Oh my darling, I'm so sad; I can't take it," and he starts sobbing. She puts her arms out—he's still holding the kitchen storm door open and lets it close behind him and hugs her and shuts his eyes and thinks "She never comes to me to hug, never lets me hug or kiss her anymore, never. She used to, all the time, but the last few years I have to force myself on her," and then she pulls away and says "I'm so sorry for you, Daddy. Uncle Dan was such a nice man," and he says "I know, thank you, so nice in saying that and what you did. But I want to walk now, my darling. Don't take offense, but I just want to walk back and forth and around, thank you," and squeezes her hand and walks toward the road, mumbling "Not Dan; not today; it can't be. My poor brother dead, but it can't be. Oh no, oh no, I can't live without him, I just can't," and drops to his knees and slaps the driveway with his hands and sobs and slams the driveway with his fists and screams "No, no, no, it can't be," and lies on his chest with his arms spread out and cheek on the ground and Anita yells "Mom, Mom, come outside; Daddy's on the ground," and runs to him and says "Daddy, get up, you'll get dirty," and he says "I can't, I can't, I'm too heartsick," and she puts her hands under his arms and tries to lift him up.